MATHEMATICAL RECREATIONS OF LEWIS CARROLL

In Two Volumes

Symbolic Logic *and* The Game of Logic
Pillow Problems *and* A Tangled Tale

•

MATHEMATICAL RECREATIONS OF LEWIS CARROLL

PILLOW PROBLEMS

AND

A TANGLED TALE

both books bound as one

BY

LEWIS CARROLL

DOVER PUBLICATIONS, INC., NEW YORK

Published in Canada by General Publishing Company, Ltd., 30 Lesmill Road, Don Mills, Toronto, Ontario.

Published in the United Kingdom by Constable and Company, Ltd., 10 Orange Street, London WC 2.

This Dover edition, first published in 1958. is an unabridged and unaltered republication of the following two books by Lewis Carroll:

Pillow-Problems (Part 2 of *Curiosa Mathematica*), as published by Macmillan and Company, Ltd., in 1895.

A Tangled Tale, as originally published by Macmillan and Company, Ltd., in 1885.

International Standard Book Number: 0-486-20493-6
Library of Congress Catalog Card Number: 58-14299

Manufactured in the United States of America
Dover Publications, Inc.
180 Varick Street
New York, N. Y. 10014

PILLOW-PROBLEMS

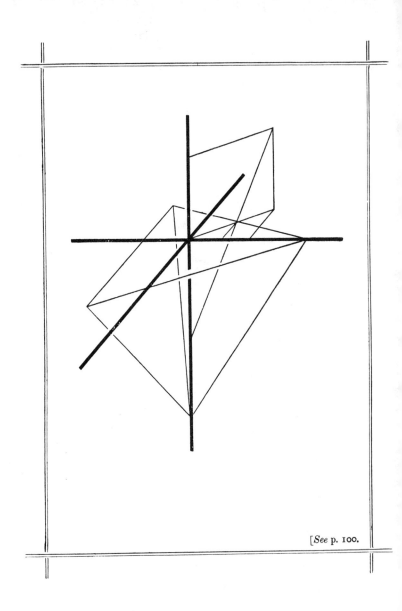

[*See* p. 100.

PILLOW-PROBLEMS

THOUGHT OUT DURING
WAKEFUL HOURS

BY

CHARLES L. DODGSON, M.A.

Student and late Mathematical Lecturer
of Christ Church, Oxford

FOURTH EDITION

DOVER PUBLICATIONS, INC.
NEW YORK • NEW YORK

PREFACE TO FOURTH EDITION.

I take this opportunity of explaining *why* it is that (as stated in the Note to p. xix) I have used the symbols ⌒ and ◠ to represent the words 'sine' and 'cosine'.

The use of *some* symbols needs, I suppose, no more justification than the use of + and − to represent 'plus' and 'minus'.

These particular symbols are derived from the old theory of Trigonometry, in which sines, cosines, &c. were actual *lines*.

In this diagram, OP being taken as the unit of length, PN is the *sine* of the angle NOP, and ON its *cosine*.

In each of my two symbols I have retained the semicircle : in the symbol ⌒, I have merely moved PN to the middle ; and, in the symbol ◠, I have lengthened ON, taking it a little *beyond* the curve, in order to avoid confusion with the existing symbol for 'semicircle'.

I also take this opportunity of adding a sort of Corollary (lately thought out) to the solution of Problem 59 (see p. 84).

If a, b, c be given lengths, they must, in order that the Tetrahedron may be *possible*, fulfil certain conditions, as follows :—

(1) they have to form the sides of a Triangle : hence any two of them must be greater than the third ;

(2) the three angles of this Triangle have to form a *solid* angle : hence any two of these angles must be together greater than the third : hence any two of them must be together greater than 90° : hence any *one* of them must be *less* than 90° : hence the *cosine* of any one of them must be greater than O : i.e. $b^2 + c^2 - a^2$ must be greater than O, &c. : hence a, b, c must be such that the *squares* of any two of them are together greater than the *square* of the third.

For example, the lengths 2, 3, 4 would *not* do as the given lengths, since, although fulfilling the *first* condition, by having $2 + 3 > 4$, they fail to fulfil the *second*, as $2^2 + 3^2$ is *not* $> 4^2$.

C. L. D.

CH CH , OXFORD.
March, 1895.

PREFACE TO SECOND EDITION.

THE principal changes, made in this Second Edition of " Pillow-Problems ", are as follows:—

(1) After the numeral, which precedes each Question, Answer, or Solution, references are given to the pages at which the corresponding matter may be found.

(2) Some of the Solutions have been re-arranged, and duplicate-diagrams have been inserted, in order that every portion of text may have its illustrative diagram visible along with it, and that the reader may thus be saved the trouble, and the strain on his temper, involved in turning a leaf backwards and forwards while referring from the one to the other.

(3) In the title of the book, the words " sleepless nights " have been replaced by " wakeful hours ".

This last change has been made in order to allay the anxiety of kind friends, who have written to me to express their sympathy in my broken-down state of health, believing that I am a sufferer from chronic " insomnia ", and that it is as a remedy for that exhausting malady that I have recommended mathematical calculation.

The title was not, I fear, wisely chosen ; and it certainly *was* liable to suggest a meaning I did not intend to convey,

viz. that my " nights" are very often *wholly* "sleepless ".
This is by no means the case: I have never suffered from
" insomnia ": and the over-wakeful hours, that I have had
to spend at night, have often been simply the result of
the over-sleepy hours I have spent during the preceding
evening ! Nor is it as a remedy for *wakefulness* that I
have suggested mathematical calculation ; but as a remedy
for the *harassing thoughts* that are apt to invade a wholly-
unoccupied mind. I hope the new title will express my
meaning more lucidly.

To state the matter logically, the dilemma which my
friends *suppose* me to be in has, for its two horns, the
endurance of a sleepless night, and the adoption of some
recipe for inducing sleep. Now, so far as *my* experience
goes, no such recipe has any effect, unless when you
are sleepy : and mathematical calculation would be more
likely to delay, than to hasten, the advent of sleep.

The *real* dilemma, which I have had to face, is this :
given that the brain is in so wakeful a condition that,
do what I will, I am *certain* to remain awake for the next
hour or so, I must choose between two courses, viz. either
to submit to the fruitless self-torture of going through
some worrying topic, over and over again, or else to
dictate to myself some topic sufficiently absorbing to keep
the worry at bay. A mathematical problem *is*, for me,
such a topic ; and is a benefit, even if it lengthens the
wakeful period a little. I believe that an hour of calculation
is much better for me than half-an-hour of worry.

The reader will, I think, be interested to see a curiously
illogical solution which has been proposed, by a correspon-

dent of the *Educational Times*, for Problem 61, viz. " Prove
that, if any 3 Numbers be taken, which cannot be arranged
in *A. P.*, and whose sum is a multiple of 3, the sum of their
squares is also the sum of another set of 3 squares, the
2 sets having no common term."

The proposed solution is as follows :—

" Let $3m$, $21m$, $30m$ be the three Numbers ; then
$$3m + 21m + 30m = 3 \times 18m.$$

Also $(3m)^2 + (21m)^2 + (30m)^2 = (6m)^2 + (15m)^2 + (33m)^2$
$$= (5m)^2 + (13m)^2 + (34m)^2 = (10m)^2 + (17m)^2 + (31m)^2$$
$$= (14m)^2 + (23m)^2 + (25m)^2 . "$$

Now, if we denote, by ' a ', the property " which cannot
be arranged in *A. P.*, and whose sum is a multiple of 3,"
and, by ' β ', the property " the sum of whose squares is
also the sum of another set of 3 squares, the 2 sets having
no common term," we see that all, that this writer has succeeded in proving, is that *certain selected Numbers*, which
have property ' a ', have also property ' β ' : but this does
not prove my Theorem, viz. that *any Numbers whatever*,
which have property ' a ', have also property ' β '.   If his
argument were arranged in a syllogistic form, it would be
found to assume a quite untenable Major Premiss, viz.
" that, which is true of *certain selected Numbers* which have
property ' a ', is true of *any Numbers whatever* which have
property ' a '."

C. L. D.

Ch. Ch., Oxford.
September, 1893.

INTRODUCTION.

———

NEARLY all of the following seventy-two Problems are veritable " Pillow-Problems ", having been solved, in the head, while lying awake at night. (I have put on record the exact dates of some.) No. 37 and one or two others belong to the daylight, having been solved while taking a solitary walk ; but every one of them was worked out, to the very end, before drawing any diagram or writing down a single word of the solution. I generally wrote down the *answer*, first of all : and *afterwards* the question and its solution. For example, in No. 70, the very first words I wrote down were as follows :—"(1) down back-edge ; up again ; down again ; and so on ; (2) about ·7 of the way down the back-edge ; (3) about 18° 18′ ; (4) about 14°." These answers are not quite correct ; but at least they are *genuine*, as the results of *mental* work *only*. " A poor thing, Sir, but mine own ! "

My motive, for publishing these Problems, with their mentally-worked solutions, is most certainly *not* any desire to display powers of mental calculation. Mine, I feel sure, are nothing out-of-the-way ; and I have no doubt there are many mathematicians who could produce, mentally, much shorter and better solutions. It is not for such persons that I intend my little book; but rather for the much larger class of *ordinary* mathematicians, who perhaps have never tried this resource, when mental occupation was needed, and who will, I hope, feel encouraged—by seeing what can be done, after a little practice, by one of *average* mathematical powers—to try the experiment for themselves, and find in it as much advantage and comfort as I have done.

The word "comfort" may perhaps sound out of place, in connection with so entirely *intellectual* an occupation; but it will, I think, come home to many who have known what it is to be haunted by some worrying subject of thought, which no effort of will is able to banish. Again and again I have said to myself, on lying down at night, after a day embittered by some vexatious matter, "I will *not* think of it any more! I have gone through it all, thoroughly. It can do no good whatever to go through it again. I *will* think of something else!" And in another ten minutes I have found myself, once more, in the very thick of the miserable business, and torturing myself, to no purpose, with all the old troubles.

Now it is not possible—this, I think, all psychologists will admit—by any effort of volition, to carry out the resolution "I will *not* think of so-and-so." (Witness the common trick, played on a child, of saying "I'll give you a penny, if you'll stand in that corner for five minutes, and *not once* think of strawberry-jam." No human child ever yet won the tempting wager!) But it *is* possible—as I am most thankful to know—to carry out the resolution "I *will* think of so-and-so." Once fasten the attention upon a subject so chosen, and you will find that the worrying subject, which you desire to banish, is *practically* annulled. It may recur, from time to time—just looking in at the door, so to speak ; but it will find itself so coldly received, and will get so little attention paid to it, that it will, after a while, cease to be any worry at all.

Perhaps I may venture, for a moment, to use a more serious tone, and to point out that there are mental troubles, much worse than mere worry, for which an absorbing subject of thought may serve as a remedy. There are sceptical thoughts, which seem for the moment to uproot the firmest faith ; there are blasphemous thoughts, which dart unbidden into the most reverent souls ; there are unholy thoughts, which torture, with their hateful presence, the fancy that would fain be pure. Against all these some real mental *work* is a most helpful ally. That " unclean spirit " of the parable, who brought back with him seven others more wicked than himself, only did so because he found the chamber " swept and garnished ", and its owner sitting with folded hands : had he found it all alive with the " busy hum " of active *work*, there would have been scant welcome for him and his seven !

My purpose—of giving this encouragement to others— would not be so well fulfilled had I allowed myself, in writing out my solutions, to *improve* on the work done in my head. I felt it to be much more important to set down *what had actually been done in the head*, than to supply shorter or neater solutions, which perhaps would be much harder to do without paper. For example, a Long-Multiplication sum (say the multiplying together of two numbers of 7 digits) is no doubt best done, on *paper*, by beginning at the unit-end, and writing out 7 rows of figures, and adding up the columns in the usual way. But it would be very difficult indeed—to *me* quite impossible—to do such a thing in the *head*. The only chance seems to be to begin with the *millions*, and get *them* properly grouped ; then the hundred-thousands, adding the results to the previous one ; and so on. Very often it seems to happen, that the easiest *mental* process looks decidedly lengthy and round-about when committed to paper.

When I first tried this plan, easy geometrical problems were all I could manage ; and, even in these, I had to pause from time to time, in order to re-draw the diagram, which *would* persist in getting ' rubbed-out '. Algebraical problems I avoided at first, owing to the provoking fact that, if one single co-efficient escaped the memory, there was no resource but to begin the calculation all over again. But I soon got over both these difficulties, and found myself able to remember fairly large numerical co-efficients, and also to retain, in the mind's eye, fairly complex diagrams, even to the extent of *finding my way* from one part of the diagram to another. The *lettering* of the diagrams proved such a troublesome thing to keep in the memory, that I almost gave up using it, and learned to recognise Points by their *situation* only. In my MS. of No. 53, I find the following memorandum :—

" I had never set myself this Problem before the week ending Ap. 6, 1889. I tried it, two or three nights, lying awake ; and finally worked it out on the night of Ap. $\frac{6}{7}$.

All the conclusions were worked out mentally before any use was made of pen and paper. While working it, I did not give *names* to any Points, except *A, B, C,* and *P* : I merely thought of them by their positions (e. g. 'the foot of the perpendicular from *P* on *BC*')."

If any of my readers should feel inclined to reproach me with having worked too uniformly in the region of Common-place, and with never having ventured to wander out of the beaten tracks, I can proudly point to my one Problem in 'Transcendental Probabilities'—a subject in which, I believe, *very* little has yet been done by even the most enterprising of mathematical explorers. To the casual reader it may seem abnormal, and even paradoxical ; but I would have such a reader ask himself, candidly, the question "Is not Life itself a Paradox ?"

To give the Reader some idea of the process of construction of these Problems, I will give the biography of No. 63. The history of one is, to a great extent, the history of all.

It was begun during the night of Sept. $\frac{3}{4}$, 1890, and completed during the following night. The idea had occurred to me, a short time previously, that something interesting might be found in the subject of what I may call 'partially-regular' Solids. The 'regular' Solids are provokingly few in number ; and it would be hopeless to find any question, connected with them, that has not already been exhaustively analysed : some also of the 'partially-regular' Solids (e. g. rhomboidal crystals) have probably been similarly treated ; but there seemed to be room for the invention of other such Solids.

Accordingly, I devised a Solid enclosed, above and below, by 2 equal and parallel Squares, having their centres in the same vertical line, and the upper one twisted round so that its sides should be parallel to the diagonals of the lower Square. Then I imagined the upper one raised until its corners formed the vertices of 4 equilateral Triangles, whose bases were the sides of the lower one. The Solid, thus obtained, was evidently enclosed by 2 Squares and 8 equilateral Triangles: and the Problem I set myself was to obtain its *Volume.*

There was no great difficulty in proving that the distance between the 2 Squares (taking each side as equal to ' 2 ') was $2^{\frac{3}{4}}$. But, when I looked about for some Trigonometrical method for calculating the Volume, despair soon seized upon me! A calculable Prism could be cut out of the *middle* of the Solid, I saw: but the outlying projections completely baffled me. After a while, the happy idea occurred to me of trying Algebraical Geometry, and regarding each facet as the base of a Pyramid, having its vertex at the centre of the Solid, which I decided to take as the Origin. I saw at once that I could calculate the coordinates of all the vertical Points, thence obtain equations to the Planes containing the facets, and thence calculate their distances from the Origin, which would be the altitudes of the Pyramids. Also it was evident that a sample Pyramid would suffice. I worked out a value for the Volume, that first night; but the thing got into a tangle, and I felt pretty sure I had got it wrong.

The next night I began again, and worked it all through from the beginning. In the morning the *answer* was clear in my memory, and I wrote it down at once ; and did not write out the Problem, and its solution, until later in the day, when I was well pleased to find the written proof confirm the result I had arrived at in the hours of darkness.

It is not, perhaps, much to be wondered at that, when these Problems came to be re-written and arranged for publication, a good many mistakes were discovered. Some were so bad as quite to spoil the solutions in which they occurred : these Problems I have omitted altogether. The others I have corrected, in the solutions as given in Chapter III : but, that I may not be credited with an amount of accuracy, as a computator, which I am well aware I do not possess, I here append a list of them.

In No. 7, in the denominator ' $2 \frown A$ ', I forgot the ' 2 '.*

In No. 10, I failed to notice that the 3 coins might *also* be a half-crown and 2 shillings.

In No. 13, in the last line but one, I put ' $2bc \cdot ca$ ', instead of ' $4bc \cdot ca$ '.

In No. 32, I brought out the arithmetical value as ' 358520 ', instead of ' 358550 '.

In No. 38, I got the decimal wrong, making it ·476 instead of ·478, and thus brought out the answer as ·042 instead of ·044.

In No. 44, I said that the denominator would be of the form $(10^n - 1) \cdot 10^m$. This last factor is superfluous : i. e. $m = 0$.

---

* In the trigonometrical Problems, I have used the symbols $\frown$ and $\frown$, to represent the words ' sine ' and ' cosine '.

In No. 50, I made a mistake near the end, bringing out $\frac{41}{108}$, instead of $\frac{50}{108}$.

In No. 55, I put 'tan' for 'sin'.

In No. 57, in the last paragraph, I replaced the denominator '$a \frown B \frown C$' by (what I imagined to be its equivalent) '$2m$'. Apparently I was under the delusion that '$a \frown B \frown C$' was the same thing as '$\frown A . b c$'!

In No. 70, section (3), I forgot to add in the ·45, thus making the answer half a degree wrong. And, in section (4), I forgot to add in the 53, thus again making the answer half a degree wrong.

Let me, in conclusion, gratefully acknowledge the valuable assistance I have received from Mr. F. G. Brabant, M.A., of Corpus Christi College, Oxford, who has most patiently and carefully gone through my proofs, first working out each result independently, and has thus detected many mistakes which had escaped my notice. He has also supplied, for No. 59, a much neater answer than mine, viz. $\dfrac{abc}{3} . \sqrt{\triangle A \triangle B \triangle C}$.

Other mistakes may perchance, having eluded us both, await the penetrating glance of some critical reader, to whom the joy of discovery, and the intellectual superiority which he will thus discern, in himself, to the author of this little book, will, I hope, repay to some extent the time and trouble its perusal may have cost him!

C. L. D.

CH. CH., OXFORD.
May, 1893.

CONTENTS.

—◆—

SUBJECTS CLASSIFIED.

———♦♦———

ARITHMETIC. No. 31.

ALGEBRA:—
    Equational Problems. Nos. 8, 25, 39, 52, 68.
    Series. Nos. 21, 32.
    Indeterminate Equations. No. 47.
    Properties of Numbers. Nos. 1, 14, 29, 44, 61.
    Chances. Nos. 5, 10, 16, 19, 23, 27, 38, 41, 45, 50, 58, 66.

PURE GEOMETRY, PLANE. Nos. 2, 3, 9, 15, 17, 18, 20, 24, 26, 30, 34, 35, 36, 40, 46, 51, 57, 62, 64, 71.

TRIGONOMETRY:—
    Plane. Nos. 4. 6, 7, 11, 12, 13, 18, 22, 28, 37, 42, 43, 48, 54, 55, 56, 57, 60, 65, 69.
    Solid. Nos. 49, 59, 63, 70.

ALGEBRAICAL GEOMETRY:—
    Plane. No. 53.
    Solid. No. 67.

DIFFERENTIAL CALCULUS:—
    Maxima and Minima. No. 33.

TRANSCENDENTAL PROBABILITIES. No. 72.

PILLOW-PROBLEMS.

CHAPTER I.

Questions.

1. (28)*

Find a general formula for two squares whose sum = 2.

[24/3/84

2. (29)

In a given Triangle to place a line parallel to the base, such that the portions of sides, intercepted between it and the base, shall be together equal to the base.

3. (30)

If the sides of a Tetragon pass through the vertices of a Parallelogram, and if three of them are bisected at those vertices: prove that the fourth is so also.

4. (30)

In a given acute-angled Triangle inscribe a Triangle, whose sides make, at each of the vertices, equal angles with the sides of the given Triangle.   [19/4/76

---

* The numerals, placed in parentheses, indicate the pages where the corresponding matter may be found.

5. (19, 31)

A bag contains one counter, known to be either white or
black. A white counter is put in, the bag shaken, and
a counter drawn out, which proves to be white. What is
now the chance of drawing a white counter?   [8/9/87

6. (19, 32)

Given lengths of lines drawn, from vertices of Triangle,
to middle points of opposite sides, to find its sides and
angles.

7. (19, 33)

Given 2 adjacent sides, and the included angle, of a
Tetragon; and that the angles, at the other ends of these
2 sides, are right: find (1) remaining sides, (2) area.

[4 or 5/89

8. (20, 34)

Some men sat in a circle, so that each had 2 neighbours;
and each had a certain number of shillings. The first had
1/ more than the second, who had 1/ more than the third,
and so on. The first gave 1/ to the second, who gave 2/ to
the third, and so on, each giving 1/ more than he received,
as long as possible. There were then 2 neighbours, one of
whom had 4 times as much as the other. How many men
were there? And how much had the poorest man at first?

[3/89

9. (35)

Given two Lines meeting at a Point, and given a Point
lying within the angle contained by them: draw, from the
given Point, two lines, at right angles to each other, and

forming with the given Lines and the line joining their intersection to the given Point, two equal Triangles.

[11/76

10. (20, 36)

A triangular billiard-table has 3 pockets, one in each corner, one of which will hold only one ball, while each of the others will hold two. There are 3 balls on the table, each containing a single coin. The table is tilted up, so that the balls run into one corner, it is not known which. The 'expectation', as to the contents of the pocket, is 2/6. What are the coins? [8/90

11. (20, 36)

A Triangle ABC has another $A'B'C'$ inscribed in it, so that $\angle BA'C' = \angle CB'A' = \angle AC'B' = \theta$; thus making it

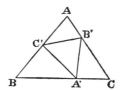

similar to the first Triangle. Find ratio between homologous sides. And solve for "$\theta = 90°$".

The Triangles can be proved similar thus :—

$$\angle C'A'B' + \angle B'A'C = \text{supp. of } \theta,$$
$$\angle B'A'C + \angle A'CB' = \text{supp. of } \theta;$$

∴ these pairs are equal; ∴ $\angle C'A'B' = C$.

Hence $\angle A'B'C' = A$, and $\angle B'C'A' = B$.

Let $C'A' = ka$; ∴ $A'B' = kb$, and $B'C' = kc$. We have to find k. [31/3/82

12. (20, 37)

Given the semi-perimeter and the area of a Triangle, and also the volume of the cuboid whose edges are equal to the sides of the Triangle : find the sum of the squares of its sides.   [23/1/91

13. (20, 38)

Given the lengths of the radii of two intersecting Circles, and the distance between their centres: find the area of the Tetragon formed by the tangents at the points of intersection.   [3/89

14. (39)

Prove that 3 times the sum of 3 squares is also the sum of 4 squares.   [2/12/81

15. (39)

If a Figure be such that the opposite angles of every inscribed Tetragon are supplementary : the Figure is a Circle.   [3/91

16. (20, 40)

There are two bags, one containing a counter, known to be either white or black ; the other containing 1 white and 2 black. A white is put into the first, the bag snaken, and a counter drawn out, which proves to be white. Which course will now give the best chance of drawing a white— to draw from one of the two bags without knowing which it is, or to empty one bag into the other and then draw ?

[10/87

17. (40)

In a given Triangle place a line parallel to the base, such that if, from its ends, lines be drawn, parallel to the

sides and terminated by the base, they shall be together
equal to the first line.   [3/89

18. $(21, 41)$

Find a Point, in the base of a given Triangle, such that,
if from it perpendiculars be dropped upon the sides, the
line joining their extremities shall be parallel to the base.
(1) Trigonometrically. (2) Geometrically.   [11/89

19. $(21, 42)$

There are 3 bags ; one containing a white counter and a
black one, another two white and a. black, and the third
3 white and a black. It is not known in what order the
bags are placed. A white counter is drawn from one of
them, and a black from another. What is the chance
of drawing a white counter from the remaining bag ?

20. (43)

In the base of a given Triangle find a Point such that if
from it two lines be drawn, terminated by the sides, one
being perpendicular to the base and one to the left-hand
side, they shall be equal.   [5/88

21. $(21, 44)$

Sum, (1) to n terms, (2) to 100 terms, the series
$$1 . 3 . 5 + 2 . 4 . 6 + \&c.$$ [7/4/89

22. $(21, 45)$

Given the 3 'altitudes' of a Triangle : find its (1) sides,
(2) angles, (3) area.   [4/6/89

23. $(21, 46)$

A bag contains 2 counters, each of which is known to be
black or white. 2 white and a black are put in, and 2

white and a black drawn out. Then a white is put in, and a white drawn out. What is the chance that it now contains 2 white?   [25/9/87

24. (21, 47)

If, from the vertices of a triangle ABC, the lines AD, BE,

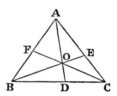

CF be drawn, intersecting at O: find the ratio $\dfrac{DO}{DA}$ in terms of the two ratios $\dfrac{EO}{EB}$, $\dfrac{FO}{FC}$.

[5/86

25. (22, 48)

If 'ϵ', 'a', 'λ' represent proper fractions; and if, in a certain hospital, 'ϵ' of the patients have lost an eye, 'a' an arm, and 'λ' a leg: what is the least possible number who have lost all three?   [7/2/76

26. (48)

Within a given Triangle place a similar Triangle, whose area shall have to its area a given ratio less than unity, whose sides shall be parallel to its sides, and whose vertices shall be equidistant from its vertices.   [4/89

27. (22, 50)

There are 3 bags, each containing 6 counters; one contains 5 white and one black; another, 4 white and 2 black; the third, 3 white and 3 black. From two of the bags (it is not known which) 2 counters are drawn, and prove to be black and white. What is the chance of drawing a white counter from the remaining bag? [4/3/80

28. (22, 50)

If the sides of a given Triangle, taken cyclically, be divided in extreme and mean ratio ; and if the Points be joined : find the ratio which the area of the Triangle, so formed, has to the area of the given Triangle. [12/78

29. (51)

Prove that the sum of 2 different squares, multiplied by the sum of 2 different squares, gives the sum of 2 squares in 2 different ways. [3/12/81

30. (52)

In a given Triangle, to place a line parallel to the base, such that if from its extremities lines be drawn, to the base, parallel to the sides, they shall be together double of the inscribed Line. [15/3/89

31. (22, 53)

On July 1, at 8 a.m. by my watch, it was $8h.\ 4m.$ by my clock. I took the watch to Greenwich, and, when it said ' noon ', the true time was $12h.\ 5m.$ That evening, when the watch said ' $6h.$', the clock said ' $5h.\ 59m.$'

On July 30, at 9 a.m. by my watch, it was $8h.\ 57m.$ by my clock. At Greenwich, when the watch said ' $12h.\ 10m.$', the true time was $12h.\ 5m.$ That evening, when the watch said ' $7h.$' the clock said ' $6h.\ 58m.$'

My watch is only wound up for each journey, and goes

uniformly during any one day : the clock is always going, and goes uniformly.

How am I to know when it is *true* noon on July 31 ?

$$\left[\frac{14}{3}/89\right.$$

32. $(22, 53)$

Sum the Series $1 . 5 + 2 . 6 +$ &c. (1) to n terms ; (2) to 100 terms. $\left[\frac{7}{4}/89\right.$

33. (54)

Inscribe in a given Circle the maximum Tetragon having 2 parallel sides, one double the other.

34. (55)

From a given Point draw 2 Lines, one to the centre of a given Circle, and the other cutting off from it a Segment containing an angle equal to that between the Lines.

$$\left[21/12/74\right.$$

35. (56)

With a given Triangle, to describe a Circle, cutting each side in two points, such that, if radii be drawn perpendicular to the sides, they are divided by the sides in given ratios. $\left[11/76\right.$

36. (57)

In a given Triangle, to draw a line, from a Point on one side of it, to a Point on the other side, perpendicular to one of these sides, and equal to the sum of the portions, of these sides, intercepted between it and the base. $\left[3/89\right.$

37. $(\overset{1}{2}2, 58)$

Two given Circles intersect, so that their common chord subtends angles of 30° and 60° at their centres. What fraction of the smaller Circle is within the larger ? $\left[12/91\right.$

38. (22, 60)

There are 3 bags, '*A*', '*B*', and '*C*'. '*A*' contains 3 red counters, '*B*' 2 red and one white, '*C*' one red and 2 white. Two bags are taken at random, and a counter drawn from each: both prove to be red. The counters are replaced, and the experiment is repeated with the same two bags: one proves to be red. What is the chance of the other being red?   [3/76

39. (22, 60)

A and *B* begin, at 6 a. m. on the same day, to walk along a road in the same direction, *B* having a start of 14 miles, and each walking from 6 a. m. to 6 p. m. daily. *A* walks 10 miles, at a uniform pace, the first day, 9 the second, 8 the third, and so on: *B* walks 2 miles, at a uniform pace, the first day, 4 the second, 6 the third, and so on. When and where are they together?   [16/3/78

40. (61)

In a given Triangle, whose base-angles are acute, draw two lines, at right angles to the base, and together equal to the line drawn, from the vertex, at right angles to the base, and such that

(1) they are equidistant from the line drawn from the vertex;

(2) they are equidistant from the ends of the base.

[5/76

41. (23, 62)

My friend brings me a bag containing four counters, each of which is either black or white. He bids me draw two, both of which prove to be white. He then says

" I meant to tell you, before you began, that there was at least *one* white counter in the bag. However, you know it now, without my telling you. Draw again."

(1) What is now my chance of drawing white?

(2) What would it have been, if he had not spoken?

[9/87

42. (23, 63)

If the angles of a given Triangle be bisected, and if lines be drawn, through its vertices, at right angles to the bisectors, so as to form a fresh Triangle : find the ratio of the area of this Triangle to the area of the given Triangle.   [17/5/78

43. (65)

From the ends of the base of a given Triangle draw two lines, intersecting, terminated by the sides, and forming an isosceles Triangle at the base, and a Tetragon, equal to it, at the vertex.   [2/82

44. (66)

If a, b be two numbers prime to each other, a value may be found for n which will make $(a^n - 1)$ a multiple of b.   [18/3/81

45. (23, 67)

If an infinite number of rods be broken : find the chance that one at least is broken in the middle.   [5/84

46. (68)

In a given Triangle, whose base is divided at a given Point, inscribe a Triangle, having its angles equal to given angles, and having an assigned vertex at the given Point.   [19/11/87

47. (23, 69)

Solve the 2 Indeterminate Equations

$$\left. \begin{aligned} \frac{x}{y} &= x - z \; ; \\[2mm] \frac{x}{z} &= x - y \; ; \end{aligned} \right\} \qquad \begin{aligned} &(1) \\[2mm] &(2) \end{aligned}$$

and find the limits, if any, between which the *real* values lie.   [12/90

48. (70)

If semicircles be described, externally, on the sides of a given Triangle ; and if their common tangents be drawn ; and if their lengths be a, β, γ : prove that

$$\left(\frac{\beta\gamma}{a} + \frac{\gamma a}{\beta} + \frac{a\beta}{\gamma} \right)$$

is equal to the semiperimeter of the Triangle.   [9/2/81

49. (23, 72)

If four equilateral Triangles be made the sides of a square Pyramid : find the ratio which its volume has to that of a Tetrahedron made of the Triangles.   [16/11/86

50. (23, 72)

There are 2 bags, H and K, each containing 2 counters : and it is known that each counter is either black or white. A white counter is added to bag H, the bag is shaken up, and one counter transferred (without looking at it) to bag K, where the process is repeated, a counter being transferred to bag H. What is now the chance of drawing a white counter from bag H?

51. (74)

From a given Point, in one side of a given Triangle, to draw a line, terminated by the other side, so that, if from its ends lines be drawn at right angles to the base, their sum shall be equal to the first line. [12/81

52. (23, 75)

Five beggars sat down in a circle, and each piled up, in a heap before him, the pennies he had received that day : and the five heaps were equal.

Then spake the eldest and wisest of them, unfolding, as he spake, an empty sack.

"My friends, let me teach you a pretty little game ! First, I name myself ' Number One,' my left-hand neighbour ' Number Two,' and so on to ' Number Five.' I then pour into this sack the whole of my earnings for the day, and hand it on to him who sits next but one on my left, that is, ' Number Three.' *His* part in the game is to take out of it, and give to his two neighbours, so many pennies as represent their names (that is, he must give four to ' Number Four ' and two to ' Number Two '); he must then put *into* the sack half as much as it contained when he received it ; and he must then hand it on just as I did, that is, he must hand it to him who sits next but one on his left—who will of course be ' Number Five.' *He* must proceed in the same way, and hand it on to 'Number Two,' from whom the sack will find its way to ' Number Four,' and so to me again. If any player cannot furnish, from his own heap, the whole of what he has to put into the sack, he is at liberty to draw upon any of the other heaps, *except mine* ! "

The other beggars entered into the game with much enthusiasm: and in due time the sack returned to 'Number One,' who put into it the two pennies he had received during the game, and carefully tied up the mouth of it with a string. Then, remarking "it is a *very* pretty little game," he rose to his feet, and hastily quitted the spot. The other four beggars gazed at each other with rueful countenances. Not one of them had a penny left!

How much had each at first?   [16/2/89

53. (24, 76)

In a triangular billiard-table, a Point is given by its trilinear co-ordinates. A ball, starting from the given Point, strikes the three sides, and returns to the starting-point. Find, in terms of the trilinear co-ordinates and of the angles of the Triangle, the Point where the ball strikes the second side.   [6/4/89

54. (24, 78)

Cut off, from a given Triangle, by lines parallel to the sides, 3 Triangles, so that the remaining Hexagon may be equilateral. Also find the lengths of its sides in terms of the sides of the given Triangle: and the ratios in which the sides of the given Triangle are divided.   [18/4/86

55. (79)

Given three cylindrical towers on a Plane: find a Point, on the Plane, from which they shall look the same width.   [20/12/74

56. (24, 80)

Given the 3 altitudes of a Triangle: construct it.

[27/6/84

57. (25, 80)

In a given Triangle describe three Squares, whose bases shall lie along the sides of the Triangle, and whose upper edges shall form a Triangle;

(1) geometrically; (2) trigonometrically.   [27/1/91

58. (25, 83)

Three Points are taken at random on an infinite Plane. Find the chance of their being the vertices of an obtuse-angled Triangle.   [20/1/84

59. (25, 84)

Given a Tetrahedron, having every edge equal to the opposite edge, so that its facets are all (when looked at from the outside) identically equal : find its volume in terms of its edges.   [8/90

60. (25, 87)

Given a Triangle ABC, and that its base BC is divided at D in the ratio m to n : find the angles BAD, CAD.

[21/3/90

61. (89)

Prove that, if any 3 Numbers be taken, which cannot be arranged in $A. P.$, and whose sum is a multiple of 3, the sum of their squares is also the sum of another set of 3 squares, the 2 sets having no common term.   [1/12/81

62. (91)

Given two Lines meeting at a Point, and given a Point lying within the angle contained by them : draw a line, through the given Point, and forming, with the given Lines, the least possible Triangle.   [12/76

63. (26, 92)

Given 2 equal Squares, in different horizontal planes, having their centres in the same vertical line, and so placed that the sides of each are parallel to the diagonals of the other, and at such a distance apart that, by joining neighbouring vertices, 8 equilateral Triangles are formed : find the volume of the solid thus enclosed.   [3, 4/9/90

64. (94)

Given a Triangle, and a Point within it such that its distance from one of the sides is less than its distance from either of the others : describe a Circle, with given Point as centre, such that its intercepts on the sides may be equal to the sides of a right-angled Triangle.   [18/12/74

65. (95)

How many shapes are there for Triangles which have all their angles aliquot parts of 360° ?   [5/89

66. (26, 97)

Given that there are 2 counters in a bag, as to which all that was originally known was that each was either white or black.   Also given that the experiment has been tried, a certain number of times, of drawing a counter, looking at it, and replacing it ; that it has been white every time ; and that, as a result, the chance of drawing white, next time, is $\dfrac{a}{a+\beta}$.   Also given that the same experiment is repeated m times more, and that it still continues to be white every time.   What would then be the chance of drawing white ?   [9/89

67. (26, 100)

If a regular Tetrahedron be placed, with one vertex downwards, in a socket which exactly fits it, and be turned round its vertical axis, through an angle of 120°, raising it only so much as is necessary, until it again fits the socket: find the Locus of one of the revolving vertices.   [27/1/72

68. (26, 101)

Five friends agreed to form themselves into a Wine-Company (Limited). They contributed equal amounts of wine, which had been bought at the same price. They then elected one of themselves to act as Treasurer; and another of them undertook to act as Salesman, and to sell the wine at 10 % over cost-price.

The first day the Salesman drank one bottle, sold some, and handed over the receipts to the Treasurer.

The second day he drank none, but pocketed the profits on one bottle sold, and handed over the rest of the receipts to the Treasurer.

That night the Treasurer visited the Cellars, and counted the remaining wine. "It will fetch just £11," he muttered to himself as he left the Cellars.

The third day the Salesman drank one bottle, pocketed the profits on another, and handed over the rest of the receipts to the Treasurer.

The wine was now all gone: the Company held a Meeting, and found to their chagrin that their profits (i. e. the Treasurer's receipts, less the original value of the wine) only cleared 6*d.* a bottle on the whole stock. These profits had accrued in 3 equal sums on the 3 days (i. e. the Treasurer's receipts for the day, less the original value of the wine taken out during the day, had come to the same amount every time); but of course only the Salesman knew this.

(1) How much wine had they bought? (2) At what price?   [28/2/89

69. (26, 102)

If, from each of the angles of a given Triangle ABC, taken cyclically, a certain proper fraction of it be cut off, the arithmetical values of the 3 fractions being represented by 'k, l, m'; and if it be given that the Triangle, formed by the lines so drawn, is similar to the given one, the angle, formed by the lines drawn from B and C, being equal to A, and so on: find k, l, m, as similar functions of a single variable. Also find the ratio which each side of the second Triangle bears to the corresponding side of the first.   [8/89

70. (27, 105)

Let an equilateral and equiangular Tetrahedron be placed with one facet in front: and suppose a series of triangles, equal to that facet, constructed in the Plane containing that facet, and having a base common with it; and that they are all wrapped round the Tetrahedron as far as they will go. Find (1) the locus of their vertices; (2) the situation of the vertex of the one whose left-hand base-angle is 15°; (3) the left-hand base-angle of the one which (wrapped round towards the right) covers portions of all four facets of the Tetrahedron, and whose vertex coincides with *its* vertex; (4) the left-hand base-angle of the one which (similarly treated) occupies all four facets, and then the front and right-hand facet for the second time, and whose vertex coincides with the distal vertex of the base of the Tetrahedron.

71. (108)

In a given Triangle place a Hexagon having its opposite sides equal and parallel, and three of them lying along the sides of the Triangle, and such that its diagonals intersect in a given Point.   [14/12/74

72. (27, 109)

A bag contains 2 counters, as to which nothing is known except that each is either black or white. Ascertain their colours without taking them out of the bag.   [8/9/87

CHAPTER II.

Answers.

---

5. $(2, 31)$

Two-thirds.

6. $(2, 32)$

Calling the sides '$2a$', '$2b$', '$2c$', and the lines 'a', 'β', 'γ', we have

$$a^2 = \frac{-a^2 + 2\beta^2 + 2\gamma^2}{9},$$

$$\frown A = \frac{5a^2 - \beta^2 - \gamma^2}{2\sqrt{2a^2 - \beta^2 + 2\gamma^2} \cdot \sqrt{2a^2 + 2\beta^2 - \gamma^2}}.$$

7. $(2, 33)$

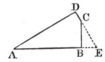

Let AB, AD be given sides, and B, D the right $\angle$s; and let $AB = b$, $AD = d$.

(1) $\quad BC = \dfrac{d - b \frown A}{\frown A}$; $\quad CD = \dfrac{b - d \frown A}{\frown A}$;

(2) $\quad$ area $= \dfrac{2bd - (b^2 + d^2) \frown A}{2 \frown A}$.

8. (2, 34)

7 men; 2 shillings.

10. (3, 36)

Either 2 florins and a sixpence; or else a half-crown and 2 shillings.

11. (3, 36)

The required ratio is equal to

$$\frac{\frown A \frown B \frown C}{\frown \theta \left(1 + \smile A \smile B \smile C\right) + \smile \theta \frown A \frown B \frown C}.$$

If $\theta = 90°$, this $= \dfrac{\frown A \frown B \frown C}{1 + \smile A \smile B \smile C}.$

12. (4, 37)

If $s =$ semi-perimeter, $m =$ area, $v =$ volume; then

$$a^2 + b^2 + c^2 = 2 \cdot \left(s^2 - \frac{v}{s} - \frac{m^2}{s^2}\right).$$

13. (4, 38)

If '$2M$' $=$ area of Tetragon whose vertices are the Centres and the Points of intersection; and if its sides be 'a', 'b', and its diagonal, joining the Centres, 'c': required area

$$= \frac{32 M^3}{\left(b^2 + c^2 - a^2\right) \cdot \left(c^2 + a^2 - b^2\right)}.$$

16. (4, 40)

The first course gives chance $= \frac{1}{2}$; the second, $\frac{5}{12}$. Hence the first is best.

18. $(5, 41)$

(1) Divide base BC, at E, so that $\dfrac{BE}{EC} = \dfrac{\frown 2C}{\frown 2B}$.

(2) At B, C, make right angles ABD, ACD; and join AD cutting BC at E, which is the required Point.

19. $(5, 42)$

Eleven-seventeenths.

21. $(5, 44)$

(1) $\dfrac{n \cdot \overline{n+1} \cdot \overline{n+4} \cdot \overline{n+5}}{4}$;   (2) 27,573,000.

22. $(5, 45)$

Calling the given altitudes ' a, β, γ '; and the fraction

$$\dfrac{2\,a^2\,\beta^2\,\gamma^2 \cdot (a^2 + \beta^2 + \gamma^2) - (\beta^4\,\gamma^4 + \gamma^4\,a^4 + a^4\,\beta^4)}{4\,a^4\,\beta^4\,\gamma^4} \cdot k^2 \,,$$

(1) $a = \dfrac{1}{k a}$, &c.;

(2) $\frown A = k\,\beta\gamma$, &c.;

(3) area $= \dfrac{1}{2\,k}$.

23. $(5, 46)$

Two-fifths.

24. $(6, 47)$

$\dfrac{DO}{DA} + \dfrac{EO}{EB} + \dfrac{FO}{FC} = 1$; whence any one can be found in terms of the other two.

25. (6, 48)

$\epsilon + a + \lambda - 2$.

27. (6, 50)

Seventeen-twentyfifths.

28. (7, 50)

$7 - 3\sqrt{5}$.

31. (7, 53)

When the clock says '$12h.\ 2m.\ 29\frac{277}{288}\ sec.$'

32. (8, 53)

(1) $\dfrac{n \cdot (n+1) \cdot (2n+13)}{6}$;

(2) 358550.

37. (8, 58)

$\dfrac{4 + \sqrt{3}}{12} - \dfrac{1 + \sqrt{3}}{2\pi}$; i. e. about ·044.

38. (9, 60)

Fortynine-seventytwoths.

39. (9, 60)

They meet at end of $2d.\ 6h.$, and at end of $4d.$: and the distances are 23 miles, and 34 miles.

41. $(9, 62)$

(1) Seven-twelfths. (2) One-half.

42. $(10, 63)$

$$\frac{abc}{2\,(s-a)\,.\,(s-b)\,.\,(s-c)}$$

45. $(10, 67)$

·6321207 &c.

47. $(11, 69)$

One set of values is 0, 0, 0.

A 2nd set is $x = y = 0$; z has any value.

A 3rd is $x = z = 0$; y has any value.

And the 4th set is $x = \dfrac{k^2}{k-1}, y = z = k$; where k has any value.

If x has any positive value less than 4, y and z are unreal.

49. $(11, 72)$

Two.

50. $(11, 72)$

Seventeen-twentysevenths.

52. $(12, 75)$

$2l.$ $18s.$ $0d.$

53. (13, 76)

The portion, cut off from the second side, is equal to

$$\frac{(a \frown C + \gamma \frown A)\ (2\gamma \triangle A + \beta)}{a \triangle C + \gamma \triangle A + \beta} + \frac{\beta \triangle A + \gamma \triangle 2A}{\frown A}.$$

54. (13, 78)

Side AB must be divided at D, G, so that

$$AD : DG : GB :: \frac{1}{a} : \frac{1}{c} : \frac{1}{b};$$

and similarly for the other sides. Also each side of the

Hexagon $= \dfrac{1}{\dfrac{1}{a} + \dfrac{1}{b} + \dfrac{1}{c}}.$

56. (13, 80)

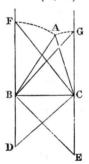

Draw BC, CE, BD equal to the given altitudes, so as to form right $\angle$s at B and C: and produce DB, EC. Join DC, and draw $CF \perp$ to it. Join EB, and draw $BG \perp$ to it. With centre B, and distance BF, describe a circle : with centre C, and distance CG describe another : let them meet at A : and join AB, AC. Triangle ABC may be proved to be similar to required Triangle. The rest of the construction is obvious.

57. (14, 80)

(1) *Geometrically.*

If Squares be described externally on the sides of the given Triangle; and if their outer edges be produced to form a new Triangle; and if the sides of the given Triangle be divided similarly to those of the new Triangle: their central portions will be the bases of the required Squares.

(2) *Trigonometrically.*

If a, b, c be the sides of the given Triangle, and m its area; and if x, y, z be the sides of the required Squares: then

$$\frac{a}{x} = \frac{b}{y} = \frac{c}{z} = \frac{a^2 + b^2 + c^2}{2m} + 1.$$

58. (14, 83)

$$\frac{3}{8 - \dfrac{6\sqrt{3}}{\pi}}.$$

59. (14, 84)

Calling lengths of the 3 pairs of edges 'a, b, c', and the corresponding ∠s, in each facet, 'A, B, C'; volume =

$$\frac{abc}{6} \cdot \sqrt{1 - (\triangle^2 A + \triangle^2 B + \triangle^2 C) + 2\triangle A \triangle B \triangle C}.$$

60. (14, 87)

$$\text{Cot } BAD = \frac{(m + n)\cot A + n\cot B}{m};$$

$$\text{similarly, cot } CAD = \frac{(m + n)\cot A + m\cot C}{n}.$$

63. $\left(15,\ 92\right)$

If each side of each Square $= 2$, the volume $=$

$$\frac{8\,.\,2^{\frac{1}{4}}\,.\,\left(\sqrt{2}+1\right)}{3}.$$

66. $\left(15,\ 97\right)$

$$\frac{2^m.\left(a-\beta\right)+\beta}{2^m.\left(a-\beta\right)+2\,\beta}.$$

67. $\left(16,\ 100\right)$

If the centre of the horizontal facet be taken as the Origin, and if the X-axis pass through one of the vertices of that facet, and the Y-axis be parallel to the opposite edge of that facet, and the Z-axis be perpendicular to that facet: and if the altitude (measured downwards) of the Tetrahedron be called ' h ', and the intercept on the X-axis be called ' a ': the Equations to the Locus are

$$\left(x+\sqrt{3}\,.\,y\right).\left(h-z\right) = ah\,;$$
$$x^2+y^2 = a^2.$$

68. $\left(16,\ 101\right)$

(1) 5 dozen ;   (2)   8/4 a bottle.

69. $\left(17,\ 102\right)$

(1) $k = \dfrac{\theta-B}{A}$; $l = \dfrac{\theta-C}{B}$; $m = \dfrac{\theta-A}{C}$.

(2) Calling new Triangle ' $A'B'C'$ ',

$$\frac{a'}{a} = \frac{b'}{b} = \frac{c'}{c} = 2 \smallfrown \theta.$$

70. (17, 105)

(1) Down the back-edge; up again; and so on.
(2) about ·7 of the way down the back-edge. (3) About
18·65°. (4) About 14·53°.

72. (18, 109)

One is black, and the other white.

CHAPTER III.

Solutions.

———◆———

1. (1)

Let u, v be the Nos.

Then $u^2 + v^2 = 2$.

Evidently '$(1+k), (1-k)$' is a form for the squares.

Also, if we write '$2m^2$' for '2' (which will not interfere with the problem, as we can divide by m^2, and get $\dfrac{u^2}{m^2} + \dfrac{v^2}{m^2} = 2$),

the above form becomes '$(m^2+k), (m^2-k)$'.

Now, as these are *squares*, their resemblance to

$$'(a^2+b^2+2\,ab), (a^2+b^2-2\,ab)'$$

at once suggests itself; so that the problem depends on the known one of finding a, b, such that (a^2+b^2) is a square; and we can then take $2\,ab$ as k.

A general form for this is

$$a = x^2 - y^2,$$
$$b = 2\,xy;$$
$$\therefore\ a^2 + b^2 = (x^2 + y^2)^2;$$

$\therefore$ the formula '$u^2 + v^2 = 2m^2$' becomes

$$(x^2 - y^2 + 2\,xy)^2 + (x^2 - y^2 - 2\,xy)^2 = 2\,(x^2 + y^2)^2;$$

i.e. $\left(\dfrac{x^2 - y^2 + 2\,xy}{x^2 + y^2}\right)^2 + \left(\dfrac{x^2 - y^2 - 2\,xy}{x^2 + y^2}\right)^2 = 2.$

Q. E. F.

2. (1)

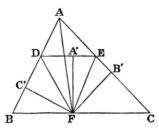

(Analysis.)

Let ABC be the Triangle, and DE the required line, so that $BD + CE = BC$.

From BC cut off BF equal to BD; then $CF = CE$.

Join DF, EF.

Now $\angle BDF = \angle BFD = [\text{by I. 29}] \angle FDE$;

Similarly $\angle CEF = \angle FED$;

∴ $\angle$s BDE, CED, are bisected by DF, EF, and F is centre of $\odot$ escribed to $\triangle ADE$.

Drop, from F, $\perp$s on BD, DE, EC; then these $\perp$s are equal.

Hence, if AF be joined, it bisects $\angle A$.

Hence construction.

(Synthesis.)

Bisect $\angle A$ by AF: from F draw FB', FC', $\perp AC$, AB: also draw $FA' \perp BC$ and equal to FB': and through A' draw $DE \perp FA'$, i. e. $\parallel BC$. Then DE shall be line required.

∵ $\angle$s at A', B', C', are right, and $FA' = FB' = FC'$,

∴ $\angle$s BDE, CED, are bisected by DF, EF.

Now $\angle BFD = \angle FDA'$; ∴ it $= \angle BDF$; ∴ $BF = BD$;

Similarly $CF = CE$; ∴ $BC = BD + CE$.

Q. E. F.

3. (1)

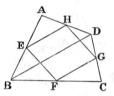

Let *ABCD* be the Tetragon; and let the 3 sides, *AB*, *BC*, *CD*, be bisected by vertices of the Parallelogram *EFGH*.

Join *BD*.

∵, in Triangle *BCD*, sides *BC*, *CD* are bisected at *F* and *G*,

∴ *FG* is parallel to *BD*;

but *EH* is parallel to *FG*;

∴ *EH* is parallel to *BD*;

∴ Triangles *AEH*, *ABD* are similar;

now *AE* is half of *AB*;

∴ *AH* is half of *AD*.

Q. E. D.

4. (1)

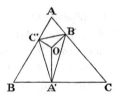

Let *ABC* be the given Triangle, and *A'B'C'* the required Triangle, so that ∠*BA'C'* = ∠*CA'B'*, &c.

Evidently *A'C'*, *A'B'* are equally inclined to a line drawn, from A', $\perp BC$; and so of the others : i.e. these $\perp$s bisect the $\angle$s at A', B', C' ;

$\therefore$ they meet in the same Point. Draw them; let them meet at O; and call the $\angle C'A'B'$ ' $2\,a$ ', and so on.

Now $(\beta+\gamma) = \pi - \angle B'OC' = A$;

$\therefore 2A = 2\,(\beta+\gamma) = \pi - 2\,a$;

$\therefore a = 90° - A$;

$\therefore \angle BA'C' = A.$

Similarly, $\angle BC'A' = C.$

$\therefore$ Triangle $BC'A'$ is similar to Triangle BCA ; and so of the others ;

$$\therefore \quad BA' = \frac{c}{a}\,.\,BC' = \frac{c}{a}\,.\,(c - AC'),$$

$$= \frac{c}{a}\,.\,\Big(c - \frac{b}{c}\,.\,AB'\Big),$$

$$= \frac{c^2}{a} - \frac{b}{a}\,.\,(b - CB'),$$

$$= \frac{c^2}{a} - \frac{b^2}{a} + \frac{b}{a}\,.\,\frac{a}{b}\,.\,CA',$$

$$= \frac{c^2}{a} - \frac{b^2}{a} + a - BA';$$

$$\therefore 2\,BA' = \frac{c^2 + a^2 - b^2}{a} = \frac{2\,ca \,\frown B}{a};$$

$$\therefore BA' = c \frown B ;$$

$\therefore A'$ is foot of $\perp$ drawn, from A, to BC. Hence the construction is obvious.

$$\text{Q. E. F.}$$

5. $(2,\ 19)$

At first sight, it would appear that, as the state of the bag, *after* the operation, is necessarily identical with its state *before* it, the chance is just what it then was, viz. $\frac{1}{2}$. This, however, is an error.

The chances, *before* the addition, that the bag contains (*a*) 1 white (*b*) 1 black, are (*a*) $\frac{1}{2}$ (*b*) $\frac{1}{2}$. Hence the chances, *after* the addition, that it contains (*a*) 2 white (*b*) 1 white, 1 black, are the same, viz. (*a*) $\frac{1}{2}$ (*b*) $\frac{1}{2}$. Now the probabilities, which these 2 states give to the observed event, of drawing a white counter, are (*a*) certainty (*b*) $\frac{1}{2}$. Hence the chances, after drawing the white counter, that the bag, before drawing, contained (*a*) 2 white, (*b*) 1 white, 1 black, are proportional to (*a*) $\frac{1}{2}$. 1 (*b*) $\frac{1}{2}$. $\frac{1}{2}$; i.e. (*a*) $\frac{1}{2}$ (*b*) $\frac{1}{4}$; i.e. (*a*) 2 (*b*) 1. Hence the chances are (*a*) $\frac{2}{3}$ (*b*) $\frac{1}{3}$. Hence, after the removal of a white counter, the chances, that the bag now contains (*a*) 1 white (*b*) 1 black, are for (*a*) $\frac{2}{3}$ and for (*b*) $\frac{1}{3}$.

Thus the chance, of now drawing a white counter, is $\frac{2}{3}$.

Q. E. F.

6. (2, 19)

Call sides ' $2a$, $2b$, $2c$ ', and lines in question ' α, β, γ '.

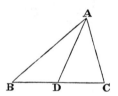

Now $\triangle ADB + \triangle ADC = 0$;

$$\therefore \quad \frac{a^2 + a^2 - 4c^2}{2\,aa} + \frac{a^2 + a^2 - 4b^2}{2\,aa} = 0 ;$$

$$\therefore \quad 2a^2 + 2a^2 - 4b^2 - 4c^2 = 0 ;$$

$$\therefore \quad a^2 = -a^2 + 2b^2 + 2c^2.$$

Similarly, $\quad \beta^2 = 2a^2 - b^2 + 2c^2$;

$$\gamma^2 = 2a^2 + 2b^2 - c^2.$$

To eliminate b, c, let us multiply by k, l, m, so taken that

$$2k - l + 2m = 0,$$

and $\quad 2k + 2l - m = 0 \;;$

$$\therefore \; 3(l - m) = 0 \;; \text{ i. e. } l = m \;;$$

$$\therefore \; 2k = -l = -m \;;$$

hence we may make $k = -1, \; l = 2, \; m = 2 \;;$

$$\therefore \; -a^2 + 2\beta^2 + 2\gamma^2 = 9a^2 \;;$$

i. e. $\quad a^2 = \dfrac{-a^2 + 2\beta^2 + 2\gamma^2}{9} \;;$

$\therefore \; BC$ (which $= 2a$) $= \frac{2}{3}\sqrt{-a^2 + 2\beta^2 + 2\gamma^2}$, &c.,

which gives lengths of sides.

Also $\; \angle A = \dfrac{b^2 + c^2 - a^2}{2bc}$

$$= \dfrac{2a^2 - \beta^2 + 2\gamma^2 + 2a^2 + 2\beta^2 - \gamma^2 + a^2 - 2\beta^2 - 2\gamma^2}{2 \cdot \sqrt{2a^2 - \beta^2 + 2\gamma^2} \cdot \sqrt{2a^2 + 2\beta^2 - \gamma^2}}$$

$$= \dfrac{5a^2 - \beta^2 - \gamma^2}{\text{den.}} \;; \text{ and so for other angles.}$$

Q. E. F.

7. (2, 19)

Let AB, AD be given sides, and B, D the right $\angle$s; and let $AB = b$, $AD = d$.

Produce DC to meet AB-produced at E.

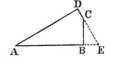

Now $AE = AD \cdot \sec A = d \sec A \;;$

$\therefore \; BE = d \sec A - b.$

Also $BC = BE \cdot \tan E = (d \sec A - b) \cdot \cot A,$

$$= \dfrac{d - b \, \angle A}{\frown A} \;;$$

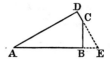

similarly, $CD = \dfrac{b - d \frown A}{\frown A}$; which answers (1).

Also area $= \frac{1}{2} \cdot (AB \cdot BC + AD \cdot DC)$,

$$= \frac{1}{2} \cdot \frac{b \cdot (d - b \frown A) + d \cdot (b - d \frown A)}{\frown A},$$

$$= \frac{2\,bd - (b^2 + d^2)\,\frown A}{2 \frown A}; \text{ which answers (2).}$$

Q. E. F.

8. (2, 20)

Let m = No. of men, k = No. of shillings possessed by the last (i. e. the poorest) man. After one circuit, each is a shilling poorer, and the moving heap contains m shillings. Hence, after k circuits, each is k shillings poorer, the last man now having nothing, and the moving heap contains mk shillings. Hence the thing ends when the last man is again called on to hand on the heap, which then contains $(mk + m - 1)$ shillings, the penultimate man now having nothing, and the first man having $(m - 2)$ shillings.

It is evident that the first and last man are the only 2 neighbours whose possessions can be in the ratio '4 to 1'. Hence either

$$mk + m - 1 = 4\,(m - 2),$$

or else $\qquad 4\,(mk + m - 1) = m - 2.$

The first equation gives $mk = 3m - 7$, i. e. $k = 3 - \dfrac{7}{m}$, which evidently gives no integral values other than $m = 7$, $k = 2$.

The second gives $4mk = 2 - 3m$, which evidently gives no positive integral values.

Hence the answer is ' 7 men ; 2 shillings '.

9. (2)

Let AB, AC, be the given Lines, and P the given Point ;

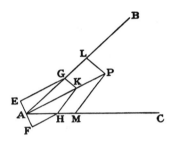

and join AP.

Through A draw EAF, $\perp AP$, and bisected at A ; from E, F, draw EG, FH, parallel to AP, and meeting AB, AC, at G, H ; join GH, and on it describe a semicircle cutting AP at K ; and join KG, KH. Then $\angle GKH$ is a right angle. From P draw PL, PM, parallel to KG, KH.

Now Triangle APL has, to Triangle AKG, the duplicate ratio of AP to AK ;

but so also has triangle APM to Triangle AKH ;

also Triangles AKG, AKH, are equal, being on the same base AK, and having equal altitudes AE, AF ;

$\therefore$ Triangles APL, APM are equal : and $\angle LPM$ is evidently equal to $\angle GKH$; $\therefore$ it is a right angle.

Q. E. F.

10. (3, 20)

Call them x, y, z; and let $x + y + z = s$.

The chance, that the pocket contains 2 balls, is $\frac{2}{3}$; and, if it does, the 'expectation' is the average value of

$$(y + z), \ (z + x), \ (x + y) \ ; \ \text{i. e. it is } \frac{2s}{3}.$$

Also the chance, that it contains only one, is $\frac{1}{3}$; and, if it does, the 'expectation' is $\dfrac{s}{3}$.

Hence total 'expectation' $= \dfrac{4s}{9} + \dfrac{s}{9} = \dfrac{5s}{9}.$

$$\therefore \ \frac{5s}{9} = 30d. \ ; \quad \therefore \ s = 54d. = 4/6.$$

Hence the coins must be 2 florins and a sixpence; or else a half-crown and 2 shillings.

Q. E. F.

11. (3, 20)

Now $\dfrac{BA'}{A'C'} = \dfrac{\frown (B + \theta)}{\frown B}$; and $\dfrac{A'C}{A'B'} = \dfrac{\frown \theta}{\frown C}.$

$\therefore \ \ BA = \dfrac{\frown (B + \theta)}{\frown B} \cdot ka$; and $A'C = \dfrac{\frown \theta}{\frown C} \cdot kb$

but $BA' + A'C = a$; $\ \therefore \ k$

$$= \frac{a}{\dfrac{a \cdot \frown (B + \upsilon)}{\frown B} + \dfrac{b \frown \theta}{\frown C}} = \frac{\frown A}{\dfrac{\frown A \ \frown (B + \theta)}{\frown B} + \dfrac{\frown B \frown \theta}{\frown C}}$$

$$= \frac{\frown A \frown B \frown C}{\frown A \ \frown (B + \theta) \frown C + \frown^2 B \frown \theta}$$

$$= \frac{\frown A \frown B \frown C}{\frown A \frown C (\frown B \smile \theta + \smile B \frown \theta) + (1 - \smile^2 B) \frown \theta}$$

$$= \frac{\frown A \frown B \frown C}{\frown \theta + \frown \theta (\frown A \frown C \smile B - \smile^2 B) \atop + \smile \theta \frown A \frown B \frown C}$$

$$= \frac{\frown A \frown B \frown C}{\frown \theta + \frown \theta \smile B (\frown A \frown C + \smile (A + C)) \atop + \smile \theta \frown A \frown B \frown C}$$

$$= \frac{\frown A \frown B \frown C}{\frown \theta (1 + \smile A \smile B \smile C) + \smile \theta \frown A \frown B \frown C}.$$

Q. E. F.

COR. Let $\theta = 90°$; then $k = \dfrac{\frown A \frown B \frown C}{1 + \smile A \smile B \smile C}.$

12. (4, 20)

Let $s = $ semi-perimeter, $m = $ area, $v = $ volume.

We know that $m = \sqrt{s \cdot (s-a) \cdot (s-b) \cdot (s-c)}$;

$\therefore \quad m^2 = s \cdot (s-a) \cdot (s-b) \cdot (s-c)$;

$\therefore \quad \dfrac{m^2}{s} = s^3 - s^2 \cdot (a+b+c) + s \cdot (bc + ca + ab) - abc$;

$\qquad = s^3 - 2s^3 + s \cdot (bc + ca + ab) - v$;

$\therefore \quad \dfrac{m^2}{s^2} + \dfrac{v}{s} + s^2 = bc + ca + ab$;

$\therefore \quad 2 \cdot \left(\dfrac{m^2}{s^2} + \dfrac{v}{s} + s^2 \right) = (a+b+c)^2 - (a^2+b^2+c^2)$;

$\qquad = 4s^2 - (a^2+b^2+c^2)$;

$\therefore \quad a^2 + b^2 + c^2 = 2 \cdot \left(s^2 - \dfrac{v}{s} - \dfrac{m^2}{s^2} \right).$

Q. E. F.

13. $\left(4, \, 20\right)$

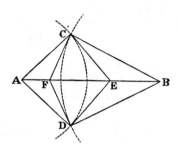

Let A, B, be the centres of the Circles; C, D, their points of intersection; and $CFDE$ the Tetragon whose area is required.

Let the sides of the Triangle ABC be a, b, c; and its ∠s a, β, γ.

Then $CE = b \cdot \tan a$, and $CF = a \cdot \tan \beta$.

Also $\angle FCE = \angle ACE + \angle FCB - \gamma = \pi - \gamma$;

$\therefore \frown FCE = \frown \gamma$.

Hence area of Triangle $FCE = \frac{1}{2} \cdot ab \cdot \tan a \cdot \tan \beta \cdot \frown \gamma$;

$\therefore$ area of Tetragon $= \dfrac{ab \frown a \frown \beta \frown \gamma}{\triangle a \triangle \beta}$.

Now, writing ' M ' for area of Triangle ABC, we have

$$\frown a = \frac{2M}{bc}, \ \frown \beta = \frac{2M}{ca}, \ \frown \gamma = \frac{2M}{ab};$$

$\therefore$ area of Tetragon $= ab \cdot \dfrac{8M^3}{a^2 b^2 c^2} \cdot \dfrac{4bc \cdot ca}{(b^2 + c^2 - a^2)(c^2 + a^2 - b^2)}$;

$$= \frac{32M^3}{(b^2 + c^2 - a^2) \cdot (c^2 + a^2 - b^2)}.$$

Q. E. F.

14. (4)

This simply expresses the identity

$3 (a^2 + b^2 + c^2)$

$= (a+b+c)^2 + (b^2 - 2bc + c^2) + (c^2 - 2ca + a^2) + (a^2 - 2ab + b^2);$

$= (a+b+c)^2 + (b-c)^2 + (c-a)^2 + (a-b)^2.$

Q. E. D.

Numerical Examples (not thought out).

$$3 (1^2 + 2^2 + 3^2) = 6^2 + 1^2 + 2^2 + 1^2.$$
$$3 (1^2 + 3^2 + 7^2) = 11^2 + 4^2 + 6^2 + 2^2.$$

15. (4)

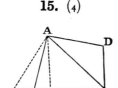

Let $ABCD$ be an inscribed Tetragon.   Join AC: and about Triangle ACD describe a Circle.

Now, if this Circle does not pass through B, let it cut CB, or CB produced, in B' or B''.   Join AB', AB''.

Then $\angle AB'C$, or $\angle AB''C$, is supplementary to $\angle ADC$;

∴ it $= \angle ABC$; which is absurd;

∴ this Circle does pass through B.

The same thing may be proved for any other Point on that portion, of the perimeter of the given Figure, which lies on the same side of AC as the Point D.

Similarly for the other portion.

Hence the Figure is a Circle.

Q. E. D.

16. (4, 20)

The 'a priori' chances of possible states of first bag are 'W, $\frac{1}{2}$; B, $\frac{1}{2}$'. Hence chances, after putting W in, are 'WW, $\frac{1}{2}$; WB, $\frac{1}{2}$'. The chances, which these give to the 'observed event', are 1, $\frac{1}{2}$. Hence chances of possible states 'W, B', after the event, are proportional to 1, $\frac{1}{2}$; i.e. to 2, 1; i.e. their actual values are $\frac{2}{3}$, $\frac{1}{3}$.

Now, in first course, chance of drawing W is $\frac{1}{2} \cdot \frac{2}{3} + \frac{1}{2} \cdot \frac{1}{3}$; i.e. $\frac{1}{2}$.

And, in second course, chances of possible states '$WWBB$, $WBBB$' are $\frac{2}{3}$, $\frac{1}{3}$: hence chance of drawing W is $\frac{2}{3} \cdot \frac{1}{2} + \frac{1}{3} \cdot \frac{1}{4}$; i.e. $\frac{5}{12}$.

Hence *first* course gives best chance.

Q. E. F.

17. (4)

(*Analysis.*)

Let ABC be the given Triangle, and DE the line required.

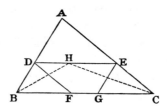

From D, E, draw DF, EG, parallel to the sides. Then $DF + EG = DE$.

Because BE is a Parallelogram, $\therefore DB = EG$;

similarly $EC = DF$;

$\therefore DB + EC = DE$.

Hence construction.

(*Synthesis.*)

Bisect ∠s *B*, *C*, by *BH*, *CH*, meeting at *H* ; through *H* draw *DE* parallel to *BC* ; and from *D*, *E*, draw *DF*, *EG*, parallel to *AC*, *AB*.

Because *DE* is parallel to *BC*,

∴ ∠*DHB* = alternate ∠*HBF* = ∠*DBH* ;

∴ *DB* = *DH*.

Similarly *EC* = *EH*.

∴ *DB* + *EC* = *DE*.

Because *BE*, *DC* are Parallelograms,

∴ *EG* = *DB*, and *DF* = *EC* ;

∴ *DF* + *EG* = *DE*.

Q. E. F.

18. (5, 21)

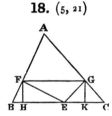

(1) Call required Point *E*. From *E* draw *EF*, *FG* ⊥ sides. Join *FG*. From *F*, *G*, draw *FH*, *GK* ⊥ *BC*. Call *BE* '*x*', and *EC* '*y*'.

Now *FH* must = *GK*.

Also *EF* = *x* ⌒ *B* ; and *FH* = *EF* ⌒ *FEH*,

= *EF* ⌒ *B*,

= *x* ⌒ *B* ⌒ *B* ;

similarly, *GK* = *y* ⌒ *C* ⌒ *C*.

But *FH* = *GK* ; ∴ *x* ⌒ *B* ⌒ *B* = *y* ⌒ *C* ⌒ *C* ;

$$\therefore \frac{x}{y} = \frac{\frown 2C}{\frown 2B}.$$

Q. E. F.

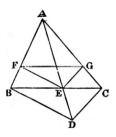

(2) At B, C, make right angles ABD, ACD; and join AD, cutting BC at E. From E draw EF, $EG \perp$ sides; and join FG.

$\therefore$ BD, FE are $\perp AB$, $\therefore$ they are $\parallel$; $\therefore$ $AF : FB :: AE : ED$;

$\therefore$ CD, GE are $\perp AC$, $\therefore$ they are $\parallel$; $\therefore$ $AG : GC :: AE : ED$;

$\therefore$ $AF : FB :: AG : GC$;

$\therefore$ FG is parallel to BC.

Q. E. F.

19. (5, 21)

Call the bags A, B, C; so that A contains a white counter and a black one; &c.

The chances of the orders ABC, ACB, BAC, BCA, CAB, CBA, are, a priori, $\frac{1}{6}$ each. Since they are equal, we may, instead of multiplying each by the probability it gives to the observed event, simply assume those probabilities as being proportional to the chances *after* the observed event.

These probabilities are :—

$$\text{for} \quad ABC, \ \tfrac{1}{2} \times \tfrac{1}{3}; \ \text{i.e.} \ \tfrac{1}{6}.$$

$$ACB, \ \tfrac{1}{2} \times \tfrac{1}{4}; \ \text{i.e.} \ \tfrac{1}{8}.$$

$$BAC, \ \tfrac{2}{3} \times \tfrac{1}{2}; \ \text{i.e.} \ \tfrac{1}{3}.$$

$$BCA, \ \tfrac{2}{3} \times \tfrac{1}{4}; \ \text{i.e.} \ \tfrac{1}{6}.$$

$$CAB, \ \tfrac{3}{4} \times \tfrac{1}{2}; \ \text{i.e.} \ \tfrac{3}{8}.$$

$$CBA, \ \tfrac{3}{4} \times \tfrac{1}{3}; \ \text{i.e.} \ \tfrac{1}{4}.$$

Hence the chances are proportional to 4, 3, 8, 4, 9, 6 ; i. e. they are these Nos. divided by 34.

Hence the chance, of drawing a white counter from the remaining bag; is

$$\tfrac{1}{34} \cdot \{4 \times \tfrac{3}{4} + 3 \times \tfrac{2}{3} + 8 \times \tfrac{3}{4} + 4 \times \tfrac{1}{2} + 9 \times \tfrac{2}{3} + 6 \times \tfrac{1}{2}\} ;$$

i. e. $\tfrac{1}{34} \times \{3 + 2 + 6 + 2 + 6 + 3\}$; i. e. $\tfrac{22}{34}$; i. e. $\tfrac{11}{17}$.

20. (5)

(*Analysis.*)

Let ABC be the given Triangle, and P the required Point. Draw $PQ \perp BC$, and $PR \perp AB$. Then $PQ = PR$.

Hence $PC \tan C = PB \frown B$;

$\therefore PC : PB :: \frown B : \tan C$, (draw AD $\perp BC$,)

$$:: \frac{AD}{AB} : \frac{AD}{DC},$$

$$:: DC : AB.$$

Hence construction.

(*Synthesis.*)

From A draw $AD \perp BC$. Produce BA to E, making AE equal to DC. Join EC. From A draw AP parallel to EC; and from P draw $PQ \perp BC$, and $PR \perp AB$.

Then
$$\frac{PQ}{PC} = \frac{AD}{DC} = \frac{AD}{AB} \cdot \frac{AB}{DC},$$
$$= \frac{PR}{PB} \cdot \frac{AB}{AE},$$
$$= \frac{PR}{PB} \cdot \frac{PB}{PC} = \frac{PR}{PC};$$
$$\therefore PQ = PR.$$

Q. E. F.

21. $\left(5,\ 21\right)$

(1) The nth term is $n \cdot \overline{n+2} \cdot \overline{n+4}$;

$\therefore$ the $(n+1)$th term is $\overline{n+1} \cdot \overline{n+3} \cdot \overline{n+5}$;

$= (n+1) \cdot (\overline{n+2}+1) \cdot (n+5)$;

$= \overline{n+1} \cdot \overline{n+2} \cdot \overline{n+5} + \overline{n+1} \cdot \overline{n+5}$

$= \overline{n+1} \cdot \overline{n+2} \cdot (\overline{n+3}+2) + \overline{n+1} \cdot (\overline{n+2}+3)$;

$= \overline{n+1} \cdot \overline{n+2} \cdot \overline{n+3} + 2 \cdot \overline{n+1} \cdot \overline{n+2} + \overline{n+1} \cdot \overline{n+2}$

$\qquad\qquad\qquad\qquad\qquad +3 \cdot \overline{n+1}$;

$= \overline{n+1} \cdot \overline{n+2} \cdot \overline{n+3} + 3 \cdot \overline{n+1} \cdot \overline{n+2} + 3 \cdot \overline{n+1}.$

$\therefore S = \dfrac{n \cdot \overline{n+1} \cdot \overline{n+2} \cdot \overline{n+3}}{4} + n \cdot \overline{n+1} \cdot \overline{n+2} + \tfrac{3}{2} \cdot n \cdot \overline{n+1} + C$;

and $C = 0$.

$\therefore S = n \cdot \overline{n+1} \cdot \left(\dfrac{n^2+5n+6}{4} + n + 2 + \tfrac{3}{2}\right)$;

$\qquad = n \cdot \overline{n+1} \cdot \dfrac{n^2+9n+20}{4} = \dfrac{n \cdot \overline{n+1} \cdot \overline{n+4} \cdot \overline{n+5}}{4}.$

Q. E. F.

(2) S, to 100 terms,

$\qquad = \dfrac{100 \cdot 101 \cdot 104 \cdot 105}{4} = 100 \cdot 101 \cdot 26 \cdot 105$;

now $101 \cdot 105 = 10{,}605$;

$\therefore\ 101 \cdot 105 \cdot 13 = 130{,}000 + 7800 + 65 = 137{,}865$;

and twice this $= 274{,}000 + 1730 = 275{,}730$;

$\therefore\ S = 27{,}573{,}000.$

Q. E. F.

22. (5, 21)

Call given altitudes 'a, β, γ'.

Now $aa = b\beta = c\gamma$;

$\therefore a \sin A = \beta \sin B = \gamma \sin C$;

$\therefore \dfrac{\sin A}{\beta\gamma} = \dfrac{\sin B}{\gamma a} = \dfrac{\sin C}{a\beta} = k \text{ (say)}$;

$\therefore \sin A = k\beta\gamma, \quad \sin B = k\gamma a, \quad \sin C = ka\beta$.

Now $\sin(A+B) = \sin C$;

$\therefore \sin A \cos B + \cos A \sin B = \sin C$;

$\therefore \sin A \cos B = \sin C - \cos A \sin B$;

$\therefore \sin^2 A\,(1 - \sin^2 B) = \sin^2 C + \sin^2 B\,(1 - \sin^2 A)$
$$- 2 \sin C \cos A \sin B;$$

$\therefore \sin^2 A - \sin^2 A\,\sin^2 B = \sin^2 C + \sin^2 B - \sin^2 A\,\sin^2 B$
$$- 2 \sin B \sin C \cos A;$$

$\therefore \sin^2 A - \sin^2 B - \sin^2 C = -2 \sin B \sin C \cos A$;

$\therefore$, squaring, $(\sin^4 A + \&\text{c.}) - 2 \sin^2 A\,\sin^2 B - 2 \sin^2 A\,\sin^2 C$
$$+ 2 \sin^2 B\,\sin^2 C = 4 \sin^2 B\,\sin^2 C\,(1 - \sin^2 A);$$

$\therefore (\sin^4 A + \&\text{c.}) - 2'(\sin^2 B\,\sin^2 C + \&\text{c.})$
$$+ 4 \sin^2 A\,\sin^2 B\,\sin^2 C = 0;$$

$\therefore$, substituting for $\sin A$, &c., and dividing by k^4,

$(\beta^4\gamma^4 + \&\text{c.}) - 2 a^2\beta^2\gamma^2.\,(a^2 + \&\text{c.}) + 4k^2 a^4\beta^4\gamma^4 = 0$;

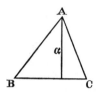

$$\therefore \; k^2 = \frac{2\,a^2\,\beta^2\,\gamma^2\,(a^2 + \&c.) - (\beta^4\,\gamma^4 + \&c.)}{4\,a^4\,\beta^4\,\gamma^4}.$$

Now $\frown A = k\beta\gamma$, &c.; which answers (2).

Also $a = b \frown C$; and similarly $\gamma = a \frown B$;

$$\therefore \; a = \frac{\gamma}{\frown B} = \frac{\gamma}{k\gamma a} = \frac{1}{ka}, \text{ \&c.; which answers (1).}$$

Also area $= \dfrac{bc \frown A}{2} = \dfrac{1}{2} \cdot \dfrac{1}{k\beta} \cdot \dfrac{1}{k\gamma} \cdot k\beta\gamma = \dfrac{1}{2\,k}$;

which answers (3).   Q. E.

23. (5, 21)

The original chances, as to states of bag, are

$$\text{for} \quad 2\ W \quad . \quad . \quad . \quad . \quad . \quad \tfrac{1}{4};$$
$$1\ W,\ 1\ B \quad . \quad . \quad . \quad \tfrac{1}{2};$$
$$2\ B \quad . \quad . \quad . \quad . \quad . \quad \tfrac{1}{4}.$$

$\therefore$ the chances, after adding $2\ W$ and $1\ B$, are

$$\text{for} \quad 4\ W,\ 1\ B . \quad . \quad . \quad . \quad \tfrac{1}{4};$$
$$3\ W,\ 2\ B . \quad . \quad . \quad . \quad \tfrac{1}{2};$$
$$2\ W,\ 3\ B . \quad . \quad . \quad . \quad \tfrac{1}{4}.$$

Now the chances, which these give to the observed event, drawing $2\ W$ and $1\ B$, are $3, \tfrac{3}{5}, \tfrac{3}{10}$.

$\therefore$ the chances, after this event, are proportional to $\tfrac{3}{20}, \tfrac{3}{10}, \tfrac{3}{40}$

i. e. to 2, 4, 1.   Hence they are $\tfrac{2}{7}, \tfrac{4}{7}, \tfrac{1}{7}$.

Hence the chances, as to states, now are

$$\text{for} \quad 2\ W \quad . \quad . \quad . \quad . \quad . \quad \tfrac{2}{7}\,;$$
$$1\ W,\ 1\ B \quad . \quad . \quad . \quad . \quad \tfrac{4}{7}\,;$$
$$2\ B \quad . \quad . \quad . \quad . \quad . \quad \tfrac{1}{7}.$$

$\therefore$ the chances, after adding 1 W, are

$$\text{for} \quad 3\ W \quad . \quad . \quad . \quad . \quad . \quad \tfrac{2}{7}\,;$$
$$2\ W,\ 1\ B \quad . \quad . \quad . \quad . \quad \tfrac{4}{7}\,;$$
$$1\ W,\ 2\ B \quad . \quad . \quad . \quad . \quad \tfrac{1}{7}.$$

Now the chances, which these give to the observed event, of drawing 1 W, are 1, $\tfrac{2}{3}$, $\tfrac{1}{3}$.

$\therefore$ the chances, after this event, are proportional to $\tfrac{2}{7}$, $\tfrac{8}{21}$, $\tfrac{1}{21}$;

i. e. to 6, 8, 1.   Hence they are $\tfrac{6}{15}$, $\tfrac{8}{15}$, $\tfrac{1}{15}$.

Hence the chance, that the bag now contains 2 white, is $\tfrac{6}{15}$; i. e. $\tfrac{2}{5}$.

Q. E. F.

24. $\left(6,\ 21\right)$

Because $\dfrac{DO}{OA} = \dfrac{\triangle DOC}{\triangle OAC} = \dfrac{\triangle DOB}{\triangle OAB} = \dfrac{\triangle OBC}{\triangle OCA + \triangle OAB};$

$\therefore \quad \dfrac{DO}{DA} = \dfrac{\triangle OBC}{\triangle ABC}.$

Similarly, $\dfrac{EO}{EB} = \dfrac{\triangle OCA}{\triangle ABC}$, and $\dfrac{FO}{FC} = \dfrac{\triangle OAB}{\triangle ABC}.$

Hence $\dfrac{DO}{DA} + \dfrac{EO}{EB} + \dfrac{FO}{FC} = 1.$

Q. E. F.

25. (6, 22)

Let ' E ' mean 'having lost an eye ', ' A ' 'having lost an arm ', and ' L ' 'having lost a leg '.

Then the state of things which gives the least possible number of those who, being E and A, are also L, may evidently be found by arranging the patients in a row, so that the EA-class may begin from one end of the row, and the L-class from the other end, and counting the portion where they overlap; and, the smaller the EA-class, the smaller will be this common portion : hence we must make the EA-class a minimum.

This may be done by re-arranging the patients, so that the E-class may begin from one end of the row, and the A-class from the other : and the least possible number for the EA-class is the common portion, i. e. $(\epsilon - \overline{1-a})$, i. e. $(\epsilon + a - 1)$.

Then, as already shown, the least possible number for the EAL-class is the common portion, i. e. $(\epsilon + a - 1 - \overline{1 - \lambda})$, i. e. $(\epsilon + a + \lambda - 2)$.

Q. E. F.

26. (6)

(*Analysis.*)

Let ABC be the given Triangle, and $A'B'C'$ the required one ; and let the ratio, which $B'C'$ has to BC, be ' k ' ; so that k is less than 1.

Since $BB' = CC'$, and that BC, $B'C'$, are parallel, it may easily be proved, by dropping perpendiculars from B', C', upon BC, which must necessarily be equal, that $\angle$s $B'BC$, $C'CB$, are equal.

Similarly, $\angle$s $A'AC$, $C'CA$, are equal ; and so are $\angle$s $A'AB$, $B'BA$.

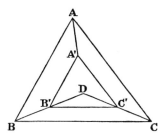

Call $\angle B'BC$ 'θ'; then $\angle C'CB = \theta$;

$\therefore \angle C'CA = C - \theta = \angle A'AC$;

$\therefore \angle A'AB = A - (C - \theta) = \angle B'BA$.

Now $\angle$s $B'BC$, $B'BA$, together $= B$;

$\therefore \theta + A - (C - \theta) = B$;

$\therefore 2\theta = B + C - A = 180° - 2A$;

$\therefore \theta = 90° - A$.

Hence, if BB', CC', be produced to meet at D, Triangle DBC will be isosceles, with a vertical $\angle$ equal to $2A$.

Now, if a Circle be drawn about ABC, and its centre joined to B and C, the Triangle, so formed, will fulfil the same conditions;

hence the centre of this Circle will be D;

hence the construction.

(Synthesis.)

Bisect the sides, and draw perpendiculars, meeting at D. Join D to the vertices B, C. From DB cut off $DB' = k \cdot DB$. From B' draw $B'C'$ parallel to BC.

Then $B'C'$ is easily proved equal to $k \cdot BC$.

And if, from B', C', parallels to AB, AC, be drawn, it may easily be proved that they meet on DA, and that they are respectively equal to $k \cdot AB$, $k \cdot AC$.

Q. E. F.

27. (6, 22)

Call the bags A, B, C.

If remaining bag be A, chance of observed event $= \frac{1}{2}$ chance of drawing white from B and black from $C + \frac{1}{2}$ chance of drawing black from B and white from C:

i. e. it $= \frac{1}{2} \cdot \{\frac{2}{3} \times \frac{1}{2} + \frac{1}{3} \times \frac{1}{2}\} = \frac{1}{4}$.

Similarly, if remaining bag be B, it is $\frac{1}{2} \cdot \{\frac{5}{6} \cdot \frac{1}{2} + \frac{1}{6} \cdot \frac{1}{2}\} = \frac{1}{4}$; and, if it be C, it is $\frac{1}{2} \cdot \{\frac{5}{6} \cdot \frac{1}{3} + \frac{1}{6} \cdot \frac{2}{3}\} = \frac{7}{36}$.

$\therefore$ chances of remaining bag being A, B, or C, are as $\frac{1}{4}$ to $\frac{1}{4}$ to $\frac{7}{36}$; i. e. as 9 to 9 to 7. $\therefore$ they are, in value, $\frac{9, 9, 7}{25}$.

Now, if remaining bag be A, chance of drawing white from it is $\frac{5}{6}$; $\therefore$ chance, on this issue, is $\frac{5}{6} \cdot \frac{9}{25} = \frac{3}{10}$; similarly, for B, it is $\frac{2}{3} \cdot \frac{9}{25} = \frac{6}{25}$; and, for C, $\frac{1}{2} \cdot \frac{7}{25} = \frac{7}{50}$. And entire chance of drawing white from the remaining bag is the sum of these; i. e. $\frac{15 + 12 + 7}{50} = \frac{34}{50} = \frac{17}{25}$.

28. (7, 22)

Let ABC be the given Triangle; and let its sides be divided internally at A', B', C', in extreme and mean ratio.

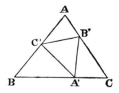

And let M be the area of ABC.

Let $BA' = x$; then $x^2 = a \cdot (a-x)$;

i. e. $x^2 + ax - a^2 = 0$;

$\therefore x = \dfrac{-a \pm a\sqrt{5}}{2} = \dfrac{a}{2} \cdot (\sqrt{5} - 1)$, the other sign being excluded by the terms of the question.

Then area of Triangle $AB'C'$

$$= \tfrac{1}{2} \cdot \frac{c}{2} \cdot (\sqrt{5}-1) \cdot \{b - \frac{b}{2} \cdot (\sqrt{5}-1)\} \cdot \sin A,$$

$$= \tfrac{1}{8} \cdot (\sqrt{5}-1)(3-\sqrt{5}) \, bc \cdot \sin A,$$

$$= \tfrac{1}{4} \cdot (4\sqrt{5}-8) \cdot M = (\sqrt{5}-2) \cdot M.$$

Similarly for $BC'A'$ and $CA'B'$.

Hence the sum of these 3 Triangles $= 3 \cdot (\sqrt{5}-2) \cdot M$, and area of Triangle $A'B'C' = (7-3\sqrt{5}) \cdot M$.

Q. E. F.

29. (7)

This may be deduced from the identity

$$(a^2+b^2) \cdot (c^2+d^2) = a^2c^2 + b^2d^2 + a^2d^2 + b^2c^2.$$

$(a^2+b^2) \cdot (c^2+d^2) = a^2c^2 + b^2d^2 + a^2d^2 + b^2c^2 ;$

$$= a^2c^2 + b^2d^2 + 2\,acbd + a^2d^2 + b^2c^2 - 2\,adbc, \left.\right\}$$

or else $\quad = a^2c^2 + b^2d^2 - 2\,acbd + a^2d^2 + b^2c^2 + 2\,adbc ; \left.\right\}$

i. e. $\qquad = (ac+bd)^2 + (ad-bc)^2, \left.\right\}$

or else $\qquad = (ac-bd)^2 + (ad+bc)^2. \left.\right\}$

Now, if these last 2 sets are *identical*, $(ac+bd)$ must $= (ad+bc)$; for it cannot $= (ac-bd)$;

i. e., $a\,(c-d) - b\,(c-d)$ must $= 0$;

i. e., $(a-b) \cdot (c-d)$ must $= 0$;

i. e., one or other of the first 2 sets is the sum of 2 *identical* squares.

Hence, contranominally, if *each* of the original sets consists of 2 *different* squares, their product gives the sum of 2 squares in 2 *different* ways.

Q. E. D.

30. (7)

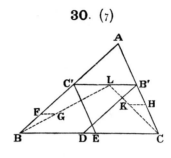

(*Analysis.*)

Let ABC be the Triangle: and suppose $B'C'$ so placed that $B'D$, $C'E$, drawn parallel to the sides, shall together $= 2\,B'C'$.

By Euc. I. 34, $B'D = C'B$, and $C'E = B'C$:

$$\therefore\ B'C + C'B = 2\,B'C'.$$

Hence, if $B'L$ be cut off equal to half $B'C$, $C'L =$ half $C'B$.

Hence construction.

(*Synthesis.*)

In BC' take any point F: draw FG, $\parallel BC$, and equal to half BF: and join BG.

Similarly, in CB' take any point H: draw HK, $\parallel BC$, and equal to half HC: and join CK.

Produce BG, CK, to meet at L: and through L draw $C'B' \parallel BC$: and from B', C', draw $B'D$, $C'E$, $\parallel$ the sides.

$\because\ FG =$ half FB; $\therefore$, by similar Triangles, $C'L =$ half $C'B$;

Similarly $B'L =$ half $B'C$;

$\therefore\ C'B' =$ half sum of $C'B$, $B'C$; i. e. $C'B + B'C = 2\,B'C'$.

But, by Euc. I. 34, $C'B = B'D$, and $B'C = C'E$;

$\therefore\ B'D + C'E = 2\,B'C'$.

Q. E. F.

31. $(7, 22)$

On July 1, watch gained on clock $5\,m.$ in $10\,h.$; i. e. $\frac{1}{2}m.$ per hour; i. e. $2\,m.$ in $4\,h.$ Hence, when watch said 'noon', clock said '$12\,h.$ $2\,m.$'; i. e. clock was $3\,m.$ slow of true time, when *true* time was $12\,h.$ $5\,m.$

On July 30, watch lost on clock $1\,m.$ in $10\,h.$; i.e. $6\,sec.$ per hour; i. e. $19\,sec.$ in $3\,h.$ $10\,m.$ Hence, when watch said '$12\,h.$ $10\,m.$', clock said '$12\,h.$ $7\,m.$ $19\,sec.$'; i. e. clock was $2\,m.$ $19\,sec.$ fast of *true* time, when true time was $12\,h.$ $5\,m.$

Hence clock gains, on *true* time, $5\,m.$ $19\,sec.$ in 29 days; i. e. $319\,sec.$ in 29 days; i. e. $11\,sec.$ per day; i. e. $\dfrac{11}{24 \times 12}$ $sec.$ in $5\,m.$

Hence, while *true* time goes $5\,m.$, watch goes $5\,m.$ $\frac{11}{288}\,sec.$

Now, when *true* time is $12\,h.$ $5\,m.$ on July 31, clock is $(2\,m.\ 19\,sec. + 11\,sec.)$ fast of it; i. e. says '$12\,h.$ $7\frac{1}{2}\,m.$' Hence, if *true* time be put $5\,m.$ back, clock must be put $5\,m.$ $\frac{11}{288}\,sec.$ back ; i. e. must be put back to $12\,h.$ $2\,m.$ $29\frac{277}{288}\,sec.$

Hence, on July 31, when clock indicates this time, it is *true* noon.

Q. E. F.

32. $(8, 22)$

The nth term is $n.(n+4)$;

$\therefore$ the $(n+1)$th term is $(n+1).(n+5) = (n+1).\{(n+2)+3\}$,
$$= (n+1).(n+2)+3\,(n+1);$$

$\therefore S_n = \dfrac{n.(n+1).(n+2)}{3} + 3.\dfrac{n.(n+1)}{2} + C;$ and $C = 0;$

$\therefore S_n = n.(n+1).\left(\dfrac{n+2}{3}+\dfrac{3}{2}\right) = \dfrac{n.(n+1).(2n+13)}{6}.$

Q. E. F.

Also $S_{100} = \dfrac{100 \cdot 101 \cdot 213}{6} = \dfrac{100 \cdot 101 \cdot 71}{2} = \dfrac{100 \cdot 7171}{2}$

$$= \dfrac{717100}{2} = 358550.$$

Q. E. F.

33. (8)

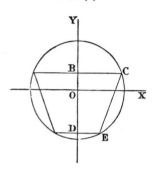

Let $DE = x$; $\therefore BC = 2x$.

Area $= 3x \cdot (\sqrt{r^2 - x^2} + \sqrt{r^2 - 4x^2}) = $ max.

let $v = x \cdot (\sqrt{r^2 - x^2} + \sqrt{r^2 - 4x^2}) = $ max.

$\therefore \dfrac{dv}{dx} = \sqrt{r^2 - x^2} + \sqrt{r^2 - 4x^2} - x^2 \cdot \left(\dfrac{1}{\sqrt{r^2 - x^2}} + \dfrac{4}{\sqrt{r^2 - 4x^2}} \right)$
$$= 0;$$

$\therefore (r^2 - x^2) \cdot \sqrt{r^2 - 4x^2} + (r^2 - 4x^2) \cdot \sqrt{r^2 - x^2}$
$$= x^2 \cdot (4\sqrt{r^2 - x^2} + \sqrt{r^2 - 4x^2});$$

$\therefore (r^2 - 2x^2) \cdot \sqrt{r^2 - 4x^2} = -(r^2 - 8x^2) \cdot \sqrt{r^2 - x^2};$

$\therefore r^4 - 4(r^2 x^2 + 4x^4) \cdot (r^2 - 4x^2)$
$$= (r^4 - 16r^2 x^2 + 64x^4) \cdot (r^2 - x^2);$$

$\therefore r^6 - 8r^4 x^2 + 20r^2 x^4 - 16x^6$
$$= r^6 - 17r^4 x^2 + 80r^2 x^4 - 64x^6;$$

∴, omitting r^6, and dividing by x^2,

$$48x^4 - 60r^2x^2 + 9r^4 = 0;$$

i. e. $16x^4 - 20r^2x^2 + 3r^4 = 0;$

∴ $\dfrac{x^2}{r^2} = \dfrac{20 \pm \sqrt{208}}{3^2} = \dfrac{5 - \sqrt{13}}{8}$ (upper sign being inadmissible,

though this was not thought out.)   Q. E. F.

34. (8)

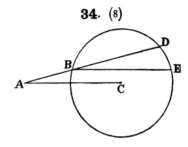

(*Analysis.*)

Let A be the given Point, and C the centre of the given Circle. Join AC, and let ABD be the required Line. From B draw the Chord BE parallel to AC. Then $\angle DBE = \angle A$. Hence Arc DE = Arc BD; i.e. Arc BE is bisected by D; i. e. D is on perpendicular from C.

(*Synthesis.*)

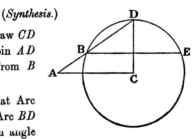

Join AC. From C draw CD perpendicular to AC. Join AD cutting Circle at B. From B draw BE parallel to AC.

It is easily proved that Arc BD = Arc DE. Hence Arc BD subtends, in the Circle, an angle $= \angle DBE = \angle A$.

                    Q. E. F.

35. (8)

Let ABC be the given Triangle; and let the portions of the radii, outside the Triangle, have to the radius the given ratios

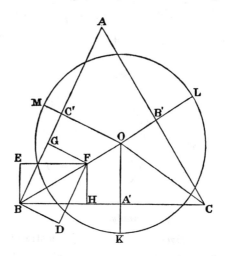

$k : 1, \; l : 1, \; m : 1.$ (N.B. $k, l, m,$ are supposed to be proper fractions.)

From B draw $BD \perp BA$, and $BE \perp BC$; and make BD have, to BE, the ratio $1 - m : 1 - k$. Through D draw DF parallel to BA, and EF parallel to BC; and join BF. From F draw FG $\perp BA$, and $FH \perp BC$.

Then $FG : FH :: 1 - m : 1 - k.$

Similarly, draw CO so that the $\perp$s, drawn from any Point of it to CA and CB, are in the ratio $1 - l : 1 - k$; and produce BF to meet it at O.

From O draw OA', OB', OC', $\perp$ the sides.

Then $OA' : OB' : OC' :: 1 - k : 1 - l : 1 - m.$

Produce OA' to K, so that $OK : OA' :: 1 : 1 - k.$

With centre *O*, and distance *OK*, describe a Circle; and
produce *OB'*, *OC'*, to meet it at *L*, *M*.

Now $OK : OA' :: 1 : 1-k$;

       $OA' : OB' :: 1-k : 1-l$;

   $\therefore \ OK : OB' :: \ 1 \ : 1-l$;

Similarly, $OK : OC' :: 1 : 1-m$.

But $A'K : OK :: OK - OA' : OK :: k : 1$.

Similarly $B'L : \text{radius} :: l : 1$, and $C'M : \text{radius} :: m : 1$.

                                        Q. E. F.

36. (8)

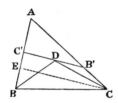

(Analysis.)

Let *B'C'* be required Line : and let $\angle$ at *C'* be right.

Cut off *C'D* equal to *C'B* : then $DB' = B'C$.

Join *DB*, *DC* : then $\angle DBC' = 45°$, and $\angle B'DC = \angle B'CD$.

From *C* draw $CE \perp AB$.

Then $\angle B'DC = \angle DCE$; $\therefore \ \angle B'CD = \angle DCE$.

(Synthesis.)

Hence construction. Draw $CE \perp AB$: bisect $\angle ACE$: at *B*
make $\angle ABD = 45°$. Let these lines meet at *D*. Through *D*
draw $B'DC' \perp AB$.

Then $\angle C'DB = \pi - (\angle DC'B + \angle C'BD) = 45° = \angle C'BD$;

$\therefore \ C'D = C'B$.

Also $\angle B'DC = \angle DCE = \angle DCB'$;

$\therefore DB' = B'C$;

$\therefore C'B' =$ sum of BC', CB'.

Q. E. F.

Limits of possibility:—

$\angle A$ must not be $> 90°$;

$\angle B$ must not be $< 45°$;

$\angle C$ must not be $<$ half complement of A,

i. e. not $< \left(45° - \dfrac{A}{2} \right)$.

37. (8, 22)

Let BC be the common chord, and A, D, the centres.

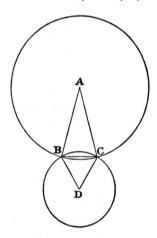

Let $\angle A = 30°$, and $\angle D = 60°$.

And let BC (which $= DB = DC$) $= 1$.

And let $AB = x$.

Now $\quad \triangle A = \dfrac{\sqrt{3}}{2} = \dfrac{2x^2 - 1}{2x^2}$;

$\therefore \dfrac{\sqrt{3}}{2} = 1 - \dfrac{1}{2x^2}$; $\therefore \dfrac{1}{2x^2} = \dfrac{2 - \sqrt{3}}{2}$;

$\therefore x^2 = \dfrac{1}{2 - \sqrt{3}} = 2 + \sqrt{3}$;

$\therefore$ areas of Circles are $\pi \cdot (2 + \sqrt{3})$ and π ;

$\therefore$ areas of Sectors are $\pi \cdot \dfrac{2 + \sqrt{3}}{12}$ and $\dfrac{\pi}{6}$;

$\therefore$ their sum $= \pi \cdot \dfrac{4 + \sqrt{3}}{12}$.

Again, area of Triangle $ABC = \frac{1}{2} \cdot (2 + \sqrt{3}) \cdot \frac{1}{2}$,

$$= \dfrac{2 + \sqrt{3}}{4} ;$$

also area of Triangle $DBC = \dfrac{\sqrt{3}}{4}$;

$\therefore$ their sum $= \dfrac{2 + 2\sqrt{3}}{4} = \dfrac{1 + \sqrt{3}}{2}$.

Now the portion, of the smaller Circle, that is within the larger one, is the difference between these two sums ;

$\therefore$ it $= \pi \cdot \dfrac{4 + \sqrt{3}}{12} - \dfrac{1 + \sqrt{3}}{2}$.

Hence its ratio, to the area of the smaller Circle, is this sum divided by π ;

$\therefore$ it $= \dfrac{4 + \sqrt{3}}{12} - \dfrac{1 + \sqrt{3}}{2\pi}$,

$= \dfrac{5 \cdot 732}{12} - \dfrac{2 \cdot 732}{\left(\frac{44}{7}\right)} = \cdot 478 - \dfrac{\cdot 248}{\left(\frac{4}{7}\right)}$,

$= \cdot 478 \quad \dfrac{1 \cdot 736}{4} = \cdot 478 - \cdot 434 = \cdot 044$.

Q. E. F.

38. (9, 22)

Taking, in order, the bag from which this unknown counter is drawn, the bag from which a red one was twice drawn, and the remaining bag, we see that there are six possible arrangements of '*A*', '*B*', and '*C*': viz.—

(1)	*ABC*,	(4)	*BCA*,
(2)	*ACB*,	(5)	*CAB*,
(3)	*BAC*,	(6)	*CBA*.

Now the chance of the observed event is, in case (1), $1 \times \frac{4}{9} = \frac{4}{9}$; in case (2), $1 \times \frac{1}{9} = \frac{1}{9}$; in case (3), $\frac{2}{3} \times 1 = \frac{2}{3}$; in case (4), $\frac{2}{3} \times \frac{1}{9} = \frac{2}{27}$; in case (5), $\frac{1}{3} \times 1 = \frac{1}{3}$; and in case (6), $\frac{1}{3} \times \frac{4}{9} = \frac{4}{27}$.

Hence the chances of existence, for these 6 states, are proportional to '12, 3, 18, 2, 9, 4'. Hence their actual values are '$\frac{1}{4}$, $\frac{1}{16}$, $\frac{3}{8}$, $\frac{1}{24}$, $\frac{3}{16}$, $\frac{1}{12}$'.

Hence the chance of the unknown counter being red is the sum of $\frac{1}{4} \times 1$, $\frac{1}{16} \times 1$, $\frac{3}{8} \times \frac{2}{3}$, $\frac{1}{24} \times \frac{2}{3}$, $\frac{3}{16} \times \frac{1}{3}$, $\frac{1}{12} \times \frac{1}{3}$;

i.e. it is $\dfrac{36 + 9 + 36 + 4 + 9 + 4}{9 \times 16}$; which $= \dfrac{98}{9 \times 16} = \frac{49}{72}$.

Q. E. F.

39. (9, 22)

Let $x = $ no. of days.

Then $(2 \times 10 - \overline{x-1}) \cdot \dfrac{x}{2} = 14 + \{2 \times 2 + \overline{x-1} . 2\} \cdot \dfrac{x}{2}$;

i.e. $\dfrac{21x}{2} - \dfrac{x^2}{2} = 14 + x + x^2$;

$\therefore 3x^2 - 19x + 28 = 0$; $\therefore x = \dfrac{19 \pm 5}{6} = 4$ or $\dfrac{7}{3}$.

Now the above solution has taken no account of the *discontinuity* of increase, or decrease of pace, and is the true solution only on the supposition that the increase or decrease is *continuous,* and such as to coincide with the above data at the end of each day.   Hence '4' is a correct answer; but '$\frac{7}{3}$' only indicates that a meeting occurs *during the third day.*   To find the hour of this, let $y =$ no. of hours.

Now in 2 days A has got to the end of 19 miles, B to the end of $(14 + 6)$, i. e. 20.

∴ $19 + y \cdot \frac{8}{12} = 20 + y \cdot \frac{6}{12}$

i. e. $y \cdot \frac{2}{3} = 1 + y \cdot \frac{1}{2}$;   ∴ $y = 6$.

Hence they meet at end of $2\,d.\ 6\,h.$, and at end of $4\,d.$: and the distances are 23 miles, and 34 miles.

Q. E. F.

40. (9)

(1) Let ABC be the given Triangle, and AD the line from

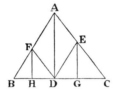

the vertex.

From D draw DE, DF, parallel to the sides; and from E and F draw EG, FH, $\perp BC$.

Then Triangles FBD, EDC, are similar to ABC;

∴ $FH : AD :: BD : BC$,

and $EG : AD :: DC : BC$;

∴ $(FH + EG) : AD :: BC : BC$;

∴ $FH + EG = AD$.

Also, ∵ Triangles AED, AFD, are equal and on the same base AD,

∴ their altitudes are equal; i. e. $DH = DG$.

Q. E. F.

(2) Let ABC be the given Triangle, and AD the line from the vertex.

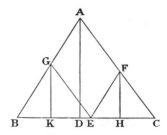

Make $CE=BD$; from E draw EF, EG, parallel to the sides; and from F, G, draw FH, GK, $\perp BC$.

Then Triangles GBE, FEC, are similar to ABC;

$\therefore\ GK:AD::BE:BC$,

and $FH:AD::EC:BC$;

$\therefore\ (GK+FH):AD::BC:BC$;

$\therefore\ GK+FH = AD$.

Also $BK:BE::BD:BC$;

$\therefore\quad BK:DC::EC:BC$;

$\qquad\qquad ::HC:DC$;

$\therefore\ BK = HC$.

Q. E. F.

41. (9, 23)

(1) As there was certainly at least one W in the bag at first, the 'a priori' chances for the various states of the bag, '$WWWW$, $WWWB$, $WWBB$, $WBBB$,' were '$\frac{1}{8}$, $\frac{3}{8}$, $\frac{3}{8}$, $\frac{1}{8}$'.

These would have given, to the observed event, the chances '1, $\frac{1}{2}$, $\frac{1}{6}$, 0'.

Hence the chances, after the event, for the various states, are proportional to '$\frac{1}{8}\cdot1$, $\frac{3}{8}\cdot\frac{1}{2}$, $\frac{3}{8}\cdot\frac{1}{6}$'; i.e .to '$\frac{1}{8}$, $\frac{3}{16}$, $\frac{1}{16}$'; i.e. to '2, 3, 1'. Hence their actual values are '$\frac{1}{3}$, $\frac{1}{2}$, $\frac{1}{6}$'.

Hence the chance, of now drawing W, is '$\frac{1}{3}\cdot1+\frac{1}{2}\cdot\frac{1}{2}$'; i.e. it is $\frac{7}{12}$.

Q. E. F.

(2) If he had not spoken, the 'a priori' chances for the states '$WWWW$, $WWWB$, $WWBB$, $WBBB$, $BBBB$', would have been $\dfrac{'1, 4, 6, 4, 1'}{16}$.

These would have given, to the observed event, the chances '$1, \frac{1}{2}, \frac{1}{6}, 0, 0$'.

Hence the chances, after the event, for the various states, are proportional to '$\frac{1}{16} \cdot 1, \frac{1}{4} \cdot \frac{1}{2}, \frac{1}{6} \cdot \frac{3}{8}$'; i. e. to '$1, 2, 1$'. Hence their actual values are '$\frac{1}{4}, \frac{1}{2}, \frac{1}{4}$'.

Hence the chance, of now drawing W, is '$\frac{1}{4} \cdot 1 + \frac{1}{2} \cdot \frac{1}{2}$'; i. e. it is $\frac{1}{2}$.

Q. E. F.

42. (10, 23)

Let ABC be the given Triangle. Bisect its angles, and draw ⊥s to them, forming the Triangle $A'B'C'$.

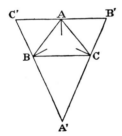

Now $\angle CBA' = 90° - \dfrac{B}{2}$; and so of the others.

$$\therefore \quad A' = 180° - (CBA' + BCA') = \frac{B + C}{2} = 90° - \frac{A}{2};$$

$$\therefore \quad BA' = a \cdot \frac{\triangle \frac{C}{2}}{\triangle \frac{A}{2}}.$$

Similarly, $BC' = c \cdot \dfrac{\triangle \frac{A}{2}}{\triangle \frac{C}{2}}$;

$\therefore A'C' = \dfrac{a \triangle^2 \frac{C}{2} + c \triangle^2 \frac{A}{2}}{\triangle \frac{A}{2}\, \triangle \frac{C}{2}} = \dfrac{a \cdot \dfrac{s \cdot (s-c)}{ab} + c \cdot \dfrac{s \cdot (s-a)}{bc}}{\dfrac{s}{b} \cdot \sqrt{\dfrac{(s-a) \cdot (s-c)}{ac}}}$,

$= \dfrac{s-c+s-a}{\frown \frac{B}{2}} = \dfrac{b}{\frown \frac{B}{2}}$.

Similarly, $A'B' = \dfrac{c}{\frown \frac{C}{2}}$;

$\therefore$ area of $A'B'C' = \dfrac{bc \triangle \frac{A}{2}}{2 \frown \frac{B}{2} \frown \frac{C}{2}}$;

$\therefore \dfrac{\text{area of } A'B'C'}{\text{area of } ABC} = \dfrac{bc \triangle \frac{A}{2}}{2 \frown \frac{B}{2} \frown \frac{C}{2}} \quad \dfrac{2}{bc \frown A}$,

$= \dfrac{\triangle \frac{A}{2}}{\frown \frac{B}{2} \frown \frac{C}{2} \cdot 2 \frown \frac{A}{2} \triangle \frac{A}{2}}$,

$= \dfrac{1}{2 \frown \frac{A}{2} \frown \frac{B}{2} \frown \frac{C}{2}}$,

$= \dfrac{abc}{2\,(s-a) \cdot (s-b) \cdot (s-c)}$.

Q. E. F.

43. (10)

Let ABC be the given Triangle; and let BFD, CFE, be the

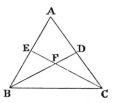

required lines, so that $FB = FC$, and Tetragon $AEFD =$ Triangle FBC. And call the angle FBC 'θ'. It will suffice to calculate this angle.

Because Triangle $FBC =$ Tetragon $AEFD$,

$\therefore$ Triangle $DBC =$ Triangle AEC,

$\qquad = $ Triangle ABC $-$ Triangle EBC;

$\therefore$ Triangles DBC, EBC, together $=$ Triangle ABC;

$$\therefore \; \tfrac{1}{2} \cdot \frac{a^2}{\cot\theta + \cot C} + \tfrac{1}{2} \cdot \frac{a^2}{\cot\theta + \cot B} = \tfrac{1}{2} \cdot \frac{a^2}{\cot B + \cot C};$$

$$\therefore \; \frac{1}{\cot\theta + \cot C} + \frac{1}{\cot\theta + \cot B} = \frac{1}{\cot B + \cot C};$$

$$\therefore \; \frac{2\cot\theta + (\cot B + \cot C)}{\cot^2\theta + \cot\theta \cdot (\cot B + \cot C) + \cot B \cot C} = \text{do.};$$

$\therefore \; \cot^2\theta + \cot\theta \cdot (\cot B + \cot C) + \cot B \cot C$

$$= 2\cot\theta \cdot (\cot B + \cot C) + (\cot B + \cot C)^2;$$

$\therefore \; \cot^2\theta - \cot\theta \cdot (\cot B + \cot C)$

$$- (\cot^2 B + \cot B \cot C + \cot^2 C) = 0;$$

$\therefore \; \cot\theta = \tfrac{1}{2} \cdot \{\cot B + \cot C$

$$\pm \sqrt{(5\cot^2 B + 6\cot B \cot C + 5\cot^2 C)}\}.$$

$$\text{Q. E. F.}$$

44. $\left(\text{10}\right)$

Let k be a No. not containing 2 or 5 as a factor, i. e. let it be prime to 10. Then, if $\frac{1}{k}$ be reduced to a circulating decimal, and that to a vulgar fraction, the digits of the denominator will be a certain number of 9's; i. e. it will be of the form $(\text{10}^n - 1)$.

And since this fraction $= \frac{1}{k}$, and that k is prime to 10, and so prime to 10^m, the factor $(\text{10}^n - 1)$ must be a multiple of k.

This evidently holds good in any other scale of notation. Hence, if a be the radix of the scale of notation, and b a No. prime to a, a value may be found for n, which will make $(a^n - 1)$ a multiple of b.

Q. E. D.

EXAMPLES (not thought out).

(1) With radix 10, find a value, for n, which will make $(\text{10}^n - 1)$ a multiple of 7.

$$\tfrac{1}{7} = \cdot\dot{1}4285\dot{7} = \frac{142857}{\text{10}^6 - 1}.$$

Ans. $n = 6$.

(2) Let the two given Nos. be 8, 9.

Taking 8 as radix, we get $\tfrac{1}{9} = \cdot\dot{0}\dot{7} = \dfrac{7}{8^2 - 1}.$

Ans. $n = 2$.

(3) Let the two given Nos. be 7, 13.

Taking 7 as radix, we get

$$\tfrac{1}{13} = \cdot\dot{0}35245631 42\dot{1} = \frac{35245631421}{7^{12} - 1}.$$

Ans. $n = 12$.

45. (10, 23)

Divide each rod into $(n+1)$ parts, where n is assumed to be odd, and the n points of division are assumed to be the only points where the rod will break, and to be equally frangible.

The chance of one failure is $\dfrac{n-1}{n}$;

$\therefore$ „ „ n failures is $\left(\dfrac{n-1}{n}\right)^n$

$$= \left(1 - \dfrac{1}{n}\right)^n.$$

Now, if $m = \dfrac{1}{n}$; then, when $n = \dfrac{1}{0}$, $m = 0$;

$\therefore$ the chance that no rod is broke in the middle $= (1-m)^{\frac{1}{m}}$, when $m = 0$;

i. e. it approaches the limit $(1-0)^{\frac{1}{0}}$.

And Ans. $= 1 - (1-0)^{\frac{1}{0}}$.

Now $(1+0)^{\frac{1}{0}} = e$. Hence if, in the series for e, we call the sum of the odd terms 'a', and of the even terms 'b'; then $e = a + b$; and $(1-0)^{\frac{1}{0}} = a - b = 2a - e$.

Q. E. F.

[N. B. What follows here was *not* thought out.]

Now $a = 1 + \dfrac{1}{\lfloor 2} + \dfrac{1}{\lfloor 4} + \&c.$

$\qquad 1 = 1$

$\qquad \dfrac{1}{\lfloor 2} = \cdot 5$

$\qquad \dfrac{1}{\lfloor 4} = \quad \cdot 04166666 \ \&c.$

$$\frac{1}{\lfloor 6} = \cdot 00138888 \ \&c.$$

$$\frac{1}{\lfloor 8} = \cdot 00002480 \ \&c.$$

$$\frac{1}{\lfloor 10} = \cdot 00000027 \ \&c.$$

$$\therefore \quad a = 1 \cdot 5430806 \ \&c.$$

$$\therefore 2a = 3 \cdot 0861612 \ \&c.$$

$$e = 2 \cdot 7182818 \ \&c.$$

$$\therefore (1-0)^{\frac{1}{6}} = \cdot 3678793 \ \&c.$$

$$\therefore \text{Ans.} = 1 - (1-0)^{\frac{1}{6}} = \cdot 6321207 \ \&c.$$

46. (10)

Let *ABC* be the given Triangle, and *D* the given Point.

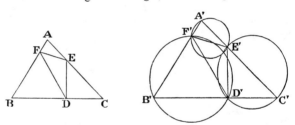

If we make a Triangle $D'E'F'$, having its angles equal to the given angles, and having D' as its assigned vertex, the Problem may be solved, if we can circumscribe, about the Triangle $D'E'F'$, a Triangle similar to *ABC*.

Now we can construct, on $E'F'$, $F'D'$, $D'E'$, segments of Circles containing angles equal to *A*, *B*, *C*. Hence the Problem may be solved, if we can place, in these Circles, a line $B'D'C'$, divided in the same proportion as *BDC*.

This Lemma may be solved as follows. Let ' G, H, be the

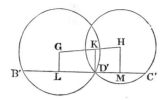

centres of the Circles. Join GH, and divide it, at K, proportionally to BDC.

Join KD'; through D' draw $B'D'C' \perp KD'$; and from G, H, draw GL, HM, $\perp B'C'$.

Now it may be easily proved that

$$LD' : D'M :: GK : KH :: BD : DC.$$

But $B'D'$, $D'C'$, are doubles of LD', $D'M$;

$$\therefore B'D' : D'C' :: BD : DC.$$

Q. E. F.

[The construction is now obvious, viz. to join $B'F'$, $C'E'$, and produce them to meet, on the third Circle (as they may be easily proved to do), at A'; then to divide AB, AC, at F and E, proportionally to $A'F'B'$, $A'E'C'$; and then to join DE, DF.]

<h2 align="center">47. (11, 23)</h2>

By inspection, ' $\circ$, $\circ$, $\circ$ ' are one set of values.

Subtracting, we get $x \cdot \left(\dfrac{1}{y} - \dfrac{1}{z} \right) = y - z$;

$\therefore x = yz \cdot \dfrac{y-z}{z-y} = -yz$, unless $y = z$, in which case $x = \dfrac{\circ}{\circ}$.

Now, by (1), $x = xy - yz$;

$\therefore$, when $y \neq z$, $x = xy + x$;

$\therefore xy = \circ$, unless x be infinite.

Similarly, by (2), $xz = $ o, unless x be infinite.

Hence, if x be finite, and if $y \neq z$, either x or $y = $ o, and also either x or $z = $ o; i. e. either $x = $ o, or else $y = z = $ o. But the latter is excluded by our hypothesis. Hence $x = $ o. Hence $yz = $ o; i. e. either y or $z = $ o, and the other may take any value.

This gives us 2 more sets of values, viz.

$$x = y = \text{o} \; ; \; z \text{ has any value} \; ;$$

$$x = z = \text{o} \; ; \; y \text{ has any value.}$$

We have now to ascertain what happens when $y = z$.

By (1), $\dfrac{x}{y} = x - y$;

$\therefore y^2 = x \cdot (y - 1)$; i.e. $x = \dfrac{y^2}{y - 1}$.

Similarly, by (2), $x = \dfrac{z^2}{z - 1}$.

This gives us a 4th set of values, viz. $x = \dfrac{k^2}{k-1}$, $y = z = k$; where k has any value.

Now y and z may evidently have *any* real values, but x is restricted by the equation

$$y^2 - xy + x = \text{o},$$

in which y cannot be real, unless $(x^2 - 4x) > $ o. Hence x may have any negative value, and any positive value that is not less than 4; but it cannot have any positive value, less than 4, without making y unreal.   Q. E. F.

48. (11)

Let ABC be the given Triangle, A', B', C', the centres of the semicircles, and DE, FG, HJ, the common tangents; so that $DE = a$, $FG = \beta$, and $HJ = \gamma$.

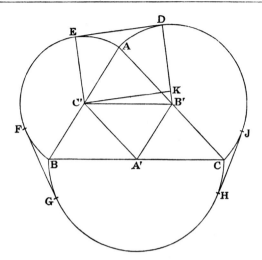

Join $B'D$, $C'E$; and from C' draw $C'K \perp B'D$. Hence $CK = a$.

Call sides of given Triangle '$2a$, $2b$, $2c$'.

Then $B'C' = a$, and $B'K = b - c$;

$\therefore C'K = \sqrt{\{a^2 - (b - c)^2\}}$;

i.e. $a = \sqrt{\{(a - b + c) \cdot (a + b - c)\}}$;

similarly, $\beta = \sqrt{\{(a + b - c) \cdot (-a + b + c)\}}$,

and $\gamma = \sqrt{\{(-a + b + c) \cdot (a - b + c)\}}$;

$\therefore \dfrac{\beta\gamma}{a} = -a + b + c$;

similarly, $\dfrac{\gamma a}{\beta} = a - b + c$,

and $\dfrac{a\beta}{\gamma} = a + b - c$;

$\therefore$ their sum $= a + b + c$,

    $=$ semi-perimeter of ABC.

Q. E. D.

49. $(\text{II},\ 23)$

Take, as unit, a side of one of the Triangles.

If the Tetrahedron be cut by a vertical Plane containing one of the slant edges, the section is a Triangle whose base is $\dfrac{\sqrt{3}}{2}$, and whose sides are $\dfrac{\sqrt{3}}{2}$, 1;

hence cosine of smaller base-angle

$$= \left(\tfrac{3}{4} + 1 - \tfrac{3}{4}\right) \cdot \frac{1}{\sqrt{3}} = \frac{1}{\sqrt{3}};$$

$\therefore$ its sine $= \dfrac{\sqrt{2}}{\sqrt{3}} =$ its altitude;

and this is the altitude of the Tetrahedron;

$\therefore$ volume of Tetrahedron $= \dfrac{1}{3} \cdot \dfrac{\sqrt{2}}{\sqrt{3}} \cdot \dfrac{\sqrt{3}}{4} = \dfrac{\sqrt{2}}{12}.$

Also altitude of Pyramid = altitude of Triangle whose base is $\sqrt{2}$, and whose sides are 1, 1;

i. e. it $= \dfrac{\sqrt{2}}{2}$;

$\therefore$ volume of Pyramid $= \dfrac{1}{3} \cdot \dfrac{\sqrt{2}}{2} = \dfrac{\sqrt{2}}{6}.$

Hence required ratio $= \dfrac{\sqrt{2}}{6} \cdot \dfrac{12}{\sqrt{2}} = 2.$

Q. E. F.

50. $(\text{II},\ 23)$

At first, the chance that bag H shall contain

2 W counters, is $\tfrac{1}{4}$.

1 W and 1 B, is $\tfrac{1}{2}$.

2 B,   is 1.

$\therefore$, after adding a W, the chance that it shall contain

$3\ W$,   is $\frac{1}{4}$.

$2\ W$, $1\ B$,   is $\frac{1}{2}$.

$1\ W$, $2\ B$,   is $\frac{1}{4}$.

hence the chance of drawing a W from it is

$$\tfrac{1}{4} \times 1 + \tfrac{1}{2} \times \tfrac{2}{3} + \tfrac{1}{4} \times \tfrac{1}{3} : \text{i. e. } \tfrac{2}{3}.$$

$\therefore$ the chance of drawing a B is $\frac{1}{3}$.

After transferring this (unseen) counter to bag K, the chance that it shall contain

$3\ W$,   is $\frac{2}{3} \times \frac{1}{4}$;   i. e. $\frac{1}{6}$.

$2\ W$, and $1\ B$, is $\frac{2}{3} \times \frac{1}{2} + \frac{1}{3} \times \frac{1}{4}$; i. e. $\frac{5}{12}$.

$1\ W$, $2\ B$, is $\frac{2}{3} \times \frac{1}{4} + \frac{1}{3} \times \frac{1}{2}$; i. e. $\frac{1}{3}$.

$3\ B$,   is $\frac{1}{3} \times \frac{1}{4}$;   i. e. $\frac{1}{12}$;

$\therefore$ the chance of drawing a W from it is

$$\tfrac{1}{6} \times 1 + \tfrac{5}{12} \times \tfrac{2}{3} + \tfrac{1}{3} \times \tfrac{1}{3} ; \qquad \text{i. e. } \tfrac{5}{9}.$$

$\therefore$ the chance of drawing a B is $\frac{4}{9}$.

Before transferring this to bag H, the chance that bag H shall contain

$2\ W$,   is $\frac{1}{4} \times 1 + \frac{1}{2} \times \frac{1}{3}$; i. e. $\frac{5}{12}$.

$1\ W$, $1\ B$, $\frac{1}{2} \times \frac{2}{3} + \frac{1}{4} \times \frac{2}{3}$; i. e. $\frac{1}{2}$.

$2\ B$, $\frac{1}{4} \times \frac{1}{3}$;   i. e. $\frac{1}{12}$.

$\therefore$, after transferring it, the chance that bag H shall contain

$3\ W$,   is $\frac{5}{12} \times \frac{5}{9}$;   i. e. $\frac{25}{108}$.

$2\ W$, $1\ B$, $\frac{5}{12} \times \frac{4}{9} + \frac{1}{2} \times \frac{5}{9}$; i. e. $\frac{50}{108}$.

$1\ W$, $2\ B$, $\frac{1}{2} \times \frac{4}{9} + \frac{1}{12} \times \frac{5}{9}$; i. e. $\frac{29}{108}$.

$3\ B$, $\frac{1}{12} \times \frac{4}{9}$;   i. e. $\frac{4}{108}$.

Hence the chance of drawing a W is

$$\tfrac{1}{108} \times \left\{ 25 \times 1 + 50 \times \tfrac{2}{3} + 29 \times \tfrac{1}{3} \right\} ; \text{ i. e. } \tfrac{17}{27}.$$

i. e. the odds are 17 to 10 on its happening.

Q. E. F.

51. (12)

Let ABC be the given Triangle, and D the given Point.

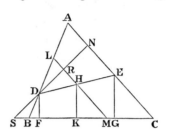

(Analysis.)

Let DE be the line required. Draw DF, EG, $\perp$ the base. Then their sum is equal to DE.

Bisect DE at H, and draw $HK \perp$ the base: then it is evident that HK is the $A. M.$ of DF, EG, and is equal to half their sum; i. e. it is equal to half of DE. Hence a Circle, drawn with centre H and at distance HD, will pass through E and K, and will touch the base at K.

Through H draw LHM parallel to AC. Then DA is evidently bisected at L. Also LM passes through the centre of the Circle. Hence, if DN be drawn $\perp LM$ (or CA), it is a chord of the Circle, and is bisected at R. Produce ND to meet the base produced at S. Hence SDN cuts the Circle, and SK touches it at K. But S can be found, and SK can then be taken, so that sq. of SK may be equal to rect. of SD, SN.

(Synthesis.)

From D draw $DN \perp AC$, and produce it to meet the base produced at S. Take SK, so that its square may be equal to rect. of SD, SN.

Bisect DA at L, and from L draw LM parallel to AC; and from K draw $KH \perp$ the base, to meet LM at H. Join DH, and produce it to meet AC at E, and draw DF, EG, $\perp$ the base.

Because $DL = LA$, and that LM is parallel to AC,

$\therefore DH = HE = HK$; $\therefore DE = 2\,HK$.

But $DF + EG = 2\,HK$; $\therefore DF + EG = DE$.

Q. E. F.

[N. B. This proof is incomplete. I have assumed, without proving it, that $DH = HK$. It may be proved thus. Because sq. of SK = rect. of SD, SN, $\therefore DN$ is a chord of a Circle which touches the base at K; $\therefore LM$, which bisects it at right angles, passes through the centre. But KH also passes through the centre; $\therefore H$ is the centre; $\therefore HD = HK$.]

52. ($_{12}$, $_{23}$)

Let x be the number of pennies each had at first.

No. (3) received x, took out $(2 + 4)$, and put in $\frac{x}{2}$; so that the sack then contained $(x \cdot \frac{3}{2} - 6)$. Let us write '$a$' for '$\frac{3}{2}$.'

No. (5) received $(xa - 6)$, took out $(4 + 1)$, and put in enough to multiply, by a, its contents when he received it. The sack now contained $(xa^2 - 6a - 5)$.

No. (2) took out $(1 + 3)$, and handed on $(xa^3 - 6a^2 - 5a - 4)$.

No. (4) took out $(3 + 5)$, and handed on
$$(xa^4 - 6a^3 - 5a^2 - 4a - 8).$$

No. (1) put in 2. The sack now contained $5x$.

Hence $xa^4 - 6a^3 - 5a^2 - 4a - 6 = 5x$;

$$\therefore \quad x = \frac{6a^3 + 5a^2 + 4a + 6}{a^4 - 5};$$

$$= \frac{(6 \cdot 3^3 + 5 \cdot 3^2 \cdot 2 + 4 \cdot 3 \cdot 2^2 + 6 \cdot 2^3) \cdot 2}{3^4 - 5 \cdot 2^4};$$

$$= \frac{(162 + 90 + 48 + 48) \cdot 2}{81 - 80} = 696 = 2l.\ 18s.\ 0d.$$

Q. E. F.

53. (13, 24)

Let ABC be the given Triangle, and P the given Point; and call its trilinear co-ordinates 'a, β, γ'.

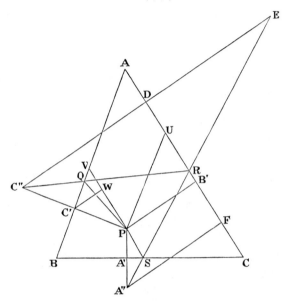

From P draw PA', PB', PC', $\perp$ the sides, and therefore equal to a, β, γ. Produce PA' and PC' to A'' and C'', making $A'A'' = PA'$, and $C'C'' = PC'$. From C'' draw $C''D \perp AC$, and produce it to E, making $DE = C''D$. Join EA'', cutting AC in R, and BC in S. Join $C''R$, cutting AB in Q. Join PQ, PS.

The path of the ball is evidently $PQRSP$; and we have to calculate the length of AR.

Now $AR = DR + AD = DR + AB' - DB'$.

First, to calculate DR.

From P draw PU, PV, parallel to AB, AC; from C' draw $C'W \perp PV$; and from A'' draw $A''F \perp AC$.

By similar Triangles, $DR : RF :: DE : A''F :: C''D : A''F$;

$\therefore DR : DF :: C''D : (C''D + A''F)$;

$\therefore DR = \dfrac{DF \cdot C''D}{C''D + A''F}.$

Now $\angle C'VP = A$; $\therefore \angle C'PV = 90° - A$;

$\therefore WP = \gamma \frown A$;

$\therefore DB'$, which $= 2\,WP$, $= 2\gamma \frown A$.

Similarly, $B'F = 2a \frown C$;

$\therefore DF = 2\,(a \frown C + \gamma \frown A)$.

Again, $C'W = \gamma \triangle A$;

$\therefore C''D$, which $= 2\,C'W + PB'$, $= 2\gamma \triangle A + \beta$.

Similarly, $A''F = 2a \triangle C + \beta$;

$\therefore C''D + A''F = 2\,(a \triangle C + \gamma \triangle A + \beta)$;

$\therefore DR = \dfrac{(a \frown C + \gamma \frown A) \cdot (2\gamma \triangle A + \beta)}{a \triangle C + \gamma \triangle A + \beta}.$

Now $AB' = B'U + UA = B'U + PV$,

$$= \beta \cot A + \gamma \operatorname{cosec} A = \frac{\beta \triangle A + \gamma}{\frown A};$$

$\therefore AB' - DB' = \dfrac{\beta \triangle A + \gamma}{\frown A} - 2\gamma \frown A,$

$$= \frac{\beta \triangle A + \gamma\,(1 - 2 \frown^2 A)}{\frown A}$$

$$= \frac{\beta \triangle A + \gamma \triangle 2A}{\frown A}.$$

Now $AR = DR + AB' - DB'$;

$\therefore AR = \dfrac{(a \frown C + \gamma \frown A) \cdot (2\gamma \triangle A + \beta)}{a \triangle C + \gamma \triangle A + \beta}$

$$+ \frac{\beta \triangle A + \gamma \frown 2A}{\frown A}.$$

Q. E. F.

54. (13, 24)

It is evident that Triangle ADE is similar to ABC.

Let 'k' = ratio $\dfrac{DE}{a} = \dfrac{AE}{b} = \dfrac{AD}{c}$.

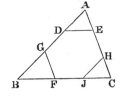

Now $DG = DE$; $\therefore$ $DG = ka$;

$\therefore$ $GB = c - ka - kc$;

$\therefore$ $\dfrac{GB}{c} = 1 - k - k \cdot \dfrac{a}{c}$;

$\therefore$ $GF \left(\text{which} = GB \cdot \dfrac{b}{c}\right) = b - kb - k \cdot \dfrac{ab}{c}$;

but $GF = DE = ka$;

$\therefore$ $b - kb - k \cdot \dfrac{ab}{c} = ka$;

$\therefore$ $bc = k \cdot (bc + ca + ab)$;

$\therefore$ $k = \dfrac{bc}{bc + ca + ab} = \dfrac{\frac{1}{a}}{\frac{1}{a} + \frac{1}{b} + \frac{1}{c}} = \dfrac{\frac{1}{a}}{m}$ (say).

Hence $AD = \dfrac{c \cdot \frac{1}{a}}{m}$; $DG = \dfrac{1}{m} = \dfrac{c \cdot \frac{1}{c}}{m}$.

$\therefore$ GB (which $= c - AD - DG) = \dfrac{c \cdot \left(m - \frac{1}{a} - \frac{1}{c}\right)}{m} = \dfrac{c \cdot \frac{1}{b}}{m}$;

$\therefore$ $AD : DG : GB :: \dfrac{1}{a} : \dfrac{1}{c} : \dfrac{1}{b}$.

Also $DE = ka = \dfrac{1}{m} = \dfrac{1}{\frac{1}{a} + \frac{1}{b} + \frac{1}{c}}$.

Q. E. F.

55. (13)

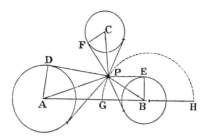

Let A, B, C be the centres of the bases of the towers; and a, b, c their radii. Suppose P the required Point; and from P draw a pair of tangents to each circle, and lines to the centres, which will evidently bisect the angles contained by the pairs of tangents.

Hence angles APD, BPE, CPF are equal;

∴ ⌢ APD = ⌢ BPE = ⌢ CPF;

i. e. $\dfrac{a}{AP} = \dfrac{b}{BP} = \dfrac{c}{CP}$;

∴ $AP : BP : CP :: a : b : c$.

Draw a Line through A, B, and on it take Points G, H, such that $AG : GB :: AH : HB :: a : b$.

Then the Semicircle, described on GH, is the locus of all Points whose distances, from A and B, are proportional to a, b.

Hence, if a Line be drawn through B, C, and a Semicircle described which shall be the locus of all Points whose distances, from B and C, are proportional to b, c; the intersection of these two Semicircles will be the Point required. Q. E. F.

[*Note*. " The locus of all Points whose distances &c.," if represented algebraically, is evidently a Circle, whose centre is on the Line through A, B, and which passes through G and H.]

56. (13, 24)

Draw BC, CE, BD, equal to the given altitudes, so as to form right ∠s at B and C: and produce DB, EC. Join DC, and draw $CF \perp$ to it. Join EB, and draw $BG \perp$ to it. With centre B, and distance BF, describe a circle: with centre C, and distance CG, describe another: let them meet at A: and join AB, AC.

Call the altitudes of ABC, 'a, β, γ'.

Now $a . BC = \beta . CA = \gamma . AB$
$\qquad$ = twice area of ABC;

also, taking BC as unit-line,

$$BC = \frac{1}{BC}, \quad CA = CG = \frac{1}{CE},$$

$$AB = BF = \frac{1}{BD};$$

$$\therefore \frac{a}{BC} = \frac{\beta}{CE} = \frac{\gamma}{BD};$$

i. e. a, β, γ are proportional to given altitudes;

∴. Triangle ABC is similar to required Triangle.

The rest of the construction is obvious. $\qquad$ Q. E. F.

57. (14, 25)

(1) *Geometrically.*

Let ABC be given Triangle.

(*Analysis.*)

Suppose the 3 Squares described, and that their upper edges form the Triangle $A'B'C'$. Join AA', BB', CC'.

Now it is evident that, if BB' be produced, the perpendiculars dropped, from any Point of it, upon AB, BC, will be proportional to $B'F$, $B'D$.

Similarly for AA' and CC'.

Hence these 3 Lines will meet at the Point from which the perpendiculars, dropped upon the sides of ABC, are proportional to $B'C'$, $C'A'$, $A'B'$.

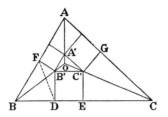

Hence, if Squares be described externally on the sides of
ABC, and if their outer edges be produced to form a new
Triangle $A''B''C''$: this Triangle, with these 3 Squares, will
form a Diagram wholly similar to that formed by the Triangle
ABC, with the 3 Squares inside it.

(*Synthesis.*)

Hence, if Squares be described externally on the sides of the
given Triangle; and if their outer edges be produced to form a
new Triangle; and if the sides of the given Triangle be divided
similarly to those of the new Triangle: their central portions
will be the bases of the required Squares.   Q. E. F.

(2) *Trigonometrically.*

Let *a*, *b*, *c* be the sides of the given Triangle, and *m* its area;
and let *x*, *y*, *z* be the sides of the required Squares.

It is evident that a Circle can be described about the
Tetragon $BDB'F$.

Hence $\angle B'BD = \angle B'FD$.

Now, in Triangle $B'FD$, we know that
$$B'D \frown D = B'F \frown F;$$

i.e. $x \frown (B' + F) = z \frown F;$

$\therefore$ $x \frown B' \smile F + x \smile B' \frown F = z \frown F.$

Now $\angle B$ is supplementary to $\angle B'$;

$\therefore$ $x \frown B \frown F = (z + x \smile B) \frown F;$

$\therefore$ $\cot F = \dfrac{z + x \smile B}{x \frown B} = \cot B'BD.$

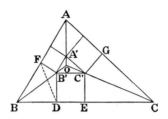

Now $BD = x \cot B'BD$;

$\therefore \quad BD = \dfrac{z + x \frown B}{\frown B}.$

Similarly, $EC = \dfrac{y + x \frown C}{\frown C}$.

But $BD + EC = a - x$;

$\therefore \quad \dfrac{z + x \frown B}{\frown B} + \dfrac{y + x \frown C}{\frown C} = a - x;$

$\therefore \quad \dfrac{x \frown (B + C) + y \frown B + z \frown C}{\frown B \frown C} = a - x;$

i. e. $\dfrac{x \frown A + y \frown B + z \frown C}{\frown B \frown C} = a - x.$

Now it is evident that these Triangles are similar; so that

$$\frac{a}{x} = \frac{b}{y} = \frac{c}{z}.$$

Hence, multiplying the last equation, throughout, by one or other of these equal fractions, we get

$$\frac{a \frown A + b \frown B + c \frown C}{\frown B \frown C} = \frac{a^2}{x} - a;$$

$$\therefore \quad \frac{a \frown A + b \frown B + c \frown C}{a \frown B \frown C} = \frac{a}{x} - 1;$$

$$\therefore \quad \frac{a}{x} = \frac{a \frown A + b \frown B + c \frown C}{a \frown B \frown C} + 1.$$

Hence, multiplying above and below by one or other of the equal fractions $\dfrac{a}{\frown A}$, $\dfrac{b}{\frown B}$, $\dfrac{c}{\frown C}$,

$$\frac{a}{x} = \frac{a^2 + b^2 + c^2}{ab \frown C} + 1 \; ;$$

$$= \frac{a^2 + b^2 + c^2}{2\,m} + 1 = \frac{b}{y} = \frac{c}{z}.$$

Q. E. F.

58. $(14, 25)$

It may be assumed that the 3 Points form a Triangle, the chance of their lying in a straight Line being (practically) *nil*.

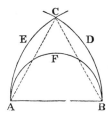

Take the longest side of the Triangle, and call it 'AB': and, on that side of it, on which the Triangle lies, draw the semicircle AFB. Also, with centres A, B, and distances AB, BA, draw the arcs BDC, AEC, intersecting at C.

Then it is evident that the vertex of the Triangle cannot fall outside the Figure $ABDCE$.

Also, if it fall inside the semicircle, the Triangle is obtuse-angled: if outside it, acute-angled. (The chance, of its falling *on* the semicircle, is practically *nil*.)

Hence required chance $= \dfrac{\text{area of semicircle}}{\text{area of fig. } ABDCE}$.

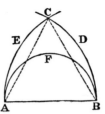

Now let $AB = 2a$: then area of semicircle $= \dfrac{\pi a^2}{2}$; and area

of Fig. $ABDCE = 2 \times$ sector $ABDC -$ Triangle ABC;

$$= 2 \cdot \frac{4\pi a^2}{6} - \sqrt{3} \cdot a^2 = a^2 \cdot \left(\frac{4\pi}{3} - \sqrt{3} \right);$$

$$\therefore \quad \text{chance} = \frac{\dfrac{\pi}{2}}{\dfrac{4\pi}{3} - \sqrt{3}} = \frac{3}{8 - \dfrac{6\sqrt{3}}{\pi}}.$$

Q. E. F.

59. $\left({}_{14}, {}_{25} \right)$

Let $KL = MN = a$,

$KN = LM = b$,

$KM = LN = c$;

and let $\angle$s LMK, MKL, KLM be equal to 'A, B, C'; and similarly for the $\angle$s of the other facets.

From K draw $KT \perp$ base-facet LMN. Also draw KR, KS, $\perp LM$, MN. And join TR, TM, TS,

It is easily proved that $\angle$s TRM, TSM are right.

The required volume is $\frac{1}{3} \cdot KT \cdot LMN$. The area of LMN is of course known. All we need is the length of KT. Now $KT^2 = KS^2 - TS^2$; and KS evidently $= c \cdot \frown B$. Hence all we need is the length of TS.

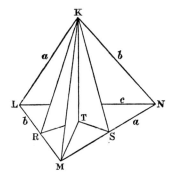

Now this requires a preliminary Lemma, in itself a very pretty problem, viz.—

LEMMA (1).

Given, in Tetragon $RMST$, sides RM, MS, and $\angle RMS$, and that $\angle$s TRM, TSM are right: find TS.

Now $\dfrac{TS}{\frown TRS} = \dfrac{TR}{\frown TSR}$;

also $TS \frown TSR + TR \frown TRS = RS$;

$\therefore \dfrac{TS}{\frown TRS} = \dfrac{TR}{\frown TSR}$,

$\qquad = \dfrac{TS \frown TSR + TR \frown TRS}{\frown TRS \frown TSR + \frown TSR \frown TRS}$,

$\qquad = \dfrac{RS}{\frown RMS} = \dfrac{MS}{\frown MRS}$;

$\therefore \dfrac{TS}{\frown MRS} = \dfrac{MS}{\frown MRS}$; i. e. $TS = MS \cot MRS$.

Q. E. F.

Hence this requires another Lemma, in order to find the value of cot MRS (or tan MRS, which will do as well, and makes a prettier problem).

LEMMA (2).

Given, in Triangle RMS, sides RM, MS, and $\angle RMS$: find tan MRS.

$$\text{Tan } MRS = \frac{\frown MRS}{\triangle MRS} = \frac{RS \frown MRS}{RS \triangle MRS},$$

$$= \frac{MS \frown RMS}{RM - MS \triangle RMS}.$$

Q. E. F.

Hence, in Tetragon $RMST$, we have by Lemma (1),

$$TS = MS \cot MRS;$$

and, by Lemma (2), $\cot MRS = \dfrac{RM - MS \triangle RMS}{MS \frown RMS}$,

$$= \frac{c \triangle A - c \triangle B \triangle C}{c \triangle B \frown C} = \frac{\triangle A - \triangle B \triangle C}{\triangle B \frown C};$$

$$\therefore\ TS = \frac{c}{\frown C} \cdot (\triangle A - \triangle B \triangle C).$$

Now $KT^2 = KS^2 - TS^2$;

$$\therefore\ \text{it} = (c \frown B)^2 - \frac{c^2}{\frown^2 C} \cdot (\triangle A - \triangle B \triangle C)^2,$$

$$= \frac{c^2}{\frown^2 C} \cdot \{(\frown B \frown C)^2 - (\triangle A - \triangle B \triangle C)^2\};$$

therefore $\quad KT = \dfrac{c}{\frown C}$ multiplied by

$$\sqrt{\frown^2 B \frown^2 C - \triangle^2 B \triangle^2 C - \triangle^2 A + 2 \triangle A \triangle B \triangle C},$$

$$= \frac{c}{\frown C} \text{ multiplied by}$$

$$\sqrt{(1 - \triangle^2 B) \cdot (1 - \triangle^2 C) - \triangle^2 B \triangle^2 C - \triangle^2 A + 2 \triangle A \triangle B \triangle C}$$

$$= \frac{c}{\frown C} \cdot \sqrt{1 - (\triangle^2 A + \triangle^2 B + \triangle^2 C) + 2 \triangle A \triangle B \triangle C},$$

which is symmetrical, as it ought to be.

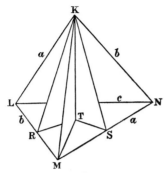

Now area of $LMN = \dfrac{ab \frown C}{2}$;

hence volume of Tetrahedron

$$= \frac{abc}{6} . \sqrt{1 - (\frown^2 A + \frown^2 B + \frown^2 C) + 2 \frown A \frown B \frown C} .$$

Q. E. F.

60. (14, 25)

Let $\angle BAD = \theta$, $\angle CAD = \phi$.

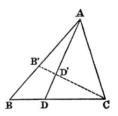

Now $\dfrac{\frown (B+\theta)}{\frown \theta} = \dfrac{c}{\left(\dfrac{ma}{m+n}\right)}$

$$= \frac{c . (m+n)}{ma} ;$$

$\therefore \frown B \cot \theta + \frown B = \dfrac{c . (m+n)}{ma}$;

$\therefore \cot \theta = \dfrac{c . (m+n)}{ma . \frown B} - \cot B,$

$$= \frac{(m+n) . (a \frown B + b \frown A) - ma \frown B}{ma \frown B} ,$$

$$= \frac{(m+n) b \frown A + na \frown B}{ma \frown B} ;$$

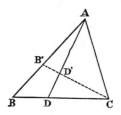

i. e. $\cot \theta = \dfrac{(m+n) \cdot \dfrac{b}{\cap B} \cdot \frown A + na \cot B}{ma}$,

$= \dfrac{(m+n)\, a \cot A + na \cot B}{ma}$,

$= \dfrac{(m+n) \cot A + n \cot B}{m}$.

Similarly, $\cot \phi = \dfrac{(m+n) \cot A + m \cot C}{n}$.

Q. E. F.

COROLLARIES.

(1) $m \cot \theta - n \cot \phi = n \cot B - m \cot C.$

(2) $\dfrac{\cot B + \cot \phi}{\cot C + \cot \theta} = \dfrac{m}{n}$.

(3) If Triangle be equilateral,

$$\cot \theta = \dfrac{m + 2n}{m} \cdot \dfrac{1}{\sqrt{3}},$$

$$\cot \phi = \dfrac{n + 2m}{n} \cdot \dfrac{1}{\sqrt{3}};$$

$$\therefore \dfrac{\cot \theta}{\cot \phi} = \dfrac{mn + 2n^2}{mn + 2m^2};$$

$$\therefore \dfrac{\tan \theta}{\tan \phi} = \dfrac{mn + 2m^2}{mn + 2n^2};$$

i. e., if $CD'B'$ be drawn $\perp$ to AD, $\dfrac{B'D'}{D'C} = \dfrac{mn + 2m^2}{mn + 2n^2}$;

e. g., if $\dfrac{m}{n} = \dfrac{1}{2}$, $\dfrac{B'D'}{D'C} = \dfrac{2}{5}$.

(4) Let $\tan A = 1$, $\tan B = 2$, $\tan C = 3$;

then $\cot \theta = \dfrac{m + n + n \cdot \frac{1}{2}}{m} = \dfrac{2m + 3n}{2m}$,

$\cot \phi = \dfrac{m + n + m \cdot \frac{1}{3}}{n} = \dfrac{3n + 4m}{3n}$;

$\therefore \dfrac{\tan \theta}{\tan \phi} = \dfrac{6mn + 8m^2}{6mn + 9n^2}$;

from which, if $\dfrac{\tan \theta}{\tan \phi}$ were given, we could find $\dfrac{m}{n}$ from a Quadratic Equation.

I tried various values, to find one which would give rational values for m and n, and found that $\frac{2}{3}$ would do, as it leads to the Quadratic

$$2 \left(6mn + 9n^2\right) - 3 \left(6mn + 8m^2\right) = 0,$$

in which $\left(B^2 - 4AC\right)$ becomes, after dividing all through by 6, $\left(1^2 + 4 \cdot 4 \cdot 3\right)$, i. e. 49.

The Quadratic is $4m^2 + mn - 3n^2 = 0$;

whence $\dfrac{m}{n} = \dfrac{-1 \pm 7}{8} = \dfrac{3}{4}$; which solves the Problem 'Given a Triangle ABC, having the tangents of its angles equal to 1, 2, 3: divide BC at D, so that, if AD be joined, and $CD'B'$ drawn $\perp$ to it, the ratio $\dfrac{B'D'}{D'C}$ may be $\dfrac{2}{3}$'. The answer is 'Divide it so that $\dfrac{BD}{DC} = \dfrac{3}{4}$'.

61. (14)

We know that the equation

$$'\left(a^2 + 4b^2 + 4c^2\right) + \left(4a^2 + b^2 + 4c^2\right) + \left(4a^2 + 4b^2 + c^2\right) = 9\left(a^2 + b^2 + c^2\right)'$$

is identically true.

Hence $a^2 + b^2 + c^2$

$= \frac{1}{9} \cdot \{(a^2 + 4\,b^2 + 4\,c^2) + (4\,a^2 + b^2 + 4\,c^2) + (4\,a^2 + 4\,b^2 + c^2)\}$;

$= \frac{1}{9} \cdot \{(a^2 + 4\,b^2 + 4\,c^2 + 8\,bc - 4\,ca - 4\,ab)$

$\qquad + (4\,a^2 + b^2 + 4\,c^2 - 4\,bc + 8\,ca - 4\,ab)$

$\qquad + (4\,a^2 + 4\,b^2 + c^2 - 4\,bc - 4\,ca + 8\,ab)\}$;

$= \frac{1}{9} \cdot \{(-a + 2\,b + 2\,c)^2 + (2\,a - b + 2\,c)^2 + (2\,a + 2\,b - c)^2\}$;

$= \left(\dfrac{-a + 2\,b + 2\,c}{3}\right)^2 + \left(\dfrac{2\,a - b + 2\,c}{3}\right)^2 + \left(\dfrac{2\,a + 2\,b - c}{3}\right)^2$.

Now $(-a + 2\,b + 2\,c) = 3\,(b + c) - (a + b + c)$;

$\therefore$, if $(a + b + c)$ be a multiple of 3, so also is $(-a + 2\,b + 2\,c)$;

$\therefore \dfrac{-a + 2\,b + 2\,c}{3}$ is an integer;

and similarly for the other 2 fractions.

Also it may be proved that, if $\dfrac{-a + 2\,b + 2\,c}{3}$ be equal to a, or b, or c, then a, b, c can be arranged in $A.\,P.$

First, let $\dfrac{-a + 2\,b + 2\,c}{3} = a$;

then $-a + 2\,b + 2\,c = 3\,a$; i.e. $b + c = 2\,a$;

secondly, let $\dfrac{-a + 2\,b + 2\,c}{3} = b$;

then $-a + 2\,b + 2\,c = 3\,b$; i.e. $2\,c = a + b$;

thirdly, let $\dfrac{-a + 2\,b + 2\,c}{3} = c$;

then $-a + 2\,b + 2\,c = 3\,c$; i.e. $2\,b = c + a$.

And similarly for the other 2 fractions.

Hence, contranominally, if a, b, c can *not* be arranged in $A.\,P.$, the 2 sets of squares have no common term.

$$\text{Q. E. D.}$$

Numerical Examples (not thought out).

a^2	b^2	c^2	$\left(\dfrac{-a+2b+2c}{3}\right)^2$	$\left(\dfrac{2a-b+2c}{3}\right)^2$	$\left(\dfrac{2a+2b-c}{3}\right)^2$
1^2	4^2	4^2	5^2	2^2	2^2
3^2	4^2	8^2	7^2	6^2	2^2
4^2	5^2	9^2	8^2	7^2	3^2

62. (14)

Let AB, AC, be the given Lines, and P the given Point.

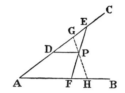

Through P draw PD parallel to AB; from DC cut off DE equal to AD; join EP, and produce it to meet AB at F.

Because $AD = DE$, and that DP is parallel to AB,

∴ $FP = PE$.

Now let GPH be any other line through P;

then $\angle PFH > \angle PEG$.

Because, in Triangles PFH, PEG, $PF = PE$, and

$\qquad \angle FPH = \angle GPE$, and $\angle PFH > \angle PEG$,

∴ $PH > PG$, and Triangle PFH > Triangle PGE.

To each add Tetragon $AFPG$;

∴ Triangle AGH > Triangle AEF.

And so of any other line through P.

Hence AEF is the least possible Triangle.

Q. E. F.

63. $\left(15,\ 26\right)$

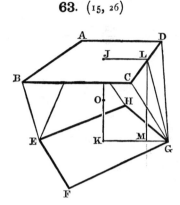

Let each side of each Square $= 2$.

Then $LG = \sqrt{3},\ MG = (\sqrt{2}-1)$;

$\therefore\ LM\,(= JK) = \sqrt{3-(2+1-2\sqrt{2})}$

$$= 2^{\frac{3}{4}};$$

$\therefore\ OJ = OK\ \ = \dfrac{1}{2^{\frac{1}{4}}}.$

Take O as origin, the X-axis $\parallel$ to AD, and the Y-axis to AB; and let JK be part of the Z-axis.

Let equation to plane containing Triangle CDG be

$$x\triangle a + y\triangle\beta + z\triangle\gamma - p = 0,$$

where p is length of perpendicular dropped, from O, upon this plane, and meeting it somewhere in LG.

Hence we can find p from equation to LG, in the XZ-plane, which will be

$$x\triangle a + z\triangle\gamma - p = 0\,;$$

now this line contains L, whose co-ordinates are $\left(1,\ \dfrac{1}{2^{\frac{1}{4}}}\right)$, and G, whose co-ordinates are $\left(\sqrt{2}, -\dfrac{1}{2^{\frac{1}{4}}}\right)$;

$$\therefore \triangle a + \frac{1}{2^{\frac{1}{4}}} \cdot \triangle \gamma - p = 0,$$

and $\sqrt{2} \cdot \triangle a - \dfrac{1}{2^{\frac{1}{4}}} \cdot \triangle \gamma - p = 0$;

$$\therefore (\sqrt{2}-1) \cdot \triangle a = \frac{2}{2^{\frac{1}{4}}} \cdot \triangle \gamma = 2^{\frac{3}{4}} \cdot \triangle \gamma;$$

$$\therefore \frac{\triangle a}{2^{\frac{3}{4}}} = \frac{\triangle \gamma}{\sqrt{2}-1} = \frac{1}{\sqrt{2^{\frac{3}{2}}+3-2^{\frac{3}{2}}}} = \frac{1}{\sqrt{3}};$$

$$\therefore \triangle a = \frac{2^{\frac{3}{4}}}{\sqrt{3}}, \ \triangle \gamma = \frac{\sqrt{2}-1}{\sqrt{3}};$$

$$\therefore p = \frac{2^{\frac{3}{4}}}{\sqrt{3}} + \frac{\sqrt{2}-1}{2^{\frac{1}{4}} \cdot \sqrt{3}} = \frac{\sqrt{2}+1}{2^{\frac{1}{4}} \cdot \sqrt{3}}.$$

Now area of $CDG = \sqrt{3}$;

$\therefore$ volume of pyramid, whose base is CDG and whose vertex

is $O, = \dfrac{\sqrt{2}+1}{3 \cdot 2^{\frac{1}{4}}}$;

and there are eight such pyramids in the solid;

$$\therefore \text{ their sum} = \frac{8\left(\sqrt{2}+1\right)}{3 \cdot 2^{\frac{1}{4}}}.$$

Also volume of pyramid, whose base is $ABCD$, and whose

vertex is $O, = \dfrac{4}{3 \cdot 2^{\frac{1}{4}}}$;

and there are 2 such pyramids in the solid;

$$\therefore \text{ their sum} = \frac{8}{3 \cdot 2^{\frac{1}{4}}};$$

$$\therefore \text{ volume of solid} = \frac{8\left(2+\sqrt{2}\right)}{3 \cdot 2^{\frac{1}{4}}} = \frac{8 \cdot 2^{\frac{1}{4}} \cdot \left(\sqrt{2}+1\right)}{3}$$

Q. E. F.

64. (15)

Let ABC be the given Triangle, and O the given Point; and

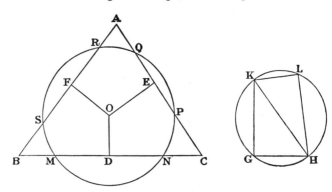

let OD, its distance from BC, be less than either OE or OF, its
distances from CA, AB.

Draw a line GH equal to OE, and $GK \perp$ it and equal to OF;
and join HK; and about the Triangle GHK describe a Circle;
and place in it a line KL equal to OD; and join LH.

Because sqs of KL, LH = sqs of KG, GH, and that KL is
less than either KG or GH, $\therefore$ LH is greater than either;

$\therefore$ a Circle, with centre O, and radius equal to LH, will cut
all three Lines, in two Points each.   Describe this Circle.

Then sqs of MD, DO = sqs of PE, EO;

also sq. of LH = sqs of RF, FO;

$\therefore$ sqs of MD, DO, LH = sqs of PE, RF, EO, FO;

but sqs of DO, LH = sqs of KL, LH,

= sqs of GH, GK = sqs of EO, FO;

$\therefore$ sq. of MD = sqs of PE, RF;

$\therefore$ 4 times sq. of MD = 4 times sqs of PE, RF;

i.e. sq. of MN = sqs of PQ, RS.

Hence MN, PQ, RS, can be sides of a right-angled Triangle.

Q. E. F.

65. ($_{15}$)

Calling the angles $\frac{1}{x}$, $\frac{1}{y}$, $\frac{1}{z}$, of 360°, we must have

$$\frac{1}{x} + \frac{1}{y} + \frac{1}{z} = \tfrac{1}{2};$$

an Indeterminate Equation with 3 unknowns.

Evidently none of them can be so small as 2.

(1) Let $x = 3$; then $\frac{1}{y} + \frac{1}{z} = \tfrac{1}{6}$.

Now, if $\frac{1}{y} = \frac{k}{k+l} \times \tfrac{1}{6}$, $\frac{1}{z}$ will $= \frac{l}{k+l} \times \tfrac{1}{6}$:

hence k can only be 1, or 2, or 3, or 6; and the same is true of l.

(N.B. It is assumed that the fractions $\dfrac{k}{k+l}$, $\dfrac{l}{k+l}$, are in their lowest terms.)

Let $\frac{1}{y}$ be $\nless \frac{1}{z}$. Then $\dfrac{k}{k+l} \nless \tfrac{1}{2}$.

Then its possible values are $\tfrac{1}{2}$, so that $\dfrac{l}{k+l} = \tfrac{1}{2}$

$$\tfrac{2}{3}, \cdot \quad \cdot \quad \cdot \quad \cdot \quad \cdot \quad \tfrac{1}{3}$$
$$\tfrac{3}{4}, \cdot \quad \cdot \quad \cdot \quad \cdot \quad \cdot \quad \tfrac{1}{4}$$
$$\tfrac{3}{5}, \cdot \quad \cdot \quad \cdot \quad \cdot \quad \cdot \quad \tfrac{2}{5}$$
$$\tfrac{6}{7}, \cdot \quad \cdot \quad \cdot \quad \cdot \quad \cdot \quad \tfrac{1}{7}.$$

This gives 5 sets of values for $\frac{1}{x}$, $\frac{1}{y}$, $\frac{1}{z}$, viz. :

$\tfrac{1}{3}, \tfrac{1}{12}, \tfrac{1}{12};$ $\tfrac{1}{3}, \tfrac{1}{9}, \tfrac{1}{18};$ $\tfrac{1}{3}, \tfrac{1}{8}, \tfrac{1}{24};$ $\tfrac{1}{3}, \tfrac{1}{10}, \tfrac{1}{15};$ $\tfrac{1}{3}, \tfrac{1}{7}, \tfrac{1}{42}.$

(2) Let $x = 4$. Then $\frac{1}{y} + \frac{1}{z} = \tfrac{1}{4}$, and, as before, k can only be 1, or 2, or 4, and the same is true of l. Hence the

possible values for $\dfrac{k}{k+l}$ are $\frac{1}{2}$, so that $\dfrac{l}{k+l}=\frac{1}{2}$

$$\frac{2}{3}, \quad . \quad . \quad . \quad . \quad . \quad \frac{1}{3}$$

$$\frac{4}{5}, \quad . \quad . \quad . \quad . \quad . \quad \frac{1}{5}$$

This gives 3 more sets of values for $\dfrac{1}{x}$, $\dfrac{1}{y}$, $\dfrac{1}{z}$, viz.

$$\tfrac{1}{4}, \tfrac{1}{8}, \tfrac{1}{8}; \quad \tfrac{1}{4}, \tfrac{1}{6}, \tfrac{1}{12}; \quad \tfrac{1}{2}, \tfrac{1}{5}, \tfrac{1}{20}.$$

(3) Let $x = 5$; then $\dfrac{1}{y} + \dfrac{1}{z} = \frac{3}{10}$.

Hence denominator must contain factor "3", and k can be only 1, or 2, or 5, or 10; and the same is true of l.

Hence possible values of $\dfrac{k}{k+l}$ are $\frac{1}{2}$, so that $\dfrac{l}{k+l}=\frac{1}{2}$

$$\frac{2}{3}, \quad . \quad . \quad . \quad . \quad . \quad \frac{1}{3}$$

$$\frac{5}{6}, \quad . \quad . \quad . \quad . \quad . \quad \frac{1}{6}.$$

This gives 2 sets of values for $\dfrac{1}{x}$, $\dfrac{1}{y}$, $\dfrac{1}{z}$, viz. :—

$$\tfrac{1}{5}, \tfrac{1}{5}, \tfrac{1}{10}; \quad \tfrac{1}{5}, \tfrac{1}{4}, \tfrac{1}{20};$$

but the latter (a fact overlooked in thinking out) we have had already.

(4) Let $x = 6$; then $\dfrac{1}{y} + \dfrac{1}{z} = \frac{1}{3}$.

Hence k can be only 1, or 3, and the same is true of l.

Hence possible values for $\dfrac{k}{k+l}$ are $\frac{1}{2}$, so that $\dfrac{l}{k+l}=\frac{1}{2}$

$$\frac{3}{4}, \quad . \quad . \quad . \quad . \quad \frac{1}{4}.$$

This gives 2 sets of values, viz. :—

$$\tfrac{1}{6}, \tfrac{1}{6}, \tfrac{1}{6}; \quad \tfrac{1}{6}, \tfrac{1}{4}, \tfrac{1}{12};$$

but the latter (a fact overlooked in thinking out) we have had already.

There is no use in giving, to x, any values greater than 6; for these would make $\frac{1}{y} + \frac{1}{z} > \frac{1}{3}$; so that one or other must be $> \frac{1}{6}$; i.e. either y or z must < 6, and we should get old values over again.

Hence there are 10 different shapes.

Q. E. F.

The 10 sets of angles (I am not certain that they were all thought out) are

$$(1) \quad 120°, \quad 30°, \quad 30°;$$
$$(2) \quad 120°, \quad 40°, \quad 20°;$$
$$(3) \quad 120°, \quad 45°, \quad 15°;$$
$$(4) \quad 120°, \quad 36°, \quad 24°;$$
$$(5) \quad 120°, \quad 51\tfrac{3}{7}°, \quad 8\tfrac{4}{7}°;$$
$$(6) \quad 90°, \quad 45°, \quad 45°;$$
$$(7) \quad 90°, \quad 60°, \quad 30°;$$
$$(8) \quad 90°, \quad 72°, \quad 18°;$$
$$(9) \quad 72°, \quad 72°, \quad 36°;$$
$$(10) \quad 60°, \quad 60°, \quad 60°.$$

66. (15, 26)

Write k for $\dfrac{a}{a+\beta}$. Now the counters must be either both white, or one white and one black. Let chance of first condition be x; hence chance of second is $(1-x)$. Hence chance of drawing white is $x \times 1 + (1-x) \times \tfrac{1}{2}$.

$$\therefore \quad x + \frac{1-x}{2} = k; \quad \therefore \quad x = 2k-1;$$
$$\therefore \quad (1-x) = 2-2k.$$

Let a counter now be drawn and prove white; then chance of 'observed event,' in 1st condition, is 1, and, in 2nd condition, $\tfrac{1}{2}$;

Hence the chances, of the existence of these two conditions, are proportional to $(2k-1) \times 1$, $(2-2k) \times \frac{1}{2}$; i.e. are proportional to $2k-1$, $1-k$;

hence these chances actually are $\dfrac{2k-1}{k}$, $\dfrac{1-k}{k}$;

hence the chance of now drawing white,

$$\text{is} \quad \frac{2k-1}{k} \times 1 + \frac{1-k}{k} \times \tfrac{1}{2};$$

$$\text{i.e.} \quad \frac{3k-1}{2k}.$$

Hence the effect of *one* repetition of the experiment has been to change k into $\dfrac{3k-1}{2k}$.

Hence a second repetition of it will change

$$\frac{3k-1}{2k} \text{ into } \frac{3 \times \dfrac{3k-1}{2k} - 1}{2 \times \dfrac{3k-1}{2k}}; \text{ i.e. into } \frac{7k-3}{6k-2}.$$

We have now to discover the law (if there is one) for the series

$$k, \quad \frac{3k-1}{2k}, \quad \frac{7k-3}{6k-2},$$

regarding these as identical functions of 1, 2, 3.

We can write the 1st and 2nd term in the form of the 3rd, thus:—

$$\frac{k-0}{0 \times k - (-1)}, \quad \frac{3k-1}{2k-0}, \quad \frac{7k-3}{6k-2}$$

and, by inspection, we see that each is of the form

$$\frac{(2^n-1) \times k - (2^{n-1}-1)}{(2^n-2) \times k - (2^{n-1}-2)},$$

where n denotes the place of the term.

Suppose this law to hold for n terms, what will be the effect of repeating the experiment once more?

We know that it changes k into $\dfrac{3k-1}{2k}$. Hence the new chance will be

$$\dfrac{3 \times \dfrac{(2^n-1) \times k-(2^{n-1}-1)}{(2^n-2) \times k-(2^{n-1}-2)} - 1}{2 \times \dfrac{(2^n-1) \times k-(2^{n-1}-1)}{(2^n-2) \times k-(2^{n-1}-2)}};$$

i. e. $\dfrac{k \times (3 \cdot 2^n - 3 - 2^n + 2) - 3 \cdot 2^{n-1} + 3 + 2^{n-1} - 2}{(2^{n+1}-2) \times k-(2^n-2)}$;

i. e. $\dfrac{(2^{n+1}-1) \times k-(2^n-1)}{(2^{n+1}-2) \times k-(2^n-2)}$;

i. e. the $\overline{n+1}|^{\text{th}}$ term of the series will follow the same law. But we know that the law holds for the 1st, 2nd, and 3rd terms. Hence it holds universally.

Hence, after m repetitions of the experiment, the chance of drawing white will be the $\overline{m+1}|^{\text{th}}$ term of the above series; i. e. it will be

$$\dfrac{(2^{m+1}-1) \times k-(2^{''}-1)}{(2^{m+1}-2) \times k-(2^m-2)}.$$

Now, for k, write $\dfrac{a}{a+\beta}$.

Then chance is $\dfrac{(2^{m+1}-1) \times a-(2^m-1) \cdot (a+\beta)}{(2^{m+1}-2) \times a-(2^m-2) \cdot (a+\beta)}$;

i. e. $\dfrac{(2^{m+1}-2^{'''}) a-(2^{'n}-1) \cdot \beta}{(2^{m+1}-2^{''}) a-(2^m-2) \cdot \beta}$;

i. e. $\dfrac{2^m \cdot (a-\beta)+\beta}{2^{'''} \cdot (a-\beta)+2\beta}$.

Q. E. F.

EXAMPLE—Let chance be $\tfrac{9}{10}$; and then let experiment be repeated 5 times more.

Here $a = 9$, $\beta = 1$;

∴ chance becomes $\dfrac{32 \times 8+1}{32 \times 8+2}$, i. e. $\tfrac{257}{258}$.

67. (16, 26)

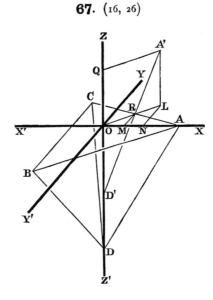

Let $ABCD$ be the socket. Revolve the Tetrahedron until the plane, in it, DOA has taken the new position $D'QA'$; and let edge DA, in its new position, meet the socket-rim AC at R. From A' draw $A'L \perp XY$-plane. Join OR, and produce it to L. And draw RM, LN, the y-ordinates of R and L.

Then co-ordinates of A' are ON, NL, LA'.

Call OM, MR, 'x', y''; and OA, OR, OD, 'a, a', h'; and $\angle XOR$ 'θ'.

It is evident that the vertical axis of the Tetrahedron always coincides with the Z-axis.

Hence A moves on the surface of a cylinder,

i. e. $x^2 + y^2 = a^2$ . . . . (1)

Now $\angle XAC = 150°$;

$\therefore$ Equation to AC is $y = -\dfrac{1}{\sqrt{3}}.(x-a)$;

i.e. $x+\sqrt{3}.y = a$ . . . . . . (2)

Also Equation to OR is $\dfrac{x}{\frown\theta} = \dfrac{y}{\frown\theta} = \delta$;

$\therefore$, at R, $\dfrac{x'}{\frown\theta} = \dfrac{y'}{\frown\theta} = a'$; . . . . (3)

$\therefore$, by (2), $a'.\frown\theta + \sqrt{3}.a'.\frown\theta = a$;

$\therefore$ $a' = \dfrac{a}{\frown\theta + \sqrt{3}.\frown\theta}$ . . . . . . (4)

Also, by similar $\triangle$s $D'QA'$, $D'OR$, $QA' : QD' :: OR \cdot OD'$

i.e. $a:h :: \dfrac{a}{\frown\theta + \sqrt{3}.\frown\theta} : h-z$;

$\therefore$ $h-z = \dfrac{h}{\frown\theta + \sqrt{3}.\frown\theta}$;

but $\frown\theta = \dfrac{x}{a}$, and $\frown\theta = \dfrac{y}{a}$;

$\therefore$ $h-z = \dfrac{ah}{x+\sqrt{3}.y}$;

i.e. $(x+\sqrt{3}.y).(h-z) = ah$ . . . . (5)

Equations (1) and (5) give the required Locus.

Q. E. F.

68. (16, 26)

Let the Nos of bottles, taken out on the 3 days, be 'x, y, z'. Let each bottle have cost $10\,v$ pence, and therefore be sold for $11\,v$ pence.

Then the Treasurer's receipts, on the 3 days, were $(x-1).11\,v$, $y.11\,v-v$, $(z-1).11\,v-v$; yielding, as profits (i.e. as remainders after deducting cost-price of bottles taken out), $xv-11\,v$, $yv-v$, $zv-12\,v$. Then these 3 quantities are equal.

Hence $y = x - 10$, and $z = x + 1$;

∴ total No. of bottles, being $(x+y+z)$, $= 3x - 9$.

Now total profits are $(x+y+z) . v - 24\,v$; i. e. $(3x-33)\,v$;

∴ profit, per bottle $= \dfrac{(3x - 33) \cdot v}{3x - 9}$; and this must $= 6$;

∴ $(x-11) . v = (x-3) . 6$.

Also $z . 11\,v = 11 \times 240$; i.e. $(x+1) . 11\,v = 11 \times 240$;

∴ $\dfrac{x - 11}{x + 1} = \dfrac{6 . (x-3)}{240}$;

∴ $(x+1) . (x-3) = 40 . (x-11)$;

∴ $x^2 - 2x - 3 = 40x - 440$;

∴ $x^2 - 42x + 437 = 0$.

Now $42^2 - 4 \times 437 = 1764 - 1748 = 16$;

∴ $x = \dfrac{42 \pm 4}{2} = 23$ or 19;

∴ No. of bottles $= 60$ or 48; but it is a multiple of 5; ∴ it $= 60$.

Also $(x+1) . 11\,v = 11 \times 240$; i.e. $24\,v = 240$;

∴ $v = 10$;

i. e. the wine was bought @ 8/4 a bottle, and sold @ 9/2 a bottle.   Q. E. F.

69. (17, 26)

§ 1. Let $\angle BAD = k . A$, $\angle CBE = l . B$, $\angle ACF = m . C$.

Then $\angle ABE = (1-l) . B$.

Now $\angle BC'D = \angle C'AB + \angle C'BA$.

i. e. $k . A + (1-l) . B = C$. . . . . (1)

Similarly, $l . B + (1-m) . C = A$; . . . . (2)

and $m . C + (1-k) . A = B$. . . . . (3)

From equations (1) and (3), l and m may be found in terms of k: but these, taken along with k, will not be *similar* functions of the single variable k. We must have k a certain function of A, B, C, and θ (say); l a similar function of B, C, A, and θ; and m a similar function of C, A, B, and θ; i.e. we must have

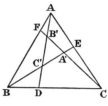

$$k = f(A,\ B,\ C,\ \theta),$$
$$l = f(B,\ C,\ A,\ \theta),$$
$$m = f(C,\ A,\ B,\ \theta).$$

Now we know, by (1), that $kA - lB = C - B$;

i.e. $A \cdot f(A,\ B,\ C,\ \theta) - B \cdot f(B,\ C,\ A,\ \theta) = C - B$.

Now, as an experiment, let

$$k \cdot A = xA + yB + zC + \theta,$$
$$l \cdot B = xB + yC + zA + \theta;$$

then $kA - lB = (x - z) \cdot A + (y - x) \cdot B + (z - y) \cdot C$;

$\therefore\ x - z = 0$; i.e. $x = z$;

$z - y = 1$; i.e. $z = y + 1$.

These conditions will be fulfilled, if we make $y = 1$, and $x = z = 2$; so that

$$kA = 2A + B + 2C + \theta,$$
$$lB = 2B + C + 2A + \theta;$$

which would make

$$f(A,\ B,\ C,\ \theta) \text{ mean } \frac{2A + B + 2C + \theta}{A}.$$

Now this may evidently be simplified by omitting $(A + B + C)$, which is constant; and we then have $k = \dfrac{A + C + \theta}{A}$; or, in a yet simpler form, by again subtracting 180°, $\quad k = \dfrac{\theta - B}{A}$.

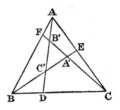

Similarly $\quad l = \dfrac{\theta - C}{B}$,

$$m = \dfrac{\theta - A}{C}.$$

Q. E. F.

§ 2. We see that $kA = \theta - B$, so that $\angle ADC$ is evidently equal to θ; and so are $\angle$s BEA, CFB.

This gives us a geometrical construction, viz. to draw lines from A, B, C, so that each makes the same angle θ with the opposite side.

§ 3. Let us now ascertain the limits within which the value of θ must lie.

We know that $kA = \theta - B$.

Now $kA \not> A$; ∴ $\theta - B \not> A$; i. e. $\theta \not> A + B$;

i. e. $\theta \not>$ the supplement of C;

and of course this is true for *each* of the three angles A, B, C; i. e. if A, B, C, be the order of the angles in a descending order of magnitude, $\theta \not>$ supplement of A.

Again $kA \not< 0$.

Hence $\theta - B \not< 0$; i. e. $\theta \not< B$;

and of course this is true for *each* angle.

Hence if A, B, C, be the order in a descending order of magnitude, $\theta \not< A$, and $\not> 180° - A$.

Q. E. F.

§ 4. We have now to ascertain the ratio which $B'C'$ bears to BC.

In Triangle ABC', whose ∠s are $(\theta - B)$, $(180° - \theta - A)$, $(180° - C)$, we have

$$AC' = \frac{AB}{\frown AC'B} \cdot \frown ABC' = \frac{c}{\frown C} \cdot \frown (\theta + A)$$

$$= \frac{a}{\frown A} \cdot \frown (\theta + A);$$

$$BC' = \frac{AB}{\frown AC'B} \cdot \frown BAC' = \frac{c}{\frown C} \cdot \frown (\theta - B)$$

$$= \frac{a}{\frown A} \cdot \frown (\theta - B)$$

∴, by symmetry, $AB' = \dfrac{a}{\frown A} \cdot \frown (\theta - A)$.

Now $B'C' = AC' - AB'$;

$$\therefore \text{ it } = \frac{a}{\frown A} \{\frown (\theta + A) - \frown (\theta - A)\},$$

$$= \frac{a}{\frown A} \cdot 2 \triangle \theta \frown A = a \, 2 \triangle \theta.$$

Hence $\dfrac{a'}{a} = \dfrac{b'}{b} = \dfrac{c'}{c} = 2 \triangle \theta.$

Q. E. F.

70. (17, 27)

Before folding the Plane containing the Triangles, the locus of their vertices is evidently a Line parallel to their common base. Hence, if the base of the Tetrahedron $= 1$, we may imagine a slip of paper, whose width is $\dfrac{\sqrt{3}}{2}$, attached to the front facet of the Tetrahedron, and wrapped round towards the right; and the upper edge of this slip will evidently be the locus of the vertices. This slip may be conveniently regarded as divided into equilateral Triangles, placed base-downwards and base-upwards alternately, and it is evident that these Triangles will successively cover the facets of the Tetrahedron, in the order 'front, right side, base, left side, front, &c.'; and its *upper* edge, made up of the bases of the inverted constituent Triangles, will evidently run as follows. Calling the successive Triangles, after the first (which occupies the front facet of the Tetrahedron), 'a' (base-up), 'β' (base-down), 'γ' (base-up), 'δ' (base-down), 'ϵ' (base-up), and so on, the locus consists of the bases of a, γ, &c. Now 'a' will occupy the right facet, its base coinciding with the back-edge of the Tetrahedron; 'β' will occupy the base of the Tetrahedron, its base coinciding with the front-edge; 'γ' will occupy the left facet, its base coinciding with the back-edge; and so on. Hence the locus runs down the back-edge; up again; and so on. Which answers Question (1).

Q. E. F.

We may therefore, in answering the other three questions, consider the slip *before* it is folded, and calculate the positions of the vertices along its *upper* edge: and the problems thus become '*plane*' ones.

(2) Gives us a right-angled Triangle, whose left-hand base-angle is $15°$, and whose altitude is $\dfrac{\sqrt{3}}{2}$ We must calculate its base, and then, deducting half the base of the initial Triangle (i. e. deducting $\frac{1}{2}$), we shall get the distance, measured along the upper edge of the slip, from the vertex of the initial Triangle to the vertex of the given Triangle; and from that we can calculate how many times we must go down and up the back-edge to reach it. Call the base of this right-angled Triangle 'x'. Then $\dfrac{\sqrt{3}}{2} \div x = \tan 15°$.

Now call $\tan 15° \;'t\;'$; then $\dfrac{2t}{1-t^2} = \tan 30° = \dfrac{1}{\sqrt{3}}$;

$\therefore\; 1-t^2 = 2\sqrt{3}\,.t;\;\; t^2 + 2\sqrt{3}\,.t - 1 = 0$;

$\therefore\; t = \dfrac{-2\sqrt{3}\pm 4}{2} =$ (rejecting negative value) $2-\sqrt{3}$.

$\therefore\; x = \dfrac{\sqrt{3}}{2(2-\sqrt{3})} \quad \dfrac{\sqrt{3}}{2}(2+\sqrt{3}) = \sqrt{3}+\tfrac{3}{2}$.

Deducting $\tfrac{1}{2}$, we get $(\sqrt{3}+1)$ as the required distance.

Now $\sqrt{3} = 1\cdot7$ &c.; $\therefore$ distance $= 2\cdot7$ &c.

Hence we must go *down* back-edge, up again, and then about 7 down again. This answers question (2).

(3) We need to go down the back-edge, and up again; i. e. we must use up the upward bases of 'a' and 'γ'. Hence the base of the required right-angled Triangle is $2\tfrac{1}{2}$. Hence the required left-hand base-angle is

$$\tan^{-1}\Big(\frac{\sqrt{3}}{2}\div\frac{5}{2}\Big);\;\; \text{i. e. } \tan^{-1}\frac{\sqrt{3}}{5}.$$

Hence, for the required base-angle, we have $\dfrac{\sin}{\cos} = \dfrac{\sqrt{3}}{5}$;

$\therefore\; \dfrac{\sin}{\sqrt{3}} = \dfrac{\cos}{5} = \dfrac{1}{\sqrt{28}};\;\; \therefore \sin = \sqrt{\dfrac{3}{28}} = \dfrac{\sqrt{84}}{28}$,

$= \dfrac{\text{rather over }9}{28};\qquad$
$\begin{array}{r|l} 7 & 9\cdot \\ \hline 4 & 1\cdot28 \text{ \&c.} \\ \hline & \cdot32 \text{ \&c.} \end{array}$

Now (by mem. tech.) $\sin^{-1}\cdot3 = 17\cdot45$ &c°.

$$\sin^{-1}\cdot4 = 23\cdot57 \text{ \&c°.}$$

and the required angle is about $\tfrac{1}{5}$ of the way from one to the other. But the difference is almost exactly $6°$. Hence we must add, to the lesser, about $1\tfrac{1}{5}$ degrees, or $1\cdot20°$. And the total will be about $18\cdot65°$.

(4) Here the right-angled Triangle has, for its base, $3\frac{1}{2}$.

∴ the required base-angle has, for its tangent,

$$\left(\frac{\sqrt{3}}{2} \div \frac{7}{2}\right); \text{ i.e. } \frac{\sqrt{3}}{7};$$

$$\therefore \frac{\sin}{\sqrt{3}} = \frac{\cos}{7} = \frac{1}{\sqrt{52}}; \quad \therefore \sin = \sqrt{\frac{3}{52}} = \text{nearly } \sqrt{\frac{1}{17}},$$

$$= \text{nearly } \frac{\sqrt{17}}{17}. \quad \text{Now } \sqrt{17} = 4.12 \text{ &c.} \quad \therefore \sin = .24 \text{ &c.}$$

Now $\sin^{-1}.2 = 11.53$ &c°.; and we must go about half-way to the next angle, viz. 17.45 &c°. The difference is about $6°$; ∴ we must add about $3°$. Hence the answer is about $14.53°$.

71. (18)

Let ABC be the given Triangle, and P the given Point.

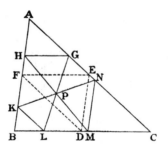

Bisect the sides of ABC at D, E, F; and join these Points.

First, let P be within the Triangle DEF.

Draw HG parallel to BC, so that its distance from BC may be double the distance of P from BC; join GP, HP, and produce them to meet BC in L, M. From L draw LK parallel to AC; join KP, and produce it to meet AC at N: join MN.

Because HG is parallel to LM,

∴ $GP = PL$, and $HP = PM$;

∵ KL is parallel to GN, and that $LP = PG$,

∴ $KP = PN$; ∴ MN is parallel to HK.

Now the Triangles PGH, PLM, are equal in all respects ;

∴ $GH = LM$. Similarly $KL = GN$, and $MN = HK$.

If P lies on FE, HG and LM vanish, and the Hexagon becomes a Parallelogram.

If P lies at D, the Hexagon becomes the line BC.

If P lies outside the Triangle DEF, the Problem is insoluble.

Q. E. F.

72. (18, 27)

We know that, if a bag contained 3 counters, 2 being black and one white, the chance of drawing a black one would be $\frac{2}{3}$; and that any *other* state of things would *not* give this chance.

Now the chances, that the given bag contains (a) BB, (β) BW, (γ) WW, are respectively $\frac{1}{4}$, $\frac{1}{2}$, $\frac{1}{4}$.

Add a black counter.

Then the chances, that it contains (a) BBB, (β) BWB, (γ) WWB, are, as before, $\frac{1}{4}$, $\frac{1}{2}$, $\frac{1}{4}$.

Hence the chance, of now drawing a black one,

$$= \tfrac{1}{4} \cdot 1 + \tfrac{1}{2} \cdot \tfrac{2}{3} + \tfrac{1}{4} \cdot \tfrac{1}{3} = \tfrac{2}{3}.$$

Hence the bag now contains BBW (since any *other* state of things would *not* give this chance).

Hence, before the black counter was added, it contained BW, i. e. one black counter and one white.

Q. E. F.

THE END.

A TANGLED TALE

"AT A PACE OF SIX MILES IN THE HOUR."

Frontispiece.

A TANGLED TALE

BY

LEWIS CARROLL

WITH SIX ILLUSTRATIONS

BY

ARTHUR B. FROST

Hoc meum tale quale est accipe.

DOVER PUBLICATIONS, INC.
NEW YORK

To My Pupil.

Beloved Pupil! Tamed by thee,
  Addish-, Subtrac-, Multiplica=tion,
Division, Fractions, Rule of Three,
  Attest thy deft manipulation!

Then onward! Let the voice of Fame
  From Age to Age repeat thy story,
Till thou hast won thyself a name
  Exceeding even Euclid's glory!

PREFACE.

THIS Tale originally appeared as a serial in *The Monthly Packet*, beginning in April, 1880. The writer's intention was to embody in each Knot (like the medicine so dexterously, but ineffectually, concealed in the jam of our early childhood) one or more mathematical questions—in Arithmetic, Algebra, or Geometry, as the case might be—for the amusement, and possible edification, of the fair readers of that Magazine.

L. C.

October, 1885.

CONTENTS.

A TANGLED TALE.

KNOT I.

EXCELSIOR.

"Goblin, lead them up and down."

THE ruddy glow of sunset was already fading into the sombre shadows of night, when two travellers might have been observed swiftly—at a pace of six miles in the hour—descending the rugged side of a mountain; the younger bounding from crag to crag with the agility of a fawn, while his companion, whose aged limbs seemed ill at ease in the heavy chain armour habitually worn by tourists in that district, toiled on painfully at his side.

As is always the case under such circumstances, the younger knight was the first to break the silence.

" A goodly pace, I trow ! " he exclaimed.   " We sped not thus in the ascent ! "

" Goodly, indeed ! " the other echoed with a groan.   " We clomb it but at three miles in the hour."

" And on the dead level our pace is——? " the younger suggested ; for he was weak in statistics, and left all such details to his aged companion.

" Four miles in the hour," the other wearily replied.   " Not an ounce more," he added, with that love of metaphor so common in old age, " and not a farthing less ! "

" 'Twas three hours past high noon when we left our hostelry," the young man said, musingly.   " We shall scarce be back by supper-time.   Perchance mine host will roundly deny us all food ! "

" He will chide our tardy return," was the grave reply, " and such a rebuke will be meet."

" A brave conceit ! " cried the other, with a merry laugh.   " And should we bid him bring us yet another course, I trow his answer will be tart ! "

" We shall but get our deserts," sighed the elder knight, who had never seen a joke in his life, and was somewhat displeased at his companion's untimely levity.   " 'Twill be nine of the clock," he added in an undertone, " by the time we regain our hostelry. Full many a mile shall we have plodded this day ! "

" How many ? How many ? " cried the eager youth, ever athirst for knowledge.

The old man was silent.

" Tell me," he answered, after a moment's thought, " what time it was when we stood together on yonder peak. Not exact to the minute ! " he added hastily, reading a protest in the young man's face. " An' thy guess be within one poor half-hour of the mark, 'tis all I ask of thy mother's son ! Then will I tell thee, true to the last inch, how far we shall have trudged betwixt three and nine of the clock."

A groan was the young man's only reply ; while his convulsed features and the deep wrinkles that chased each other across his manly brow, revealed the abyss of arithmetical agony into which one chance question had plunged him.

KNOT II.

ELIGIBLE APARTMENTS.

"Straight down the crooked lane,
And all round the square."

" LET's ask Balbus about it," said Hugh.

" All right," said Lambert.

" *He* can guess it," said Hugh.

" Rather," said Lambert.

No more words were needed : the two brothers understood each other perfectly.

Balbus was waiting for them at the hotel : the journey down had tired him, he said : so his two pupils had been the round of the place, in search of lodgings, without the old tutor who had been their inseparable companion from their childhood. They had named him after the hero of their Latin exercise-book, which overflowed with anecdotes of that versatile genius—anecdotes whose vagueness

"BALBUS WAS ASSISTING HIS MOTHER-IN-LAW TO CONVINCE THE DRAGON."

in detail was more than compensated by their sensational brilliance. " Balbus has overcome all his enemies" had been marked by their tutor, in the margin of the book, "Successful Bravery." In this way he had tried to extract a moral from every anecdote about Balbus—sometimes one of warning, as in " Balbus had borrowed a healthy dragon," against which he had written " Rashness in Specu- lation "—sometimes of encouragement, as in the words " Influence of Sympathy in United Action," which stood opposite to the anecdote " Balbus was assisting his mother-in-law to convince the dragon " —and sometimes it dwindled down to a single word, such as " Prudence," which was all he could extract from the touching record that " Balbus, having scorched the tail of the dragon, went away." His pupils liked the short morals best, as it left them more room for marginal illustrations, and in this instance they required all the space they could get to exhibit the rapidity of the hero's departure.

Their report of the state of things was dis- couraging. That most fashionable of watering- places, Little Mendip, was " chockfull" (as the boys expressed it) from end to end. But in one Square they had seen no less than four cards, in different houses, all announcing in flaming capitals "ELIGIBLE APARTMENTS." "So there's plenty of choice, after all, you see," said spokesman Hugh in conclusion.

"That doesn't follow from the data," said Balbus, as he rose from the easy chair, where he had been dozing over *The Little Mendip Gazette*. "They may be all single rooms. However, we may as well see them. I shall be glad to stretch my legs a bit."

An unprejudiced bystander might have objected that the operation was needless, and that this long, lank creature would have been all the better with even shorter legs : but no such thought occurred to his loving pupils. One on each side, they did their best to keep up with his gigantic strides, while Hugh repeated the sentence in their father's letter, just received from abroad, over which he and Lambert had been puzzling. "He says a friend of his, the Governor of——*what* was that name again, Lambert ?" ("Kgovjni," said Lambert.) "Well, yes. The Governor of——what-you-may-call-it ——wants to give a *very* small dinner-party, and he means to ask his father's brother-in-law, his brother's father-in-law, his father-in-law's brother, and his brother-in-law's father : and we're to guess how many guests there will be."

There was an anxious pause. "*How* large did he say the pudding was to be ? " Balbus said at last. " Take its cubical contents, divide by the cubical contents of what each man can eat, and the quotient——"

" He didn't say anything about pudding," said Hugh, "—and here's the Square," as they turned a corner and came into sight of the " eligible apartments."

" It *is* a Square ! " was Balbus' first cry of delight, as he gazed around him. " Beautiful ! Beau-ti-ful ! Equilateral ! *And* rectangular ! "

The boys looked round with less enthusiasm. " Number nine is the first with a card," said prosaic Lambert ; but Balbus would not so soon awake from his dream of beauty.

" See, boys ! " he cried. " Twenty doors on a side ! What symmetry ! Each side divided into twenty-one equal parts ! It's delicious ! "

" Shall I knock, or ring ? " said Hugh, looking in some perplexity at a square brass plate which bore the simple inscription " RING ALSO."

" Both," said Balbus. " That's an Ellipsis,

my boy. Did you never see an Ellipsis before ? "

" I couldn't hardly read it," said Hugh, evasively. " It's no good having an Ellipsis, if they don't keep it clean."

" Which there is *one* room, gentlemen," said the smiling landlady. "And a sweet room too ! As snug a little back-room——"

" We will see it," said Balbus gloomily, as they followed her in. " I knew how it would be ! One room in each house ! No view, I suppose ? "

" Which indeed there *is*, gentlemen ! " the landlady indignantly protested, as she drew up the blind, and indicated the back garden.

" Cabbages, I perceive," said Balbus. " Well, they're green, at any rate."

" Which the greens at the shops," their hostess explained, " are by no means dependable upon. Here you has them on the premises, *and* of the best."

" Does the window open ? " was always Balbus' first question in testing a lodging : and " Does the chimney smoke ? " his second. Satisfied on all points, he secured the refusal of the room, and they moved on to Number Twenty-five.

This landlady was grave and stern. " I've

nobbut one room left," she told them : "and it gives on the back-gyardin."

"But there are cabbages?" Balbus suggested.

The landlady visibly relented. "There is, sir," she said : "and good ones, though I say it as shouldn't. We can't rely on the shops for greens. So we grows them ourselves."

"A singular advantage," said Balbus : and, after the usual questions, they went on to Fifty-two.

"And I'd gladly accommodate you all, if I could," was the greeting that met them. "We are but mortal," ("Irrelevant!" muttered Balbus) "and I've let all my rooms but one."

"Which one is a back-room, I perceive," said Balbus : "and looking out on—on cabbages, I presume?"

"Yes, indeed, sir!" said their hostess. "Whatever *other* folks may do, *we* grows our own. For the shops——"

"An excellent arrangement!" Balbus interrupted. "Then one can really depend on their being good. Does the window open?"

The usual questions were answered satisfactorily : but this time Hugh added one of his own invention —"Does the cat scratch?"

The landlady looked round suspiciously, as if to make sure the cat was not listening, " I will not deceive you, gentlemen," she said. " It *do* scratch, but not without you pulls its whiskers ! It'll never do it," she repeated slowly, with a visible effort to recall the exact words of some written agreement between herself and the cat, "without you pulls its whiskers ! "

" Much may be excused in a cat so treated," said Balbus, as they left the house and crossed to Number Seventy-three, leaving the landlady curt-seying on the doorstep, and still murmuring to herself her parting words, as if they were a form of blessing, " ——not without you pulls its whiskers ! "

At Number Seventy-three they found only a small shy girl to show the house, who said " yes'm " in answer to all questions.

" The usual room," said Balbus, as they marched in : " the usual back-garden, the usual cabbages. I suppose you can't get them good at the shops ? "

" Yes'm," said the girl.

" Well, you may tell your mistress we will take the room, and that her plan of growing her own cabbages is simply *admirable !* "

" Yes'm," said the girl, as she showed them out.

" One day-room and three bed-rooms," said Balbus, as they returned to the hotel. " We will take as our day-room the one that gives us the least walking to do to get to it."

" Must we walk from door to door, and count the steps ? " said Lambert.

" No, no ! Figure it out, my boys, figure it out ! " Balbus gaily exclaimed, as he put pens, ink, and paper before his hapless pupils, and left the room.

" I say ! It'll be a job ! " said Hugh.

" Rather ! " said Lambert.

KNOT III.

MAD MATHESIS.

" I waited for the train."

" WELL, they call me so because I *am* a little mad, I suppose," she said, good-humouredly, in answer to Clara's cautiously-worded question as to how she came by so strange a nick-name. " You see, I never do what sane people are expected to do now-a-days. I never wear long trains, (talking of trains, that's the Charing Cross Metropolitan Station—I've something to tell you about *that*), and I never play lawn-tennis. I can't cook an omelette. I can't even set a broken limb ! *There's* an ignoramus for you ! "

Clara was her niece, and full twenty years her junior; in fact, she was still attending a High School—an institution of which Mad Mathesis spoke with undisguised aversion. " Let a woman be meek and lowly!" she would say. "None of your High Schools for me!" But it was vacation-time just now, and Clara was her guest, and Mad Mathesis was showing her the sights of that Eighth Wonder of the world—London.

"The Charing Cross Metropolitan Station!" she resumed, waving her hand towards the entrance as if she were introducing her niece to a friend. "The Bayswater and Birmingham Extension is just completed, and the trains now run round and round continuously—skirting the border of Wales, just touching at York, and so round by the east coast back to London. The way the trains run is *most* peculiar. The westerly ones go round in two hours; the easterly ones take three; but they always manage to start two trains from here, opposite ways, punctually every quarter-of-an-hour."

"They part to meet again," said Clara, her eyes filling with tears at the romantic thought.

"No need to cry about it!" her aunt grimly remarked. "They don't meet on the same line of rails, you know. Talking of meeting, an idea strikes me!" she added, changing the subject with her usual abruptness. "Let's go opposite ways

round, and see which can meet most trains.   No
need for a chaperon—ladies' saloon, you know.
You shall go whichever way you like, and we'll
have a bet about it !"

"I never make bets," Clara said very gravely.
"Our excellent preceptress has often warned
us——"

"You'd be none the worse if you did !" Mad
Mathesis interrupted.   "In fact, you'd be the
better, I'm certain !"

"Neither does our excellent preceptress approve
of puns," said Clara.   "But we'll have a match, if
you like.   Let me choose my train," she added
after a brief mental calculation, "and I'll engage
to meet exactly half as many again as you do."

"Not if you count fair," Mad Mathesis bluntly
interrupted.   "Remember, we only count the
trains we meet *on the way*.   You mustn't count
the one that starts as you start, nor the one that
arrives as you arrive."

"That will only make the difference of *one* train,"
said Clara, as they turned and entered the station.
"But I never travelled alone before.   There'll be
no one to help me to alight.   However, I don't
mind.   Let's have a match."

A ragged little boy overheard her remark, and came running after her. "Buy a box of cigar-lights, Miss!" he pleaded, pulling her shawl to attract her attention. Clara stopped to explain.

"I never smoke cigars," she said in a meekly apologetic tone. "Our excellent preceptress——," but Mad Mathesis impatiently hurried her on, and the little boy was left gazing after her with round eyes of amazement.

The two ladies bought their tickets and moved slowly down the central platform, Mad Mathesis prattling on as usual—Clara silent, anxiously re-considering the calculation on which she rested her hopes of winning the match.

"Mind where you go, dear!" cried her aunt, checking her just in time. "One step more, and you'd have been in that pail of cold water!"

"I know, I know," Clara said, dreamily. "The pale, the cold, and the moony——"

"Take your places on the spring-boards!" shouted a porter.

"What are *they* for!" Clara asked in a terrified whisper.

"Merely to help us into the trains." The elder lady spoke with the nonchalance of one quite used to the process. "Very few people can get into a carriage without help in less than three seconds, and the trains only stop for one second." At this moment the whistle was heard, and two trains rushed into the station. A moment's pause, and they were gone again ; but in that brief interval several hundred passengers had been shot into them, each flying straight to his place with the accuracy of a Minie bullet—while an equal number were showered out upon the side-platforms.

Three hours had passed away, and the two friends met again on the Charing Cross platform, and eagerly compared notes. Then Clara turned away with a sigh. To young impulsive hearts, like hers, disappointment is always a bitter pill. Mad Mathesis followed her, full of kindly sympathy.

"Try again, my love !" she said, cheerily. "Let us vary the experiment. We will start as we did before, but not to begin counting till our trains meet. When we see each other, we will say 'One !' and so count on till we come here again."

Clara brightened up. "I shall win *that*," she exclaimed eagerly, "if I may choose my train !"

Another shriek of engine whistles, another up-heaving of spring-boards, another living avalanche

plunging into two trains as they flashed by : and
the travellers were off again.

Each gazed eagerly from her carriage window,
holding up her handkerchief as a signal to her
friend. A rush and a roar. Two trains shot past
each other in a tunnel, and two travellers leaned
back in their corners with a sigh—or rather with
two sighs—of relief. " One !" Clara murmured to
herself. " Won ! It's a word of good omen. *This*
time, at any rate, the victory will be mine !"

But *was* it ?

KNOT IV.

T H E   D E A D   R E C K O N I N G.

"I did dream of money-bags to-night."

NOONDAY on the open sea within a few degrees of the Equator is apt to be oppressively warm; and our two travellers were now airily clad in suits of dazzling white linen, having laid aside the chain-armour which they had found not only endurable in the cold mountain air they had lately been breathing, but a necessary precaution against the daggers of the banditti who infested the heights. Their holiday-trip was over, and they were now on their way home, in the monthly packet which plied between the two great ports of the island they had been exploring.

Along with their armour, the tourists had laid aside the antiquated speech it had pleased them to affect while in knightly disguise, and had returned to the ordinary style of two country gentlemen of the Twentieth Century.

Stretched on a pile of cushions, under the shade of a huge umbrella, they were lazily watching some native fishermen, who had come on board at the last landing-place, each carrying over his shoulder a small but heavy sack. A large weighing-machine, that had been used for cargo at the last port, stood on the deck; and round this the fishermen had gathered, and, with much unintelligible jabber, seemed to be weighing their sacks.

"More like sparrows in a tree than human talk, isn't it?" the elder tourist remarked to his son, who smiled feebly, but would not exert himself so far as to speak. The old man tried another listener.

"What have they got in those sacks, Captain?" he inquired, as that great being passed them in his never ending parade to and fro on the deck.

The Captain paused in his march, and towered over the travellers—tall, grave, and serenely self-satisfied.

"Fishermen," he explained, "are often passengers in My ship. These five are from Mhruxi—

the place we last touched at—and that's the way they carry their money. The money of this island is heavy, gentlemen, but it costs little, as you may guess. We buy it from them by weight—about five shillings a pound. I fancy a ten pound-note would buy all those sacks."

By this time the old man had closed his eyes— in order, no doubt, to concentrate his thoughts on these interesting facts ; but the Captain failed to realise his motive, and with a grunt resumed his monotonous march.

Meanwhile the fishermen were getting so noisy over the weighing-machine that one of the sailors took the precaution of carrying off all the weights, leaving them to amuse themselves with such substitutes in the form of winch-handles, belaying-pins, &c., as they could find. This brought their excitement to a speedy end : they carefully hid their sacks in the folds of the jib that lay on the deck near the tourists, and strolled away.

When next the Captain's heavy footfall passed, the younger man roused himself to speak.

" *What* did you call the place those fellows came from, Captain ? " he asked.

" Mhruxi, sir."

" And the one we are bound for ? "

The Captain took a long breath, plunged into the word, and came out of it nobly. " They call it Kgovjni, sir."

" K—I give it up ! " the young man faintly said.

He stretched out his hand for a glass of iced water which the compassionate steward had brought him a minute ago, and had set down, unluckily, just outside the shadow of the umbrella. It was scalding hot, and he decided not to drink it. The effort of making this resolution, coming close on the fatiguing conversation he had just gone through, was too much for him : he sank back among the cushions in silence.

His father courteously tried to make amends for his *nonchalance*.

" Whereabouts are we now, Captain ? " said he, " Have you any idea ? "

The Captain cast a pitying look on the ignorant landsman. " I could tell you *that*, sir," he said, in a tone of lofty condescension, " to an inch ! "

" You don't say so ! " the old man remarked, in a tone of languid surprise.

" And mean so," persisted the Captain. " Why, what do you suppose would become of My ship, if I were to lose My Longitude and My Latitude? Could *you* make anything of My Dead Reckoning?"

"Nobody could, I'm sure!" the other heartily rejoined.

But he had overdone it.

"It's *perfectly* intelligible," the Captain said, in an offended tone, "to any one that understands such things." With these words he moved away, and began giving orders to the men, who were preparing to hoist the jib.

Our tourists watched the operation with such interest that neither of them remembered the five money-bags, which in another moment, as the wind filled out the jib, were whirled overboard and fell heavily into the sea.

But the poor fishermen had not so easily forgotten their property. In a moment they had rushed to the spot, and stood uttering cries of fury, and pointing, now to the sea, and now to the sailors who had caused the disaster.

The old man explained it to the Captain.

"Let us make it up among us," he added in conclusion. "Ten pounds will do it, I think you said?"

But the Captain put aside the suggestion with a wave of the hand.

" No, sir!" he said, in his grandest manner. " You will excuse Me, I am sure; but these are My passengers. The accident has happened on board My ship, and under My orders. It is for Me to make compensation." He turned to the angry fishermen. "Come here, my men!" he said, in the Mhruxian dialect. "Tell me the weight of each sack. I saw you weighing them just now."

Then ensued a perfect Babel of noise, as the five natives explained, all screaming together, how the sailors had carried off the weights, and they had done what they could with whatever came handy.

Two iron belaying-pins, three blocks, six holy-stones, four winch-handles, and a large hammer, were now carefully weighed, the Captain superintending and noting the results. But the matter did not seem to be settled, even then : an angry discussion followed, in which the sailors and the five natives all joined : and at last the Captain approached our tourists with a disconcerted look, which he tried to conceal under a laugh.

"It's an absurd difficulty," he said. "Perhaps one of you gentlemen can suggest something. It seems they weighed the sacks two at a time!"

"If they didn't have five separate weighings, of course you can't value them separately," the youth hastily decided.

"Let's hear all about it," was the old man's more cautious remark.

"They *did* have five separate weighings," the Captain said, "·but—Well, it beats *me* entirely!" he added, in a sudden burst of candour. "Here's the result. First and second sack weighed twelve pounds; second and third, thirteen and a half; third and fourth, eleven and a half; fourth and fifth, eight: and then they say they had only the large hammer left, and it took *three* sacks to weigh it down—that's the first, third and fifth—and *they* weighed sixteen pounds. There, gentlemen! Did you ever hear anything like *that?*"

The old man muttered under his breath "If only my sister were here!" and looked helplessly at his son. His son looked at the five natives. The five natives looked at the Captain The Captain looked at nobody: his eyes were cast down, and he seemed to be saying softly to himself "Contemplate one another, gentlemen, if such be your good pleasure. *I* contemplate *Myself!*"

KNOT V.

"Look here, upon this picture, and on this."

"And what 'made you choose the first train, Goosey?" said Mad Mathesis, as they got into the cab. "Couldn't you count better than *that?*"

"I took an extreme case," was the tearful reply. "Our excellent preceptress always says 'When in doubt, my dears, take an extreme case.' And I *was* in doubt."

"Does it always succeed?" her aunt enquired.

Clara sighed. "Not *always*," she reluctantly admitted. "And I can't make out why. One day she was telling the little girls—they make such a noise at tea, you know—'The more noise you make, the less jam you will have, and *vice versâ*.' And I thought they wouldn't know what '*vice versâ*' meant: so I explained it to them. I said 'If you make an infinite noise, you'll get no jam : and if you make no noise, you'll get an infinite lot of jam.' But our excellent preceptress said that wasn't a good instance. *Why* wasn't it ?" she added plaintively.

Her aunt evaded the question. " One sees certain objections to it," she said. " But how did you work it with the Metropolitan trains ? None of them go infinitely fast, I believe."

" I called them hares and tortoises," Clara said— a little timidly, for she dreaded being laughed at. " And I thought there couldn't be so many hares as tortoises on the Line : so I took an extreme case— one hare and an infinite number of tortoises."

" An extreme case, indeed," her aunt remarked with admirable gravity : "and a most dangerous state of things ! "

" And I thought, if I went with a tortoise, there would be only *one* hare to meet : but if I went with the hare—you know there were *crowds* of tortoises ! "

" It wasn't a bad idea," said the elder lady, as they left the cab, at the entrance of Burlington House. " You shall have another chance to-day. We'll have a match in marking pictures."

Clara brightened up.   " I should like to try again, very much," she said.   " I'll take more care this time.   How are we to play ? "

To this question Mad Mathesis made no reply : she was busy drawing lines down the margins of the catalogue.   " See," she said after a minute, " I've drawn three columns against the names of the pictures in the long room, and I want you to fill them with oughts and crosses—crosses for good marks and oughts for bad.   The first column is for choice of subject, the second for arrangement, the third for colouring.   And these are the conditions of the match.   You must give three crosses to two or three pictures.   You must give two crosses to four or five——"

" Do you mean *only* two crosses ? " said Clara. " Or may I count the three-cross pictures among the two-cross pictures ? "

"Of course you may," said her aunt.   "Any one, that has *three* eyes, may be said to have *two* eyes, I suppose ? "

Clara followed her aunt's dreamy gaze across the crowded gallery, half-dreading to find that there was a three-eyed person in sight.

" And you must give one cross to nine or ten."

"And which wins the match?" Clara asked, as she carefully entered these conditions on a blank leaf in her catalogue.

"Whichever marks fewest pictures."

"But suppose we marked the same number?"

"Then whichever uses most marks."

Clara considered. "I don't think it's much of a match," she said. "I shall mark nine pictures, and give three crosses to three of them, two crosses to two more, and one cross each to all the rest."

"Will you, indeed?" said her aunt. "Wait till you've heard all the conditions, my impetuous child. You must give three oughts to one or two pictures, two oughts to three or four, and one ought to eight or nine. I don't want you to be *too* hard on the R.A.'s."

Clara quite gasped as she wrote down all these fresh conditions. "It's a great deal worse than Circulating Decimals!" she said. "But I'm determined to win, all the same!"

Her aunt smiled grimly. "We can begin *here*," she said, as they paused before a gigantic picture, which the catalogue informed them was the "Portrait of Lieutenant Brown, mounted on his favorite elephant."

"He looks awfully conceited!" said Clara. "I don't think he was the elephant's favorite Lieutenant. What a hideous picture it is! And it takes up room enough for twenty!"

"Mind what you say, my dear!" her aunt interposed. "It's by an R.A.!"

But Clara was quite reckless. "I don't care who it's by!" she cried. "And I shall give it three bad marks!"

Aunt and niece soon drifted away from each other in the crowd, and for the next half-hour Clara was hard at work, putting in marks and rubbing them out again, and hunting up and down for suitable pictures. This she found the hardest part of all. "I *can't* find the one I want!" she exclaimed at last, almost crying with vexation.

"What is it you want to find, my dear?" The voice was strange to Clara, but so sweet and gentle that she felt attracted to the owner of it, even before she had seen her; and when she turned, and met the smiling looks of two little old ladies, whose round dimpled faces, exactly alike, seemed never to have known a care, it was as much as she could do—as she confessed to Aunt Mattie afterwards—to keep herself from hugging them both.

"I was looking for a picture," she said, "that has a good subject—and that's well arranged—but badly coloured."

The little old ladies glanced at each other in some alarm. "Calm yourself, my dear," said the one who had spoken first, "and try to remember which it was. What *was* the subject?"

"Was it an elephant, for instance?" the other sister suggested. They were still in sight of Lieutenant Brown.

"I don't know, indeed!" Clara impetuously replied. "You know it doesn't matter a bit what the subject *is*, so long as it's a good one!"

Once more the sisters exchanged looks of alarm, and one of them whispered something to the other, of which Clara caught only the one word "mad."

"They mean Aunt Mattie, of course," she said to herself—fancying, in her innocence, that London was like her native town, where everybody knew everybody else. "If you mean my aunt," she added aloud, "she's *there*—just three pictures beyond Lieutenant Brown."

"Ah, well! Then you'd better go to her, my dear!" her new friend said, soothingly. "*She'll* find you the picture you want. Good-bye, dear!"

"Good-bye, dear!" echoed the other sister, "Mind you don't lose sight of your aunt!" And the pair trotted off into another room, leaving Clara rather perplexed at their manner.

"They're real darlings!" she soliloquised. "I wonder why they pity me so!" And she wandered on, murmuring to herself "It must have two good marks, and——"

KNOT VI.

HER RADIANCY.

"One piecee thing that my have got,
Maskee* that thing my no can do.
You talkee you no sabey what?
Bamboo."

THEY landed, and were at once conducted to the Palace. About half way they were met by the Governor, who welcomed them in English—a great relief to our travellers, whose guide could speak nothing but Kgovjnian.

"I don't half like the way they grin at us as we go by!" the old man whispered to his son. "And why do they say 'Bamboo!' so often?"

"It alludes to a local custom," replied the Governor, who had overheard the question. "Such persons as happen in any way to displease Her Radiancy are usually beaten with rods."

* "*Maskee*," in Pigeon-English, means "*without.*"

"WHY DO THEY SAY 'BAMBOO!' SO OFTEN?"

The old man shuddered. "A most objectional local custom!" he remarked with strong emphasis. "I wish we had never landed! Did you notice that black fellow, Norman, opening his great mouth at us? I verily believe he would like to eat us!"

Norman appealed to the Governor, who was walking at his other side. "Do they often eat distinguished strangers here?" he said, in as indifferent a tone as he could assume.

"Not often—not ever!" was the welcome reply. "They are not good for it. Pigs we eat, for they are fat. This old man is thin."

"And thankful to be so!" muttered the elder traveller. "Beaten we shall be without a doubt. It's a comfort to know it won't be Beaten without the B! My dear boy, just look at the peacocks!"

They were now walking between two unbroken lines of those gorgeous birds, each held in check, by means of a golden collar and chain, by a black slave, who stood well behind, so as not to interrupt the view of the glittering tail, with its network of rustling feathers and its hundred eyes.

The Governor smiled proudly. "In your honour," he said, "Her Radiancy has ordered up ten thousand additional peacocks. She will, no doubt, decorate you, before you go, with the usual Star and Feathers."

"It'll be Star without the S!" faltered one of his hearers.

"Come, come! Don't lose heart!" said the other. "All this is full of charm for me."

"You are young, Norman," sighed his father; "young and light-hearted. For me, it is Charm without the C."

"The old one is sad," the Governor remarked with some anxiety. "He has, without doubt, effected some fearful crime?"

"But I haven't!" the poor old gentleman hastily exclaimed. "Tell him I haven't, Norman!"

"He has not, as yet," Norman gently explained. And the Governor repeated, in a satisfied tone, "Not as yet."

"Yours is a wondrous country!" the Governor resumed, after a pause. "Now here is a letter from a friend of mine, a merchant, in London. He and his brother went there a year ago, with a thousand pounds apiece; and on New-Year's-day they had sixty thousand pounds between them!"

"How did they do it?" Norman eagerly exclaimed. Even the elder traveller looked excited.

The Governor handed him the open letter. "Any-body can do it, when once they know how," so ran this oracular document. "We borrowed nought: we stole nought. We began the year with only a thousand pounds apiece: and last New-Year's day we had sixty thousand pounds between us—sixty thousand golden sovereigns!"

Norman looked grave and thoughtful as he handed back the letter. His father hazarded one guess. "Was it by gambling?"

"A Kgovjnian never gambles," said the Governor gravely, as he ushered them through the palace gates. They followed him in silence down a long passage, and soon found themselves in a lofty hall, lined entirely with peacocks' feathers. In the centre was a pile of crimson cushions, which almost concealed the figure of Her Radiancy—a plump little damsel, in a robe of green satin dotted with silver stars, whose pale round face lit up for a moment with a half-smile as the travellers bowed before her, and then relapsed into the exact ex-pression of a wax doll, while she languidly mur-mured a word or two in the Kgovjnian dialect.

The Governor interpreted. "Her Radiancy wel-comes you. She notes the Impenetrable Placidity

of the old one, and the Imperceptible Acuteness
of the youth."

Here the little potentate clapped her hands, and
a troop of slaves instantly appeared, carrying trays
of coffee and sweetmeats, which they offered to the
guests, who had, at a signal from the Governor,
seated themselves on the carpet.

"Sugar-plums!" muttered the old man. "One
might as well be at a confectioner's! Ask for a
penny bun, Norman!"

"Not so loud!" his son whispered. "Say something complimentary!" For the Governor was
evidently expecting a speech.

"We thank Her Exalted Potency," the old man
timidly began. "We bask in the light of her smile,
which——"

"The words of old men are weak!" the Governor
interrupted angrily. "Let the youth speak!"

"Tell her," cried Norman, in a wild burst of
eloquence, "that, like two grasshoppers in a volcano,
we are shrivelled up in the presence of Her Spang-
led Vehemence!"

"It is well," said the Governor, and translated
this into Kgovjnian. "I am now to tell you" he
proceeded, "what Her Radiancy requires of you

before you go. The yearly competition for the post of Imperial Scarf-maker is just ended; you are the judges. You will take account of the rate of work, the lightness of the scarves, and their warmth. Usually the competitors differ in one point only. Thus, last year, Fifi and Gogo made the same number of scarves in the trial-week, and they were equally light; but Fifi's were twice as warm as Gogo's and she was pronounced twice as good. But this year, woe is me, who can judge it? Three competitors are here, and they differ in all points! While you settle their claims, you shall be lodged, Her Radiancy bids me say, free of expense— in the best dungeon, and abundantly fed on the best bread and water."

The old man groaned. "All is lost!" he wildly exclaimed. But Norman heeded him not: he had taken out his note-book, and was calmly jotting down the particulars.

" Three they be," the Governor proceeded, " Lolo, Mimi, and Zuzu. Lolo makes 5 scarves while Mimi makes 2; but Zuzu makes 4 while Lolo makes 3! Again, so fairylike is Zuzu's handiwork, 5 of her scarves weigh no more than one of Lolo's; yet Mimi's is lighter still—5 of hers will but balance

3 of Zuzu's! And for warmth one of Mimi's is equal to 4 of Zuzu's; yet one of Lolo's is as warm as 3 of Mimi's!"

Here the little lady once more clapped her hands.

"It is our signal of dismissal!" the Governor hastily said. "Pay Her Radiancy your farewell compliments—and walk out backwards."

The walking part was all the elder tourist could manage. Norman simply said "Tell Her Radiancy we are transfixed by the spectacle of Her Serene Brilliance, and bid an agonized farewell to her Condensed Milkiness!"

"Her Radiancy is pleased," the Governor reported, after duly translating this. "She casts on you a glance from Her Imperial Eyes, and is confident that you will catch it!"

"That I warrant we shall!" the elder traveller moaned to himself distractedly.

Once more they bowed low, and then followed the Governor down a winding staircase to the Imperial Dungeon, which they found to be lined with coloured marble, lighted from the roof, and splendidly though not luxuriously furnished with a bench of polished malachite. "I trust you will not delay the calculation," the Governor said, ushering them in with much ceremony. " I have known great inconvenience—great and serious inconvenience—result to those unhappy ones who have delayed to execute the commands of Her Radiancy ! And on this occasion she is resolute : she says the thing must and shall be done : and she has ordered up ten thousand additional bamboos ! " With these words he left them, and they heard him lock and bar the door on the outside.

" I told you how it would end ! " moaned the elder traveller, wringing his hands, and quite forgetting in his anguish that he had himself proposed the expedition, and had never predicted anything of the sort. " Oh that we were well out of this miserable business ! "

" Courage ! " cried the younger cheerily. " *Hæc olim meminisse juvabit !* The end of all this will be glory ! "

" Glory without the L ! " was all the poor old man could say, as he rocked himself to and fro on the malachite bench. " Glory without the L ! "

KNOT VII.

PETTY   CASH.

"Base is the slave that pays."

" AUNT MATTIE ! "

" My child ? "

" *Would* you mind writing it down at once ? I shall be quite *certain* to forget it if you don't ! "

" My dear, we really must wait till the cab stops. How can I possibly write anything in the midst of all this jolting ? "

" But *really* I shall be forgetting it ! "

Clara's voice took the plaintive tone that her aunt never knew how to resist, and with a sigh the old lady drew forth her ivory tablets and prepared to record the amount that Clara had just spent at the confectioner's shop. Her expenditure was always made out of her aunt's purse, but the poor girl knew, by bitter experience, that sooner or later

"Mad Mathesis" would expect an exact account of every penny that had gone, and she waited, with ill-concealed impatience, while the old lady turned the tablets over and over, till she had found the one headed "PETTY CASH."

"Here's the place," she said at last, "and here we have yesterday's luncheon duly entered. *One glass lemonade* (Why can't you drink water, like me?) *three sandwiches* (They never put in half mustard enough. I told the young woman so, to her face; and she tossed her head—like her impudence!) *and seven biscuits. Total one-and-two-pence.* Well, now for to-day's?"

"One glass of lemonade——" Clara was beginning to say, when suddenly the cab drew up, and a courteous railway-porter was handing out the bewildered girl before she had had time to finish her sentence.

Her aunt pocketed the tablets instantly. "Business first," she said: "petty cash—which is a form of pleasure, whatever *you* may think—afterwards." And she proceeded to pay the driver, and to give voluminous orders about the luggage, quite deaf to the entreaties of her unhappy niece that she would enter the rest of the luncheon account.

A note for American readers: Knot VII. In British currency, a shilling contains twelve pence. The phrase "One and two-pence" (written 1 s. 2 d.) means "one shilling and two-pence."

"My dear, you really must cultivate a more capacious mind!" was all the consolation she vouchsafed to the poor girl. "Are not the tablets of your memory wide enough to contain the record of one single luncheon?"

"Not wide enough! Not half wide enough!" was the passionate reply.

The words came in aptly enough, but the voice was not that of Clara, and both ladies turned in some surprise to see who it was that had so suddenly struck into their conversation. A fat little old lady was standing at the door of a cab, helping the driver to extricate what seemed an exact duplicate of herself: it would have been no easy task to decide which was the fatter, or which looked the more good-humoured of the two sisters.

"I tell you the cab-door isn't half wide enough!" she repeated, as her sister finally emerged, somewhat after the fashion of a pellet from a pop-gun, and she turned to appeal to Clara. "Is it, dear?" she said, trying hard to bring a frown into a face that dimpled all over with smiles.

"Some folks is too wide for 'em," growled the cab-driver.

"Don't provoke me, man!" cried the little old

"I TELL YOU THE CAB-DOOR ISN'T HALF WIDE ENOUGH!"

lady, in what she meant for a tempest of fury. " Say another word and I'll put you into the County Court, and sue you for a *Habeas Corpus!*" The cabman touched his hat, and marched off, grinning.

" Nothing like a little Law to cow the ruffians, my dear ! " she remarked confidentially to Clara. " You saw how he quailed when I mentioned the *Habeas Corpus?* Not that I've any idea what it means, but it sounds very grand, doesn't it ? "

" It's very provoking," Clara replied, a little vaguely.

"Very ! " the little old lady eagerly repeated. " And we're very much provoked indeed. Aren't we, sister ? "

" I never was so provoked in all my life ! " the fatter sister assented, radiantly.

By this time Clara had recognised her picture-gallery acquaintances, and, drawing her aunt aside, she hastily whispered her reminiscences. " I met them first in the Royal Academy—and they were very kind to me—and they were lunching at the next table to us, just now, you know—and they tried to help me to find the picture I wanted—and I'm sure they're dear old things ! "

"Friends of yours, are they?" said Mad Mathesis. "Well, I like their looks. You can be civil to them, while I get the tickets. But do try and arrange your ideas a little more chronologically!"

And so it came to pass that the four ladies found themselves seated side by side on the same bench waiting for the train, and chatting as if they had known one another for years.

"Now this I call quite a remarkable coincidence!" exclaimed the smaller and more talkative of the two sisters—the one whose legal knowledge had annihilated the cab-driver. "Not only that we should be waiting for the same train, and at the same station—*that* would be curious enough—but actually on the same day, and the same hour of the day! That's what strikes *me* so forcibly!" She glanced at the fatter and more silent sister, whose chief function in life seemed to be to support the family opinion, and who meekly responded—

"And me too, sister!"

"Those are not *independent* coincidences ——" Mad Mathesis was just beginning, when Clara ventured to interpose.

" There's no jolting here," she pleaded meekly.
" *Would* you mind writing it down now ? "

Out came the ivory tablets once more. " What
was it, then ? " said her aunt.

" One glass of lemonade, one sandwich, one
biscuit—Oh dear me ! " cried poor Clara, the
historical tone suddenly changing to a wail of
agony.

" Toothache ? " said her aunt calmly, as she
wrote down the items. The two sisters instantly
opened their reticules and produced two different
remedies for neuralgia, each marked " unequalled."

" It isn't that ! " said poor Clara. " Thank you
very much. It's only that I *can't* remember how
much I paid ! "

" Well, try and make it out, then," said her aunt.
" You've got yesterday's luncheon to help you,
you know. And here's the luncheon we had the
day before—the first day we went to that shop—
*one glass lemonade, four sandwiches, ten bis-
cuits. Total, one-and-fivepence.*" She handed the
tablets to Clara, who gazed at them with eyes so
dim with tears that she did not at first notice
that she was holding them upside down.

The two sisters had been listening to all this

with the deepest interest, and at this junc-
ture the smaller one softly laid her hand on
Clara's arm.

"Do you know, my dear," she said coaxingly,
"my sister and I are in the very same predicament!
Quite identically the very same predicament!
Aren't we, sister?"

" Quite identically and absolutely the very——"
began the fatter sister, but she was constructing
her sentence on too large a scale, and the little one
would not wait for her to finish it.

" Yes, my dear," she resumed ; " we were lunching at the very same shop as you were—and we
had two glasses of lemonade and three sandwiches
and five biscuits—and neither of us has the least
idea what we paid.   Have we, sister?"

" Quite identically and absolutely——" murmured the other, who evidently considered that
she was now a whole sentence in arrears, and that
she ought to discharge one obligation before con-
tracting any fresh liabilities ; but the little lady
broke in again, and she retired from the conversation a bankrupt.

" *Would* you make it out for us, my dear?"
pleaded the little old lady.

"You can do Arithmetic, I trust?" her aunt said, a little anxiously, as Clara turned from one tablet to another, vainly trying to collect her thoughts. Her mind was a blank, and all human expression was rapidly fading out of her face.

A gloomy silence ensued.

KNOT VIII.

"This little pig went to market:
This little pig staid at home."

"By Her Radiancy's express command," said the Governor, as he conducted the travellers, for the last time, from the Imperial presence, "I shall now have the ecstasy of escorting you as far as the outer gate of the Military Quarter, where the agony of parting—if indeed Nature can survive the shock —must be endured! From that gate grurmstipths start every quarter of an hour, both ways——"

"Would you mind repeating that word?" said Norman. "Grurm—— ?"

"Grurmstipths," the Governor repeated. "You call them omnibuses in England. They run both ways, and you can travel by one of them all the way down to the harbour."

The old man breathed a sigh of relief; four hours of courtly ceremony had wearied him, and he had been in constant terror lest something should call into use the ten thousand additional bamboos.

In another minute they were crossing a large quadrangle, paved with marble, and tastefully decorated with a pigsty in each corner. Soldiers, carrying pigs, were marching in all directions: and in the middle stood a gigantic officer giving orders in a voice of thunder, which made itself heard above all the uproar of the pigs.

" It is the Commander-in-Chief ! " the Governor hurriedly whispered to his companions, who at once followed his example in prostrating themselves before the great man. The Commander gravely bowed in return. He was covered with gold lace from head to foot : his face wore an expression of deep misery : and he had a little black pig under each arm. Still the gallant fellow did his best, in the midst of the orders he was every moment issuing to his men, to bid a courteous farewell to the departing guests.

" Farewell, oh old one—carry these three to the

South corner—and farewell to thee, thou young one—put this fat one on the top of the others in the Western sty—may your shadows never be less—woe is me, it is wrongly done! Empty out all the sties, and begin again!" And the soldier leant upon his sword, and wiped away a tear.

" He is in distress," the Governor explained as they left the court. " Her Radiancy has commanded him to place twenty-four pigs in those four sties, so that, as she goes round the court, she may always find the number in each sty nearer to ten than the number in the last."

" Does she call ten nearer to ten than nine is ? ' said Norman.

" Surely," said the Governor. " Her Radiancy would admit that ten is nearer to ten than nine is—and also nearer than eleven is."

" Then I think it can be done," said Norman.

The Governor shook his head. " The Commander has been transferring them in vain for four months," he said. " What hope remains ? And Her Radiancy has ordered up ten thousand additional——"

" The pigs don't seem to enjoy being transferred,"

the old man hastily interrupted. He did not like the subject of bamboos.

"They are only *provisionally* transferred, you know," said the Governor. "In most cases they are immediately carried back again : so they need not mind it. And all is done with the greatest care, under the personal superintendence of the Commander-in-Chief."

"Of course she would only go *once* round ? " said Norman.

"Alas, no ! " sighed their conductor. "Round and round. Round and round. These are Her Radiancy's own words. But oh, agony ! Here is the outer gate, and we must part ! " He sobbed as he shook hands with them, and the next moment was briskly walking away.

"He *might* have waited to see us off ! " said the old man, piteously.

"And he needn't have begun whistling the very *moment* he left us ! " said the young one, severely. "But look sharp—here are two what's-his-names in the act of starting ! "

Unluckily, the sea-bound omnibus was full. "Never mind ! " said Norman, cheerily. "We'll walk on till the next one overtakes us.'

They trudged on in silence, both thinking over the military problem, till they met an omnibus coming from the sea. The elder traveller took out his watch. "Just twelve minutes and a half since we started," he remarked in an absent manner. Suddenly the vacant face brightened; the old man had an idea. "My boy!" he shouted, bringing his hand down upon Norman's shoulder so suddenly as for a moment to transfer his centre of gravity beyond the base of support.

Thus taken off his guard, the young man wildly staggered forwards, and seemed about to plunge into space: but in another moment he had gracefully recovered himself. "Problem in Precession and Nutation," he remarked — in tones where filial respect only just managed to conceal a shade of annoyance. "What is it?" he hastily added, fearing his father might have been taken ill. "Will you have some brandy?"

"When will the next omnibus overtake us? When? When?" the old man cried, growing more excited every moment.

Norman looked gloomy. "Give me time," he

said. " I must think it over." And once more
the travellers passed on in silence—a silence
only broken by the distant squeals of the
unfortunate little pigs, who were still being
provisionally transferred from sty to sty, under
the personal superintendence of the Commander-
in-Chief.

KNOT IX.

A SERPENT WITH CORNERS.

> " Water, water, every where,
>   Nor any drop to drink."

" IT'LL just take one more pebble."

" What ever *are* you doing with those buckets ? "

The speakers were Hugh and Lambert. Place, the beach of Little Mendip. Time, 1.30, P.M. Hugh was floating a bucket in another a size larger, and trying how many pebbles it would carry without sinking. Lambert was lying on his back, doing nothing.

For the next minute or two Hugh was silent, evidently deep in thought. Suddenly he started. " I say, look here, Lambert ! " he cried.

" If it's alive, and slimy, and with legs, I don't care to," said Lambert.

" Didn't Balbus say this morning that, if a body

is immersed in liquid, it displaces as much liquid
as is equal to its own bulk ? " said Hugh.

" He said things of that sort, " Lambert vaguely
replied.

" Well, just look here a minute. Here's the
little bucket almost quite immersed : so the water
displaced ought to be just about the same bulk.
And now just look at it ! " He took out the little
bucket as he spoke, and handed the big one to
Lambert. " Why, there's hardly a teacupful ! Do
you mean to say *that* water is the same bulk as the
little bucket ? "

" Course it is," said Lambert.

" Well, look here again ! " cried Hugh, triumph-
antly, as he poured the water from the big bucket
into the little one. " Why, it doesn't half fill it ! "

" That's *its* business," said Lambert. " If Balbus
says it's the same bulk, why, it *is* the same bulk,
you know."

" Well, I don't believe it," said Hugh.

" You needn't," said Lambert. " Besides, it's
dinner-time. Come along."

They found Balbus waiting dinner for them, and
to him Hugh at once propounded his difficulty.

" Let's get you helped first," said Balbus, briskly

cutting away at the joint. "You know the old proverb 'Mutton first, mechanics afterwards'?"

The boys did *not* know the proverb, but they accepted it in perfect good faith, as they did every piece of information, however startling, that came from so infallible an authority as their tutor. They ate on steadily in silence, and, when dinner was over, Hugh set out the usual array of pens, ink, and paper, while Balbus repeated to them the problem he had prepared for their afternoon's task.

"A friend of mine has a flower-garden—a very pretty one, though no great size—"

"How big is it?" said Hugh.

"That's what *you* have to find out!" Balbus gaily replied. "All *I* tell you is that it is oblong in shape—just half a yard longer than its width— and that a gravel-walk, one yard wide, begins at one corner and runs all round it."

"Joining into itself?" said Hugh.

"*Not* joining into itself, young man. Just before doing *that*, it turns a corner, and runs round the garden again, alongside of the first portion, and then inside that again, winding in and in, and each lap touching the last one, till it has used up the whole of the area."

" Like a serpent with corners ? " said Lambert.

" Exactly so.   And if you walk the whole length of it, to the last inch, keeping in the centre of the path, it's exactly two miles and half a furlong. Now, while you find out the length and breadth of the garden, I'll see if I can think out that sea-water puzzle."

" You said it was a flower-garden ? " Hugh inquired, as Balbus was leaving the room.

" I did," said Balbus.

" Where do the flowers grow ? " said Hugh.   But Balbus thought it best not to hear the question. He left the boys to their problem, and, in the silence of his own room, set himself to unravel Hugh's mechanical paradox.

" To fix our thoughts," he murmured to himself, as, with hands deep-buried in his pockets, he paced up and down the room, " we will take a cylindrical glass jar, with a scale of inches marked up the side, and fill it with water up to the 10-inch mark : and we will assume that every inch depth of jar contains a pint of water.   We will now take a solid cylinder, such that every inch of it is equal in bulk to *half* a pint of water, and plunge 4 inches of it into the water, so that the end of the cylinder

comes down to the 6-inch mark. Well, that displaces 2 pints of water. What becomes of them?
Why, if there were no more cylinder, they would
lie comfortably on the top, and fill the jar up to
the 12-inch mark. But unfortunately there *is* more
cylinder, occupying half the space between the
10-inch and the 12-inch marks, so that only *one*
pint of water can be accommodated there. What
becomes of the other pint? Why, if there were no
more cylinder, it would lie on the top, and fill the
jar up to the 13-inch mark. But unfortunately
——Shade of Newton!" he exclaimed, in sudden
accents of terror. "When *does* the water stop
rising?"

A bright idea struck him. "I'll write a little
essay on it," he said.

Balbus's Essay.

———

"When a solid is immersed in a liquid, it is well
known that it displaces a portion of the liquid
equal to itself in bulk, and that the level of the
liquid rises just so much as it would rise if a
quantity of liquid had been added to it, equal in

bulk to the solid.   Lardner says, precisely the same
process occurs when a solid is *partially* immersed :
the quantity of liquid displaced, in this case,
equalling the portion of the solid which is immersed,
and the rise of the level being in proportion.

" Suppose a solid held above the surface of a
liquid and partially immersed : a portion of the
liquid is displaced, and the level of the liquid rises.
But, by this rise of level, a little bit more of the
solid is of course immersed, and so there is a new
displacement of a second portion of the liquid, and
a consequent rise of level.   Again, this second rise
of level causes a yet further immersion, and by
consequence another displacement of liquid and
another rise.   It is self-evident that this process
must continue till the entire solid is immersed, and
that the liquid will then begin to immerse whatever
holds the solid, which, being connected with it,
must for the time be considered a part of it.   If
you hold a stick, six feet long, with its end in a
tumbler of water, and wait long enough, you must
eventually be immersed.   The question as to the
source from which the water is supplied—which
belongs to a high branch of mathematics, and is
therefore beyond our present scope—does not apply

to the sea. Let us therefore take the familiar instance of a man standing at the edge of the sea, at ebb-tide, with a solid in his hand, which he partially immerses : he remains steadfast and unmoved, and we all know that he must be drowned. The multitudes who daily perish in this manner to attest a philosophical truth, and whose bodies the unreasoning wave casts sullenly upon our thankless shores, have a truer claim to be called the martyrs of science than a Galileo or a Kepler. To use Kossuth's eloquent phrase, they are the unnamed demigods of the nineteenth century." *

" There's a fallacy *somewhere*," he murmured drowsily, as he stretched his long legs upon the sofa. " I must think it over again." He closed his eyes, in order to concentrate his attention more perfectly, and for the next hour or so his slow and regular breathing bore witness to the careful deliberation with which he was investigating this new and perplexing view of the subject.

* *Note by the writer.*—For the above Essay I am indebted to a dear friend, now deceased.

"HE REMAINS STEADFAST AND UNMOVED."

KNOT X.

CHELSEA BUNS.

"Yea, buns, and buns, and buns!"

OLD SONG.

"How very, very sad!" exclaimed Clara; and the eyes of the gentle girl filled with tears as she spoke.

"Sad—but very curious when you come to look at it arithmetically," was her aunt's less romantic reply. "Some of them have lost an arm in their country's service, some a leg, some an ear, some an eye——"

"And some, perhaps, *all!*" Clara murmured dreamily, as they passed the long rows of weather-beaten heroes basking in the sun. "Did you notice that very old one, with a red face, who was drawing a map in the dust with his wooden

leg, and all the others watching ?   I *think* it was
a plan of a battle——"

"The battle of Trafalgar, no doubt," her aunt
interrupted, briskly.

"Hardly that, I think," Clara ventured to say.
"You see, in that case, he couldn't well be
alive——"

"Couldn't well be alive!" the old lady con-
temptuously repeated.   "He's as lively as you
and me put together!   Why, if drawing a map
in the dust—with one's wooden leg—doesn't prove
one to be alive, perhaps you'll kindly mention
what *does* prove it!"

Clara did not see her way out of it.   Logic had
never been her *forte*.

"To return to the arithmetic," Mad Mathesis
resumed—the eccentric old lady never let slip an
opportunity of driving her niece into a calculation
—"what percentage do you suppose must have
lost all four—a leg, an arm, an eye, and an ear?"

"How *can* I tell?" gasped the terrified girl.
She knew well what was coming.

"You can't, of course, without *data*," her aunt
replied : "but I'm just going to give you——"

"Give her a Chelsea bun, Miss!   That's what

most young ladies likes best!" The voice was
rich and musical, and the speaker dexterously
whipped back the snowy cloth that covered his
basket, and disclosed a tempting array of the
familiar square buns, joined together in rows,
richly egged and browned, and glistening in the
sun.

"No, sir! I shall give her nothing so indigestible! Be off!" The old lady waved her parasol
threateningly : but nothing seemed to disturb the
good-humour of the jolly old man, who marched
on, chanting his melodious refrain :—

Chel - sea buns! Chel - sea buns hot!   Chel - sea   buns !

Pi - ping hot! Chel - sea buns hot!   Chel - sea   buns!

"Far too indigestible, my love!" said the old
lady. "Percentages will agree with you ever so
much better!"

Clara sighed, and there was a hungry look in her
eyes as she watched the basket lessening in the
distance : but she meekly listened to the relentless

old lady, who at once proceeded to count off the *data* on her fingers.

"Say that 70 per cent. have lost an eye—75 per cent. an ear—80 per cent. an arm—85 per cent. a leg—that'll do it beautifully. Now, my dear, what percentage, *at least*, must have lost all four?"

No more conversation occurred—unless a smothered exclamation of "Piping hot!" which escaped from Clara's lips as the basket vanished round a corner could be counted as such—until they reached the old Chelsea mansion, where Clara's father was then staying, with his three sons and their old tutor.

Balbus, Lambert, and Hugh had entered the house only a few minutes before them. They had been out walking, and Hugh had been propounding a difficulty which had reduced Lambert to the depths of gloom, and had even puzzled Balbus.

"It changes from Wednesday to Thursday at midnight, doesn't it?" Hugh had begun.

"Sometimes," said Balbus, cautiously.

"Always," said Lambert, decisively.

"*Sometimes*," Balbus gently insisted. "Six midnights out of seven, it changes to some other name."

"I meant, of course," Hugh corrected himself, "when it *does* change from Wednesday to Thursday, it does it at midnight—and *only* at midnight."

"Surely," said Balbus. Lambert was silent.

"Well, now, suppose it's midnight here in Chelsea. Then it's Wednesday *west* of Chelsea (say in Ireland or America) where midnight hasn't arrived yet : and it's Thursday *east* of Chelsea (say in Germany or Russia) where midnight has just passed by ? "

"Surely," Balbus said again. Even Lambert nodded this time.

"But it isn't midnight anywhere else ; so it can't be changing from one day to another anywhere else. And yet, if Ireland and America and so on call it Wednesday, and Germany and Russia and so on call it Thursday, there *must* be some place —not Chelsea—that has different days on the two sides of it. And the worst of it is, the people *there* get their days in the wrong order : they've got Wednesday *east* of them, and Thursday *west*—just as if their day had changed from Thursday to Wednesday ! "

"I've heard that puzzle before ! " cried Lambert. "And I'll tell you the explanation. When a ship

goes round the world from east to west, we know
that it loses a day in its reckoning : so that when
it gets home, and calls its day Wednesday, it finds
people here calling it Thursday, because we've had
one more midnight than the ship has had.   And
when you go the other way round you gain a day."

"I know all that," said Hugh, in reply to this
not very lucid explanation : "but it doesn't help
me, because the ship hasn't proper days.   One way
round, you get more than twenty-four hours to the
day, and the other way you get less : so of course
the names get wrong : but people that live on in
one place always get twenty-four hours to the day."

"I suppose there *is* such a place," Balbus said,
meditatively, "though I never heard of it.   And
the people must find it very queer, as Hugh says,
to have the old day *east* of them, and the new one
west : because, when midnight comes round to
them, with the new day in front of it and the old
one behind it, one doesn't see exactly what
happens.   I must think it over."

So they had entered the house in the state
I have described—Balbus puzzled, and Lambert
buried in gloomy thought.

"Yes, m'm, Master *is* at home, m'm," said the

stately old butler. (N.B.—It is only a butler of experience who can manage a series of three M's together, without any interjacent vowels.) "And the *ole* party is a-waiting for you in the libery."

"I don't like his calling your father an *old* party," Mad Mathesis whispered to her niece, as they crossed the hall. And Clara had only just time to whisper in reply "he meant the *whole* party," before they were ushered into the library, and the sight of the five solemn faces there assembled chilled her into silence.

Her father sat at the head of the table, and mutely signed to the ladies to take the two vacant chairs, one on each side of him. His three sons and Balbus completed the party. Writing materials had been arranged round the table, after the fashion of a ghostly banquet: the butler had evidently bestowed much thought on the grim device. Sheets of quarto paper, each flanked by a pen on one side and a pencil on the other, represented the plates—penwipers did duty for rolls of bread—while ink-bottles stood in the places usually occupied by wine-glasses. The *pièce de resistance* was a large green baize bag, which gave forth, as the old man restlessly lifted it from side to side, a charming jingle, as of innumerable golden guineas.

"Sister, daughter, sons—and Balbus—," the old man began, so nervously, that Balbus put in a gentle "Hear, hear!" while Hugh drummed on the table with his fists. This disconcerted the unpractised orator. "Sister—" he began again, then paused a moment, moved the bag to the other side, and went on with a rush, "I mean—this being—a critical occasion—more or less—being the year when one of my sons comes of age—" he paused again in some confusion, having evidently got into the middle of his speech sooner than he intended : but it was too late to go back. "Hear, hear!" cried Balbus. "Quite so," said the old gentleman, recovering his self-possession a little : "when first I began this annual custom—my friend Balbus will correct me if I am wrong—" (Hugh whispered "with a strap!" but nobody heard him except Lambert, who only frowned and shook his head at him) "—this annual custom of giving each of my sons as many guineas as would represent his age—it was a critical time—so Balbus informed me—as the ages of two of you were together equal to that of the third—

so on that occasion I made a speech——" He paused so long that Balbus thought it well to come to the rescue with the words " It was a most —— " but the old man checked him with a warning look : "yes, made a speech," he repeated. " A few years after that, Balbus pointed out—I say pointed out—" ("Hear, hear"! cried Balbus. " Quite so," said the grateful old man.) "—that it was *another* critical occasion. The ages of two of you were together *double* that of the third. So I made another speech—another speech. And now again it's a critical occasion—so Balbus says—and I am making——" (Here Mad Mathesis pointedly referred to her watch) "all the haste I can !" the old man cried, with wonderful presence of mind. " Indeed, sister, I'm coming to the point now ! The number of years that have passed since that first occasion is just two-thirds of the number of guineas I then gave you. Now, my boys, calculate your ages from the *data*, and you shall have the money ! "

" But we *know* our ages ! " cried Hugh.

" Silence, sir ! " thundered the old man, rising to his full height (he was exactly five-foot five) in his indignation. " I say you must use the *data* only! You mustn't even assume *which* it is that comes of age!" He clutched the bag as he spoke, and with tottering steps (it was about as much as he could do to carry it) he left the room.

"And *you* shall have a similar *cadeau*," the old lady whispered to her niece, "when you've calculated that percentage!" And she followed her brother.

Nothing could exceed the solemnity with which the old couple had risen from the table, and yet was it—was it a *grin* with which the father turned away from his unhappy sons? Could it be— could it be a *wink* with which the aunt abandoned her despairing niece? And were those—were those sounds of suppressed *chuckling* which floated into the room, just before Balbus (who had followed them out) closed the door? Surely not: and yet the butler told the cook—but no, that was merely idle gossip, and I will not repeat it.

The shades of evening granted their unuttered petition, and "closed not o'er" them (for the butler brought in the lamp): the same obliging shades left them a "lonely bark" (the wail of a dog, in the back-yard, baying the moon) for "awhile": but neither "morn, alas," (nor any other epoch) seemed likely to " restore " them—to that peace of mind which had once been theirs ere ever these problems had swooped upon them, and crushed them with a load of unfathomable mystery !

" It's hardly fair," muttered Hugh, " to give us such a jumble as this to work out ! "

" Fair ? " Clara echoed, bitterly. " Well ! "

And to all my readers I can but repeat the last words of gentle Clara—

Fare-well !

APPENDIX.

ANSWERS TO KNOT I.

Problem.—"Two travellers spend from 3 o'clock till 9 in walking along a level road, up a hill, and home again : their pace on the level being 4 miles an hour, up hill 3, and down hill 6.   Find   distance walked : also (within half an hour) time of reaching top of hill."

Answer.—" 24 miles : half-past 6."

Solution.—A level mile takes $\frac{1}{4}$ of an hour, up hill $\frac{1}{3}$, down hill $\frac{1}{6}$.   Hence to go and return over the same mile, whether on the level or on the hill-side, takes $\frac{1}{2}$ an hour. Hence in 6 hours they went 12 miles out and 12 back. If the 12 miles out had been nearly all level, they would have taken a little over 3 hours ; if nearly all up hill, a little under 4.   Hence $3\frac{1}{2}$ hours must be within $\frac{1}{2}$ an hour of the time taken in reaching the peak ; thus, as they started at 3, they got there within $\frac{1}{2}$ an hour of $\frac{1}{2}$ past 6.

Twenty-seven answers have come in. Of these, 9 are right, 16 partially right, and 2 wrong. The 16 give the *distance* correctly, but they have failed to grasp the fact that the top of the hill might have been reached at *any* moment between 6 o'clock and 7.

The two wrong answers are from GERTY VERNON and A NIHILIST. The former makes the distance "23 miles," while her revolutionary companion puts it at "27." GERTY VERNON says "they had to go 4 miles along the plain, and got to the foot of the hill at 4 o'clock." They *might* have done so, I grant; but you have no ground for saying they *did* so. "It was $7\frac{1}{2}$ miles to the top of the hill, and they reached that at $\frac{1}{4}$ before 7 o'clock." Here you go wrong in your arithmetic, and I must, however reluctantly, bid you farewell. $7\frac{1}{2}$ miles, at 3 miles an hour, would *not* require $2\frac{3}{4}$ hours. A NIHILIST says "Let x denote the whole number of miles; y the number of hours to hill-top; $\therefore 3y =$ number of miles to hill-top, and $x - 3y =$ number of miles on the other side." You bewilder me. The other side of *what?* "Of the hill," you say. But then, how did they get home again? However, to accommodate your views we will build a new hostelry at the foot of the hill on the opposite side, and also assume (what I grant you is *possible*, though it is not *necessarily* true) that there was no level road at all. Even then you go wrong.

You say

$$"y = 6 - \frac{x - 3\,y}{6},\ .\ .\ .\ .\ .\ \text{(i)} ;$$

$$\frac{x}{4\frac{1}{2}} = 6\ .\ .\ .\ .\ .\ .\ .\ .\ .\ .\ \text{(ii)."}$$

I grant you (i), but I deny (ii) : it rests on the assumption that to go *part* of the time at 3 miles an hour, and the rest at 6 miles an hour, comes to the same result as going the *whole* time at $4\frac{1}{2}$ miles an hour. But this would only be true if the "*part*" were an exact *half*, i.e., if they went up hill for 3 hours, and down hill for the other 3 : which they certainly did *not* do.

The sixteen, who are partially right, are AGNES BAILEY, F. K., FIFEE, G. E. B., H. P., KIT, M. E. T., MYSIE, A MOTHER'S SON, NAIRAM, A REDRUTHIAN, A SOCIALIST, SPEAR MAIDEN, T. B. C., VIS INERTIÆ, and YAK. Of these, F. K., FIFEE, T. B. C., and VIS INERTIÆ do not attempt the second part at all. F. K. and H. P. give no working. The rest make particular assumptions, such as that there was no level road—that there were 6 miles of level road—and so on, all leading to *particular* times being fixed for reaching the hill-top. The most curious assumption is that of AGNES BAILEY, who says " Let $x =$ number of hours occupied in ascent; then $\frac{x}{2} =$ hours occupied in descent; and $\frac{4\,x}{3} =$ hours occupied on the level." I suppose you were thinking of the relative *rates*, up hill and on the level; which we might express by saying that, if they went x miles up hill in a certain time, they would go $\dfrac{4x}{3}$ miles on the level *in the same time*. You have, in fact, assumed that they took *the same time* on the level that they took in ascending the hill. FIFEE assumes that, when the aged knight said they had gone "four miles in the hour" on the level, he meant that four miles was the *distance* gone, not merely the rate. This would have been—if FIFEE will excuse the slang expression—a "sell," ill-suited to the dignity of the hero.

And now "descend, ye classic Nine!" who have solved the whole problem, and let me sing your praises. Your names are BLITHE, E. W., L. B., A MARLBOROUGH BOY, O. V. L., PUTNEY WALKER, ROSE, SEA BREEZE, SIMPLE SUSAN, and MONEY SPINNER. (These last two I count as one, as they send a joint answer.) ROSE and SIMPLE SUSAN and Co. do not actually state that the hill-top was reached some time between 6 and 7, but, as they have clearly grasped the fact that a mile, ascended and descended, took the same time as two level miles, I mark them as "right." A MARLBOROUGH BOY and PUTNEY WALKER deserve honourable mention for their algebraical solutions being the only two who have perceived

that the question leads to *an indeterminate equation.*
E. W. brings a charge of untruthfulness against the aged
knight—a serious charge, for he was the very pink of
chivalry! She says "According to the data given, the
time at the summit affords no clue to the total distance.
It does not enable us to state precisely to an inch how
much level and how much hill there was on the road."
"Fair damsel," the aged knight replies, "—if, as I surmise,
thy initials denote Early Womanhood—bethink thee that
the word 'enable' is thine, not mine. I did but ask the
time of reaching the hill-top as my *condition* for further
parley. If *now* thou wilt not grant that I am a truth-
loving man, then will I affirm that those same initials
denote Envenomed Wickedness!"

CLASS LIST.

I.

A MARLBOROUGH BOY.   PUTNEY WALKER.

II.

BLITHE.	ROSE.
E. W.	SEA BREEZE.
L. B.	⎰ SIMPLE SUSAN.
O. V. L.	⎱ MONEY-SPINNER.

BLITHE has made so ingenious an addition to the problem, and SIMPLE SUSAN and Co. have solved it in such tuneful verse, that I record both their answers in full. I have altered a word or two in BLITHE'S—which I trust she will excuse; it did not seem quite clear as it stood.

"Yet stay," said the youth, as a gleam of inspiration lighted up the relaxing muscles of his quiescent features. "Stay. Methinks it matters little *when* we reached that summit, the crown of our toil. For in the space of time wherein we clambered up one mile and bounded down the same on our return, we could have trudged the *twain* on the level. We have plodded, then, four-and-twenty miles in these six mortal hours; for never a moment did we stop for catching of fleeting breath or for gazing on the scene around!"

"Very good," said the old man. "Twelve miles out and twelve miles in. And we reached the top some time between six and seven of the clock. Now mark me! For every five minutes that had fled since six of the clock when we stood on yonder peak, so many miles had we toiled upwards on the dreary mountain-side!"

The youth moaned and rushed into the hostel.

BLITHE.

The elder and the younger knight,
  They sallied forth at three ;
How far they went on level ground
  It matters not to me ;
What time they reached the foot of hill,
  When they began to mount,
Are problems which I hold to be
  Of very small account.

The moment that each waved his hat
  Upon the topmost peak—
To trivial query such as this
  No answer will I seek.
Yet can I tell the distance well
  They must have travelled o'er :
On hill and plain, 'twixt three and nine,
  The miles were twenty-four.

Four miles an hour their steady pace
  Along the level track,
Three when they climbed—but six when they
  Came swiftly striding back
Adown the hill ; and little skill
  It needs, methinks, to show,
Up hill and down together told,
  Four miles an hour they go.

For whether long or short the time
  Upon the hill they spent,
Two thirds were passed in going up,
  One third in the descent.
Two thirds at three, one third at six,
  If rightly reckoned o'er,
Will make one whole at four—the tale
  Is tangled now no more.

                    SIMPLE SUSAN.
                    MONEY SPINNER.

ANSWERS TO KNOT II.

§ 1. THE DINNER PARTY.

Problem.—" The Governor of Kgovjni wants to give a very small dinner party, and invites his father's brother-in-law, his brother's father-in-law, his father-in-law's brother, and his brother-in-law's father. Find the number of guests."

Answer.—" One."

In this genealogy, males are denoted by capitals, and females by small letters.

The Governor is E and his guest is C.

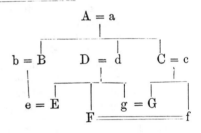

Ten answers have been received. Of these, one is wrong, GALANTHUS NIVALIS MAJOR, who insists on inviting *two* guests, one being the Governor's *wife's brother's father*. If she had taken his *sister's husband's father* instead, she would have found it possible to reduce the guests to *one*.

Of the nine who send right answers, SEA-BREEZE is the very faintest breath that ever bore the name! She simply states that the Governor's uncle might fulfill all the conditions "by intermarriages"! "Wind of the western sea," you have had a very narrow escape! Be thankful to appear in the Class-list at all! BOG-OAK and BRADSHAW OF THE FUTURE use genealogies which require 16 people instead of 14, by inviting the Governor's *father's sister's husband* instead of his *father's wife's brother*. I cannot think this so good a solution as one that requires only 14. CAIUS and VALENTINE deserve special mention as the only two who have supplied genealogies.

CLASS LIST.

I.

BEE.	M. M.	OLD CAT.
CAIUS.	MATTHEW MATTICKS.	VALENTINE.

II.

BOG-OAK.   BRADSHAW OF THE FUTURE.

III.

SEA-BREEZE.

§ 2. THE LODGINGS.

Problem.—" A Square has 20 doors on each side, which contains 21 equal parts. They are numbered all round, beginning at one corner. From which of the four, Nos. 9, 25, 52, 73, is the sum of the distances, to the other three, least ?"

Answer.—" From No. 9."

--- --- ---

Let A be No. 9, B No. 25, C No. 52, and D No. 73.

Then $AB = \sqrt{(12^2 + 5^2)} = \sqrt{169} = 13$;

$AC = 21$;

$AD = \sqrt{(9^2 + 8^2)} = \sqrt{145} = 12 +$

(N.B. *i.e.* "between 12 and 13.")

$BC = \sqrt{(16^2 + 12^2)} = \sqrt{400} = 20$;

$BD = \sqrt{(3^2 + 21^2)} = \sqrt{450} = 21 +$;

$CD = \sqrt{(9^2 + 13^2)} = \sqrt{250} = 15 +$;

Hence sum of distances from A is between 46 and 47 ; from B, between 54 and 55 ; from C, between 56 and 57 ; from D, between 48 and 51. (Why not " between 48 and 49 " ? Make this out for yourselves.) Hence the sum is least for A.

Twenty-five solutions have been received. Of these, 15 must be marked " 0," 5 are partly right, and 5 right. Of the 15, I may dismiss ALPHABETICAL PHANTOM, BOG-OAK, DINAH MITE, FIFEE, GALANTHUS NIVALIS MAJOR (I fear the cold spring has blighted our SNOWDROP), GUY, H.M.S. PINAFORE, JANET, and VALENTINE with the simple remark that they insist on the unfortunate lodgers *keeping to the pavement*. (I used the words " crossed to Number Seventy-three " for the special purpose of showing that *short cuts* were possible.) SEA-BREEZE does the same, and adds that " the result would be the same " even if they crossed the Square, but gives no proof of this. M. M. draws a diagram, and says that No. 9 is the house, " as the diagram shows." I cannot see *how* it does so. OLD CAT assumes that the house *must* be No. 9 or No. 73. She does not explain how she estimates the distances. BEE'S Arithmetic is faulty : she makes $\sqrt{169} + \sqrt{442} + \sqrt{130} = 741$. (I suppose you mean $\sqrt{741}$, which would be a little nearer the truth. But roots cannot be added in this manner. Do you think $\sqrt{9} + \sqrt{16}$ is 25, or even $\sqrt{25}$?) But AYR'S state is more perilous still : she draws illogical conclusions with a frightful calmness. After pointing out (rightly) that AC is less than BD she says, " therefore the nearest house to the other three must be A or C." And again, after pointing out (rightly) that B and D are both within the half-square containing

A, she says "therefore" AB + AD must be less than
BC + CD. (There is no logical force in either "therefore."
For the first, try Nos. 1, 21, 60, 70 : this will make your
premiss true, and your conclusion false. Similarly, for
the second, try Nos. 1, 30, 51, 71.)

Of the five partly-right solutions, RAGS AND TATTERS
and MAD HATTER (who send one answer between them)
make No. 25 6 units from the corner instead of 5.
CHEAM, E. R. D. L., and MEGGY POTTS leave openings at
he corners of the Square, which are not in the *data*:
moreover CHEAM gives values for the distances without
any hint that they are only *approximations*. CROPHI AND
MOPHI make the bold and unfounded assumption that
there were really 21 houses on each side, instead of 20 as
stated by Balbus. "We may assume," they add, "that
the doors of Nos. 21, 42, 63, 84, are invisible from the
centre of the Square"! What is there, I wonder, that
CROPHI AND MOPHI would *not* assume ?

Of the five who are wholly right, I think BRADSHAW
OF THE FUTURE, CAIUS, CLIFTON C., and MARTREB
deserve special praise for their full *analytical* solutions.
MATTHEW MATTICKS picks out No. 9, and proves it to be
the right house in two ways, very neatly and ingeniously,
but *why* he picks it out does not appear. It is an
excellent *synthetical* proof, but lacks the analysis which
the other four supply.

CLASS LIST.

I.

BRADSHAW OF THE FUTURE   CLIFTON C.
CAIUS.   MARTREB.

II.

MATTHEW MATTICKS.

III.

CHEAM.   MEGGY POTTS.
CROPHI AND MOPHI.   { RAGS AND TATTERS.
E. R. D. L.   { MAD HATTER.

A remonstrance has reached me from SCRUTATOR on
the subject of KNOT I., which he declares was "no
problem at all." "Two questions," he says, "are put.
To solve one there is no data : the other answers itself."
As to the first point, SCRUTATOR is mistaken ; there *are*
(not "is") data sufficient to answer the question. As
to the other, it is interesting to know that the question
"answers itself," and I am sure it does the question
great credit : still I fear I cannot enter it on the list
of winners, as this competition is only open to human
beings.

ANSWERS TO KNOT III.

Problem.—(1) " Two travellers, starting at the same time, went opposite ways round a circular railway. Trains start each way every 15 minutes, the easterly ones going round in 3 hours, the westerly in 2. How many trains did each meet on the way, not counting trains met at the terminus itself?" (2) "They went round, as before, each traveller counting as 'one' the train containing the other traveller. How many did each meet?"

Answers.—(1) 19. (2) The easterly traveller met 12; the other 8.

The trains one way took 180 minutes, the other way 120. Let us take the L. C. M., 360, and divide the railway into 360 units. Then one set of trains went at the rate of 2 units a minute and at intervals of 30 units; the other at the rate of 3 units a minute and at intervals of 45 units. An easterly train starting has 45 units between it and the first train it will meet: it does 2–5ths of this while the other does 3–5ths, and

918th

72

Forty-five answers have been received. Of these 12 are beyond the reach of discussion, as they give no working. I can but enumerate their names. ARDMORE, E. A., F. A. D., L. D., MATTHEW MATTICKS, M. E. T., POO-POO, and THE RED QUEEN are all wrong. BETA and ROWENA have got (1) right and (2) wrong. CHEEKY BOB and NAIRAM give the right answers, but it may perhaps make the one less cheeky, and induce the other to take a less inverted view of things, to be informed that, if this had been a competition for a prize, they would have got no marks. [N.B.—I have not ventured to put E. A.'s name in full, as she only gave it provisionally, in case her answer should prove right.]

Of the 33 answers for which the working is given, 10 are wrong; 11 half-wrong and half-right; 3 right, except that they cherish the delusion that it was *Clara* who travelled in the easterly train—a point which the data do not enable us to settle; and 9 wholly right.

The 10 wrong answers are from BO-PEEP, FINANCIER, I. W. T., KATE B., M. A. H., Q. Y. Z., SEA-GULL, THISTLEDOWN, TOM-QUAD, and an unsigned one. BO-PEEP rightly says that the easterly traveller met all trains which started during the 3 hours of her trip, as well as all which started during the previous 2 hours, *i.e.*, all which started at the commencements of 20 periods of 15 minutes each; and she is right in striking out the one she met at the moment of starting; but wrong in striking out the *last* train, for she did not meet this at the terminus, but 15 minutes before she got there. She makes the same mistake in (2). FINANCIER thinks that any train, met for the second time, is not to be counted. I. W. T. finds, by a process which is not stated, that the travellers met at the end of 71 minutes and 26½ seconds. KATE B. thinks the trains which are met on starting and on arriving

are *never* to be counted, even when met elsewhere.
Q. Y. Z. tries a rather complex algebraical solution,
and succeeds in finding the time of meeting correctly:
all else is wrong.   SEA-GULL seems to think that,
in (1), the easterly train *stood still* for 3 hours;
and says that, in (2), the travellers met at the end
of 71 minutes 40 seconds.   THISTLEDOWN nobly confesses
to having tried no calculation, but merely having drawn
a picture of the railway and counted the trains; in (1),
she counts wrong; in (2) she makes them meet in 75
minutes.   TOM-QUAD omits (1): in (2) he makes Clara
count the train she met on her arrival.   The unsigned
one is also unintelligible; it states that the travellers
go "1—24th more than the total distance to be
traversed"!   The "Clara" theory, already referred to,
is adopted by 5 of these, viz., BO-PEEP, FINANCIER,
KATE B., TOM-QUAD, and the nameless writer.

The 11 half-right answers are from BOG-OAK, BRIDGET,
CASTOR, CHESHIRE CAT, G. E. B., GUY, MARY, M. A. H.,
OLD MAID, R. W., and VENDREDI.   All these adopt
the "Clara" theory.   CASTOR omits (1).   VENDREDI
gets (1) right, but in (2) makes the same mistake as
BO-PEEP.   I notice in your solution a marvellous
proportion-sum :—"300 miles : 2 hours : : one mile : 24
seconds."   May I venture to advise your acquiring, as soon
as possible, an utter disbelief in the possibility of a ratio

existing between *miles* and *hours?* Do not be dis-
heartened by your two friends' sarcastic remarks on your
"roundabout ways." Their short method, of adding 12
and 8, has the slight disadvantage of bringing the answer
wrong : even a "roundabout" method is better than *that !*
M. A. H., in (2), makes the travellers count "one" *after*
they met, not *when* they met. CHESHIRE CAT and OLD
MAID get "20" as answer for (1), by forgetting to strike
out the train met on arrival. The others all get "18" in
various ways. BOG-OAK, GUY, and R. W. divide the trains
which the westerly traveller has to meet into 2 sets, viz.,
those already on the line, which they (rightly) make "11,"
and those which started during her 2 hours' journey (ex-
clusive of train met on arrival), which they (wrongly) make
"7"; and they make a similar mistake with the easterly
train. BRIDGET (rightly) says that the westerly traveller
met a train every 6 minutes for 2 hours, but (wrongly)
makes the number "20"; it should be "21." G. E. B.
adopts BO-PEEP's method, but (wrongly) strikes out (for
the easterly traveller) the train which started at the *com-
mencement* of the previous 2 hours. MARY thinks a train,
met on arrival, must not be counted, even when met on a
previous occasion.

The 3, who are wholly right but for the unfortunate
"Clara" theory, are F. LEE, G. S. C., and X. A. B.

And now "descend, ye classic Ten!" who have

solved the whole problem.   Your names are Aix-les-
Bains, Algernon Bray (thanks for a friendly remark,
which comes with a heart-warmth that not even the
Atlantic could chill), Arvon, Bradshaw of the Future,
Fifee, H. L. R., J. L. O., Omega, S. S. G., and Waiting
for the Train.   Several of these have put Clara, provisionally, into the easterly train : but they seem to have
understood that the data do not decide that point.

CLASS LIST.

I.

Aix-le-Bains.	H. L. R.
Algernon Bray.	Omega.
Bradshaw of the Future.	S. S. G.
Fifee.	Waiting for the train.

II.

Arvon.	J. L. O.

III.

F. Lee.	G. S. C.	X. A. B.

ANSWERS TO KNOT IV.

Problem.—"There are 5 sacks, of which Nos. 1, 2, weigh 12 lbs.; Nos. 2, 3, $13\frac{1}{2}$ lbs.; Nos. 3, 4, $11\frac{1}{2}$ lbs.; Nos. 4, 5, 8 lbs.; Nos. 1, 3, 5, 16 lbs. Required the weight of each sack."

Answer.—"$5\frac{1}{2}$, $6\frac{1}{2}$, 7, $4\frac{1}{2}$, $3\frac{1}{2}$."

The sum of all the weighings, 61 lbs., includes sack No. 3 *thrice* and each other *twice.* Deducting twice the sum of the 1st and 4th weighings, we get 21 lbs. for *thrice* No. 3, *i.e.*, 7 lbs. for No. 3. Hence, the 2nd and 3rd weighings give $6\frac{1}{2}$ lbs., $4\frac{1}{2}$ lbs. for Nos. 2, 4; and hence again, the 1st and 4th weighings give $5\frac{1}{2}$ lbs., $3\frac{1}{2}$ lbs., for Nos. 1, 5.

Ninety-seven answers have been received. Of these, 15 are beyond the reach of discussion, as they give no working. I can but enumerate their names, and I take this opportunity of saying that this is the last time I shall put on record the names of competitors who give no sort of clue to the process by which their answers were obtained. In guessing a conundrum, or in catching a flea, we do not expect the breathless victor to give us afterwards, in cold blood, a history of the mental or muscular efforts by which he achieved success; but a mathematical calculation is another thing. The names of this "mute inglorious" band are Common Sense, D. E. R., Douglas, E. L., Ellen, I. M. T., J. M. C., Joseph, Knot I, Lucy, Meek, M. F. C., Pyramus, Shah, Veritas.

Of the eighty-two answers with which the working, or some approach to it, is supplied, one is wrong: seventeen have given solutions which are (from one cause or another) practically valueless: the remaining sixty-four I shall try to arrange in a Class-list, according to the varying degrees of shortness and neatness to which they seem to have attained.

The solitary wrong answer is from Nell. To be thus "alone in the crowd" is a distinction—a painful one, no doubt, but still a distinction. I am sorry for you, my dear young lady, and I seem to hear your tearful exclamation, when you read these lines, "Ah! This is the knell of all my hopes!" Why, oh why, did you assume that the 4th and 5th bags weighed 4 lbs. each? And why did you not test your answers? However, please try again: and please don't change your *nom-de-plume*: let us have Nell in the First Class next time!

The seventeen whose solutions are practically valueless are ARDMORE, A READY RECKONER, ARTHUR, BOG-LARK, BOG-OAK, BRIDGET, FIRST ATTEMPT, J. L. C., M. E. T., ROSE, ROWENA, SEA-BREEZE, SYLVIA, THISTLEDOWN, THREE-FIFTHS ASLEEP, VENDREDI, and WINIFRED. BOG-LARK tries it by a sort of "rule of false," assuming experimentally that Nos. 1, 2, weigh 6 lbs. each, and having thus produced $17\frac{1}{2}$, instead of 16, as the weight of 1, 3, and 5, she removes "the superfluous pound and a half," but does not explain how she knows from which to take it. THREE-FIFTHS ASLEEP says that (when in that peculiar state) "it seemed perfectly clear" to her that, "3 out of the 5 sacks being weighed twice over, $\frac{3}{5}$ of $45 = 27$, must be the total weight of the 5 sacks." As to which I can only say, with the Captain, "it beats me entirely!" WINIFRED, on the plea that "one must have a starting-point," assumes (what I fear is a mere guess) that No. 1 weighed $5\frac{1}{2}$ lbs. The rest all do it, wholly or partly, by guess-work.

The problem is of course (as any Algebraist sees at once) a case of "simultaneous simple equations." It is, however, easily soluble by Arithmetic only; and, when this is the case, I hold that it is bad workmanship to use the more complex method. I have not, this time, given more credit to arithmetical solutions; but in future problems I shall (other things being equal) give the

highest marks to those who use the simplest machinery.
I have put into Class I. those whose answers seemed
specially short and neat, and into Class III. those that
seemed specially long or clumsy. Of this last set, A. C. M.,
FURZE-BUSH, JAMES, PARTRIDGE, R. W., and WAITING
FOR THE TRAIN, have sent long wandering solutions,
the substitutions having no definite method, but seeming
to have been made to see what would come of it.
CHILPOME and DUBLIN BOY omit some of the working.
ARVON MARLBOROUGH BOY only finds the weight of
one sack.

CLASS LIST.

I.

B. E. D.

C. H.

CONSTANCE JOHNSON.

GREYSTEAD.

GUY.

HOOPOE.

J. F. A.

M. A. H.

NUMBER FIVE.

PEDRO.

R. E. X.

SEVEN OLD MEN.

VIS INERTIÆ.

WILLY B.

YAHOO.

II.

AMERICAN SUBSCRIBER.

AN APPRECIATIVESCHOOLMA'AM.

AYR.

BRADSHAW OF THE FUTURE.

CHEAM.

C. M. G.

DINAH MITE.

DUCKWING.

E. C. M.

E. N. LOWRY.

ERA.

EUROCLYDON.

F. H. W.

FIFEE.

G. E. B.

HARLEQUIN.

HAWTHORN.

HOUGH GREEN.

J. A. B.

JACK TAR.

J. B. B.

KGOVJNI.

LAND LUBBER.

L. D.

MAGPIE.

MARY.

MHRUXI.

MINNIE.

MONEY-SPINNER.

NAIRAM.

OLD CAT.

POLICHINELLE.

SIMPLE SUSAN.

S. S. G.

THISBE.

VERENA.

WAMBA.

WOLFE.

WYKEHAMICUS.

Y. M. A. H.

III.

A. C. M.

ARVON MARLBOROUGH BOY.

CHILPOME.

DUBLIN BOY.

FURZE-BUSH.

JAMES.

PARTRIDGE.

R. W.

WAITING FOR THE TRAIN.

ANSWERS TO KNOT V.

Problem.—To mark pictures, giving 3 ×'s to 2 or 3, 2 to 4 or 5, and 1 to 9 or 10; also giving 3 o's to 1 or 2, 2 to 3 or 4 and 1 to 8 or 9; so as to mark the smallest possible number of pictures, and to give them the largest possible number of marks.

Answer.—10 pictures; 29 marks; arranged thus:—

```
× × × × × × × × × o
× × × × ×       o o o o
× × o o o o o o o o
```

Solution.—By giving all the ×'s possible, putting into brackets the optional ones, we get 10 pictures marked thus:—

```
× × × × × × × × × (×)
× × × × (×)
× × (×)
```

By then assigning o's in the same way, beginning at the other end, we get 9 pictures marked thus:—

```
                            (o) o
                        (o) o o o
                    (o) o o o o o o o
```

All we have now to do is to run these two wedges

as close together as they will go, so as to get the minimum number of pictures——erasing optional marks where by so doing we can run them closer, but otherwise letting them stand. There are 10 necessary marks in the 1st row, and in the 3rd; but only 7 in the 2nd. Hence we erase all optional marks in the 1st and 3rd rows, but let them stand in the 2nd.

————————

Twenty-two answers have been received. Of these 11 give no working; so, in accordance with what I announced in my last review of answers, I leave them unnamed, merely mentioning that 5 are right and 6 wrong.

Of the eleven answers with which some working is supplied, 3 are wrong. C. H. begins with the rash assertion that under the given conditions "the sum is impossible. For," he or she adds (these initialed correspondents are dismally vague beings to deal with : perhaps "it" would be a better pronoun), "10 is the least possible number of pictures" (granted) : "therefore we must either give 2 ×'s to 6, or 2 o's to 5." Why "must," oh alphabetical phantom? It is nowhere ordained that every picture "must" have 3 marks! FIFEE sends a folio page of solution, which deserved a better fate : she offers 3 answers, in each of which 10 pictures are marked, with 30 marks; in one she gives 2 ×'s to 6 pictures; in another to 7; in the 3rd she gives 2 o's to 5; thus in every case ignoring the conditions. (I pause to remark that the condition " 2 ×'s to 4 or 5 pictures " can only mean "*either* to 4 *or else* to 5 ": if, as one competitor holds, it might mean *any* number not less than 4, the words "*or* 5 " would be superfluous.) I. E. A. (I am happy to say that none of these bloodless phantoms appear this time in the class-list. Is it IDEA with the " D " left out?) gives 2 ×'s to 6 pictures. She then takes me to task for using the word "ought" instead of "nought." No doubt, to one who thus rebels against the rules laid down for her guidance, the word must be distasteful. But does not I. E. A. remember the parallel case of "adder"? That creature was originally " a nadder": then the two words took to bandying the poor "n" backwards and forwards like a shuttlecock, the final state of the game being " an adder." May not " a nought " have similarly become "an ought"? Anyhow, "oughts and crosses" is a very old game. I don't think I ever heard it called " noughts and crosses."

In the following Class-list, I hope the solitary occupant of III. will sheathe her claws when she hears how narrow an escape she has had of not being named at all. Her account of the process by which she got the answer is so meagre that, like the nursery tale of " Jack-a-Minory " (I trust I. E. A. will be merciful to the spelling), it is scarcely to be distinguished from "zero."

CLASS LIST.

I.

GUY.   OLD CAT.   SEA-BREEZE.

II.

AYR.   F. LEE
BRADSHAW OF THE FUTURE.   H. VERNON.

III.

CAT.

ANSWERS TO KNOT VI.

Problem 1.—*A* and *B* began the year with only 1,000*l*. a-piece. They borrowed nought; they stole nought. On the next New-Year's Day they had 60,000*l*. between them. How did they do it?

Solution.—They went that day to the Bank of England. *A* stood in front of it, while *B* went round and stood behind it.

_____

Two answers have been received, both worthy of much honour. ADDLEPATE makes them borrow " 0 " and steal " 0," and uses both cyphers by putting them at the right-hand end of the 1,000*l*., thus producing 100,000*l*., which is well over the mark. But (or to express it in Latin) AT SPES INFRACTA has solved it even more ingeniously: with the first cypher she turns the " 1 " of the 1,000*l*. into a " 9," and adds the result to the original sum, thus getting 10,000*l*.: and in this, by means of the other " 0," she turns the " 1 " into a " 6," thus hitting the exact 60,000*l*.

_____

CLASS LIST

I.

At Spes Infracta.

II.

Addlepate.

Problem 2.—*L* makes 5 scarves, while *M* makes 2 : *Z* makes 4 while *L* makes 3. Five scarves of *Z*'s weigh one of *L*'s; 5 of *M*'s weigh 3 of *Z*'s. One of *M*'s is as warm as 4 of *Z*'s : and one of *L*'s as warm as 3 of *M*'s. Which is best, giving equal weight in the result to rapidity of work, lightness, and warmth ?

Answer.—The order is *M, L, Z*.

Solution.—As to rapidity (other things being constant) *L*'s merit is to *M*'s in the ratio of 5 to 2 : *Z*'s to *L*'s in the ratio of 4 to 3. In order to get one set of 3 numbers fulfilling these conditions, it is perhaps simplest to take the one that occurs *twice* as unity, and reduce the others to fractions : this gives, for *L, M,* and *Z*, the marks 1, $\frac{2}{5}$, $\frac{4}{3}$. In estimating for *lightness*, we observe that the greater the weight, the less the merit, so that *Z*'s merit is to *L*'s as 5 to 1. Thus the marks for *lightness* are $\frac{1}{5}$, $\frac{5}{3}$, 1. And similarly, the marks for warmth are 3, 1, $\frac{1}{4}$. To get the

total result, we must *multiply* *L*'s 3 marks together, and
do the same for *M* and for *Z*. The final numbers are
$1 \times \frac{1}{5} \times 3$, $\frac{2}{5} \times \frac{5}{3} \times 1$, $\frac{4}{3} \times 1 \times \frac{1}{4}$; *i.e.* $\frac{3}{5}$, $\frac{2}{3}$, $\frac{1}{3}$; *i.e.* multiplying
throughout by 15 (which will not alter the proportion),
9, 10, 5; showing the order of merit to be *M, L, Z*.

Twenty-nine answers have been received, of which
five are right, and twenty-four wrong. These hapless
ones have all (with three exceptions) fallen into the
error of *adding* the proportional numbers together, for
each candidate, instead of *multiplying*. *Why* the latter
is right, rather than the former, is fully proved in text-
books, so I will not occupy space by stating it here: but
it can be *illustrated* very easily by the case of length,
breadth, and depth. Suppose *A* and *B* are rival diggers
of rectangular tanks: the amount of work done is
evidently measured by the number of *cubical feet* dug
out. Let *A* dig a tank 10 feet long, 10 wide, 2 deep:
let *B* dig one 6 feet long, 5 wide, 10 deep. The cubical
contents are 200, 300; *i.e. B* is best digger in the
ratio of 3 to 2. Now try marking for length, width, and
depth, separately; giving a maximum mark of 10 to
the best in each contest, and then *adding* the results!

Of the twenty-four malefactors, one gives no working,
and so has no real claim to be named; but I break the
rule for once, in deference to its success in Problem 1:

he, she, or it, is ADDLEPATE. The other twenty-three may be divided into five groups.

First and worst are, I take it, those who put the rightful winner *last;* arranging them as "Lolo, Zuzu, Mimi." The names of these desperate wrong-doers are AYR, BRADSHAW OF THE FUTURE, FURZE-BUSH and POLLUX (who send a joint answer), GREYSTEAD, GUY, OLD HEN, and SIMPLE SUSAN. The latter was *once* best of all; the Old Hen has taken advantage of her simplicity, and beguiled her with the chaff which was the bane of her own chickenhood.

Secondly, I point the finger of scorn at those who have put the worst candidate at the top; arranging them as " Zuzu, Mimi, Lolo." They are GRAECIA, M. M., OLD CAT, and R. E. X. " 'Tis Greece, but——."

The third set have avoided both these enormities, and have even succeeded in putting the worst last, their answer being " Lolo, Mimi, Zuzu." Their names are AYR (who also appears among the "quite too too"), CLIFTON C., F. B., FIFEE, GRIG, JANET, and MRS. SAIREY GAMP. F. B. has not fallen into the common error ; she *multiplies* together the proportionate numbers she gets, but in getting them she goes wrong, by reckoning warmth as a *de*-merit. Possibly she is " Freshly Burnt," or comes " From Bombay." JANET and MRS. SAIREY GAMP have also avoided this error: the method they have adopted is shrouded in mystery—I scarcely feel competent to criticize it. MRS. GAMP says "if Zuzu makes 4 while Lolo makes 3, Zuzu makes 6 while Lolo makes 5 (bad reasoning), while Mimi makes 2." From this she concludes "therefore Zuzu excels in speed by 1" (*i.e.* when compared with Lolo; but what about Mimi?). She then compares the 3 kinds of excellence, measured on this mystic scale. JANET takes the statement, that "Lolo makes 5 while Mimi makes 2," to prove that "Lolo makes 3 while Mimi makes 1 and Zuzu 4" (worse reasoning than MRS. GAMP'S), and thence concludes that "Zuzu excels in speed by $\frac{1}{8}$"! JANET should have been ADELINE, "mystery of mysteries!"

The fourth set actually put Mimi at the top, arranging them as "Mimi, Zuzu, Lolo." They are MARQUIS AND CO., MARTREB, S. B. B. (first initial scarcely legible: *may* be meant for "J"), and STANZA.

The fifth set consist of AN ANCIENT FISH and CAMEL. These ill-assorted comrades, by dint of foot and fin, have scrambled into the right answer, but, as their method is wrong, of course it counts for nothing. Also AN ANCIENT FISH has very ancient and fishlike ideas as to *how* numbers represent merit: she says "Lolo gains $2\frac{1}{2}$ on Mimi." Two and a half *what?* Fish, fish, art thou in thy duty?

Of the five winners I put BALBUS and THE ELDER TRAVELLER slightly below the other three—BALBUS for defective reasoning, the other for scanty working. BALBUS gives two reasons for saying that *addition* of marks is *not* the right method, and then adds " it follows that the decision must be made by *multiplying* the marks together." This is hardly more logical than to say " This is not Spring : *therefore* it must be Autumn."

CLASS LIST.

I.

DINAH MITE.   E. B. D. L.   JORAM.

II.

BALBUS.   THE ELDER TRAVELLER.

With regard to Knot V., I beg to express to VIS INERTIÆ and to any others who, like her, understood the condition to be that *every* marked picture must have *three* marks, my sincere regret that the unfortunate phrase "*fill* the columns with oughts and crosses" should have caused them to waste so much time and trouble. I can only repeat that a *literal* interpretation of " fill " would seem to *me* to require that *every* picture in the gallery should be marked. VIS INERTIÆ would have been in the First Class if she had sent in the solution she now offers.

ANSWERS TO KNOT VII.

Problem.—Given that one glass of lemonade, 3 sandwiches, and 7 biscuits, cost 1*s*. 2*d*. ; and that one glass of lemonade, 4 sandwiches, and 10 biscuits, cost 1*s*. 5*d*. : find the cost of (1) a glass of lemonade, a sandwich, and a biscuit ; and (2) 2 glasses of lemonade, 3 sandwiches, and 5 biscuits.

Answer.—(1) 8*d*. ; (2) 1*s*. 7*d*.

Solution.—This is best treated algebraically. Let $x =$ the cost (in pence) of a glass of lemonade, y of a sandwich, and z of a biscuit. Then we have $x + 3y + 7z = 14$, and $x + 4y + 10z = 17$. And we require the values of $x + y + z$, and of $2x + 3y + 5z$. Now, from *two* equations only, we cannot find, *separately*, the values of *three* unknowns : certain *combinations* of them may, however, be found. Also we know that we can, by the help of the given equations, eliminate 2 of the 3 unknowns from the quantity whose value is required, which will then contain one only. If, then, the required value is ascertainable at all, it can only be by the 3rd unknown vanishing of itself : otherwise the problem is impossible.

A note for American readers: Knot VII. In British currency, a shilling contains twelve pence. The phrase "One and two-pence" (written 1 s. 2 d.) means "one shilling and two-pence."

Let us then eliminate lemonade and sandwiches, and reduce everything to biscuits—a state of things even more depressing than "if all the world were apple-pie "— by subtracting the 1st equation from the 2nd, which eliminates lemonade, and gives $y + 3z = 3$, or $y = 3 - 3z$; and then substituting this value of y in the 1st, which gives $x - 2z = 5$, *i.e.* $x = 5 + 2z$.   Now if we substitute these values of x, y, in the quantities whose values are required, the first becomes $(5 + 2z) + (3 - 3z) + z$, *i.e.* 8: and the second becomes $2 (5 + 2z) + 3 (3 - 3z) + 5z$, *i.e.* 19. Hence the answers are (1) 8*d.*, (2) 1*s.* 7*d.*

––––––

The above is a *universal* method : that is, it is absolutely certain either to produce the answer, or to prove that no answer is possible.   The question may also be solved by combining the quantities whose values are given, so as to form those whose values are required.   This is merely a matter of ingenuity and good luck : and as it *may* fail, even when the thing is possible, and is of no use in proving it *im*possible, I cannot rank this method as equal in value with the other.   Even when it succeeds, it may prove a very tedious process.   Suppose the 26 competitors, who have sent in what I may call *accidental* solutions, had had a question to deal with where every number contained 8 or 10 digits !   I suspect it would have been a case of "silvered is the raven hair" (see

" Patience ") before any solution would have been hit on by the most ingenious of them.

Forty-five answers have come in, of which 44 give, I am happy to say, some sort of *working*, and therefore deserve to be mentioned by name, and to have their virtues, or vices as the case may be, discussed. Thirteen have made assumptions to which they have no right, and so cannot figure in the Class-list, even though, in 10 of the 12 cases, the answer is right. Of the remaining 28, no less than 26 have sent in *accidental* solutions, and therefore fall short of the highest honours.

I will now discuss individual cases, taking the worst first, as my custom is.

FROGGY gives no working—at least this is all he gives: after stating the given equations, he says " therefore the difference, 1 sandwich + 3 biscuits, = 3*d*.": then follow the amounts of the unknown bills, with no further hint as to how he got them. FROGGY has had a *very* narrow escape of not being named at all !

Of those who are wrong, VIS INERTIÆ has sent in a piece of incorrect working. Peruse the horrid details, and shudder ! She takes x (call it "y") as the cost of a sandwich, and concludes (rightly enough) that a biscuit will cost $\dfrac{3-y}{3}$. She then subtracts the second equation from the first, and deduces $3y + 7 \times \dfrac{3-y}{3} - 4y + 10 \times \dfrac{3-y}{3} = 3$.

By making two mistakes in this line, she brings out $y = \frac{3}{2}$. Try it again, oh VIS INERTIÆ! Away with INERTIÆ: infuse a little more VIS: and you will bring out the correct (though uninteresting) result, $0 = 0$! This will show you that it is hopeless to try to coax any one of these 3 unknowns to reveal its *separate* value. The other competitor, who is wrong throughout, is either J. M. C. or T. M. C.: but, whether he be a Juvenile Mis-Calculator or a True Mathematician Confused, he makes the answers $7d$. and $1s$. $5d$. He assumes, with Too Much Confidence, that biscuits were $\frac{1}{2}d$. each, and that Clara paid for 8, though she only ate 7!

We will now consider the 13 whose working is wrong, though the answer is right: and, not to measure their demerits too exactly, I will take them in alphabetical order. ANITA finds (rightly) that " 1 sandwich and 3 biscuits cost $3d$.," and proceeds "therefore 1 sandwich $= 1\frac{1}{2}d$., 3 biscuits $= 1\frac{1}{2}d$., 1 lemonade $= 6d$." DINAH MITE begins like ANITA: and thence proves (rightly) that a biscuit costs less than a $1d$.: whence she concludes (wrongly) that it *must* cost $\frac{1}{2}d$. F. C. W. is so beautifully resigned to the certainty of a verdict of " guilty," that I have hardly the heart to utter the word, without adding a " recommended to mercy owing to extenuating circumstances." But really, you know, where *are* the extenuating

circumstances ?   She begins by assuming that lemonade
is 4*d*. a glass, and sandwiches 3*d*. each, (making with
the 2 given equations, *four* conditions to be fulfilled by
three miserable unknowns !).   And, having (naturally)
developed this into a contradiction, she then tries 5*d*.
and 2*d*. with a similar result.   (N.B. *This* process might
have been carried on through the whole of the Tertiary
Period, without gratifying one single Megatherium.)   She
then, by a "happy thought," tries half-penny biscuits,
and so obtains a consistent result.   This may be a good
solution, viewing the problem as a conundrum : but it
is *not* scientific.   JANET identifies sandwiches with biscuits!
" One sandwich + 3 biscuits " she makes equal to " 4."
Four *what ?*   MAYFAIR makes the astounding assertion
that the equation, $s + 3b = 3$, " is evidently only satisfied
by $s = \dfrac{3}{2}, b = \dfrac{1}{2}$ " !   OLD CAT believes that the assumption
that a sandwich costs $1\frac{1}{2}d$. is " the only way to avoid
unmanageable fractions."   But *why* avoid them ?   Is there
not a certain glow of triumph in taming such a fraction ?
" Ladies and gentlemen, the fraction now before you is
one that for years defied all efforts of a refining nature :
it was, in a word, hopelessly vulgar.   Treating it as a
circulating decimal (the treadmill of fractions) only made
matters worse.   As a last resource, I reduced it to its
lowest terms, and extracted its square root !"   Joking

apart, let me thank OLD CAT for some very kind words
of sympathy, in reference to a correspondent (whose name
I am happy to say I have now forgotten) who had found
fault with me as a discourteous critic.   O. V. L. is
beyond my comprehension. He takes the given equations
as (1) and (2): thence, by the process [(2)—(1)] deduces
(rightly) equation (3) viz. $s + 3b = 3$: and thence again,
by the process [×3] (a hopeless mystery), deduces
$3s + 4b = 4$. I have nothing to say about it: I give it
up. SEA-BREEZE says "it is immaterial to the answer"
(why?) "in what proportion $3d$. is divided between the
sandwich and the 3 biscuits": so she assumes $s = 1\frac{1}{2}d.$,
$b = \frac{1}{2}d$. STANZA is one of a very irregular metre. At
first she (like JANET) identifies sandwiches with biscuits.
She then tries two assumptions $(s = 1, b = \frac{2}{3}$, and $s = \frac{1}{2}$
$b = \frac{5}{6})$, and (naturally) ends in contradictions. Then she
returns to the first assumption, and finds the 3 unknowns
separately : *quod est absurdum.*   STILETTO identifies
sandwiches and biscuits, as "articles." Is the word
ever used by confectioners? I fancied "What is the
next article, Ma'am ?" was limited to linendrapers. Two
SISTERS first assume that biscuits are 4 a penny, and
then that they are 2 a penny, adding that "the answer
will of course be the same in both cases." It is a dreamy

remark, making one feel something like Macbeth grasping
at the spectral dagger. " Is this a statement that I see
before me ? " If you were to say " we both walked the
same way this morning," and I were to say " *one* of you
walked the same way, but the other didn't," which of the
three would be the most hopelessly confused ? TURTLE
PYATE (what *is* a Turtle Pyate, please ?) and OLD CROW,
who send a joint answer, and Y. Y., adopt the same
method.   Y. Y. gets the equation $s + 3b = 3$: and then
says " this sum must be apportioned in one of the three
following ways." It *may* be, I grant you : but Y. Y. do
you say " must " ? I fear it is *possible* for Y. Y. to be
two Y's. The other two conspirators are less positive :
they say it " can " be so divided : but they add " either
of the three prices being right " ! This is bad grammar
and bad arithmetic at once, oh mysterious birds !

Of those who win honours, THE SHETLAND SNARK
must have the 3rd class all to himself. He has only
answered half the question, viz. the amount of Clara's
luncheon : the two little old ladies he pitilessly leaves in
the midst of their " difficulty." I beg to assure him
(with thanks for his friendly remarks) that entrance-fees
and subscriptions are things unknown in that most
economical of clubs, " The Knot-Untiers."

The authors of the 26 " accidental " solutions differ
only in the number of steps they have taken between the

data and the answers. In order to do them full justice I have arranged the 2nd class in sections, according to the number of steps. The two Kings are fearfully deliberate ! I suppose walking quick, or taking short cuts, is inconsistent with kingly dignity : but really, in reading THESEUS' solution, one almost fancied he was "marking time," and making no advance at all ! The other King will, I hope, pardon me for having altered "Coal" into "Cole." King Coilus, or Coil, seems to have reigned soon after Arthur's time. Henry of Huntingdon identifies him with the King Coël who first built walls round Colchester, which was named after him. In the Chronicle of Robert of Gloucester we read :—

> " Aftur Kyng Aruirag, of wam we habbeth y told,
> Marius ys sone was kyng, quoynte mon & bold.
> And ys sone was aftur hym, *Coil* was ys name,
> Bothe it were quoynte men, & of noble fame."

BALBUS lays it down as a general principle that "in order to ascertain the cost of any one luncheon, it must come to the same amount upon two different assumptions." (*Query.* Should not "it" be "we" ? Otherwise the *luncheon* is represented as wishing to ascertain its own cost !) He then makes two assumptions—one, that sandwiches cost nothing ; the other, that biscuits cost nothing, (either arrangement would lead to the shop being inconveniently crowded !)—and brings out the unknown luncheons as 8d. and 19d., on each assumption. He then concludes that this agreement of results " shows that the answers are correct." Now I propose to disprove his general law by simply giving *one* instance of its failing. One instance is quite enough. In logical language, in order to disprove a "universal affirmative," it is enough to prove its contradictory, which is a "particular negative." (I must pause for a digression on Logic, and especially on Ladies' Logic. The universal affirmative "everybody says he's a duck" is crushed instantly by proving the particular negative "Peter says he's a goose," which is equivalent to "Peter does *not* say he's a duck." And the universal negative "nobody calls on her" is well met by the particular affirmative "*I* called yesterday." In short, either of two contradictories disproves the other: and the moral is that, since a particular proposition is much more easily proved than a universal one, it is the wisest course, in arguing with a Lady, to limit one's *own* assertions to "particulars," and leave *her* to prove the "universal" contradictory, if she can. You will thus generally secure a *logical* victory : a *practical* victory is not to be hoped for, since she can always fall back upon the crushing remark "*that* has nothing to do with it!"—a move for which Man has not yet discovered any satisfactory answer. Now let us return to BALBUS.) Here is my "particular negative," on which to test his rule. Suppose the two recorded luncheons to have been " 2 buns, one queen-cake, 2 sausage-rolls, and a bottle of Zoëdone : total, one-and-ninepence," and " one bun, 2 queen-cakes, a sausage-roll, and a bottle of Zoëdone : total, one-and-fourpence." And suppose Clara's unknown luncheon to have been " 3 buns, one queen-cake, one sausage-roll, and 2 bottles of Zoëdone :" while the two little sisters had been indulging in " 8 buns, 4 queen-cakes, 2 sausage-rolls, and 6 bottles of Zoëdone." (Poor souls, how thirsty they must have been !) If BALBUS will kindly try this by his principle of "two assumptions," first assuming that a bun is 1d. and a queen-cake 2d., and then that a bun is 3d. and a queen-cake 3d., he will bring out the other two luncheons, on each assumption, as "one-and-nine-pence" and "four-and-ten-pence" respectively, which harmony of results, he will say, "shows that the answers are correct." And yet, as a matter of fact, the buns were 2d. each, the queen-cakes 3d., the sausage-rolls 6d., and the Zoëdone 2d. a bottle : so that Clara's third luncheon had cost one-and-sevenpence, and her thirsty friends had spent four-and fourpence !

Another remark of BALBUS I will quote and discuss : for I think that it also may yield a moral for some of my readers. He says "it is the same thing in substance whether in solving this problem we use words and call it Arithmetic, or use letters and signs and call it Algebra."

Now this does not appear to me a correct description of the two methods: the Arithmetical method is that of "synthesis" only; it goes from one known fact to another, till it reaches its goal: whereas the Algebraical method is that of "analysis:" it begins with the goal, symbolically represented, and so goes backwards, dragging its veiled victim with it, till it has reached the full daylight of known facts, in which it can tear off the veil and say " I know you ! "

Take an illustration. Your house has been broken into and robbed, and you appeal to the policeman who was on duty that night. "Well, Mum, I did see a chap getting out over your garden-wall: but I was a good bit off, so I didn't chase him, like. I just cut down the short way to the Chequers, and who should I meet but Bill Sykes, coming full split round the corner. So I just ups and says 'My lad, you're wanted.' That's all I says. And he says 'I'll go along quiet, Bobby,' he says, 'without the darbies,' he says." There's your *Arithmetical* policeman. Now try the other method. " I seed somebody a running, but he was well gone or ever *I* got nigh the place. So I just took a look round in the garden. And I noticed the foot-marks, where the chap had come right across your flower-beds. They was good big foot-marks sure-ly. And I noticed as the left foot went down at the heel, ever so much deeper than the other. And I says to myself

' The chap's been a big hulking chap : and he goes lame on his left foot.' And I rubs my hand on the wall where he got over, and there was soot on it, and no mistake. So I says to myself ' Now where can I light on a big man, in the chimbley-sweep line, what's lame of one foot ? ' And I flashes up permiscuous : and I says ' It's Bill Sykes ! ' says I." There is your *Algebraical* policeman—a higher intellectual type, to my thinking, than the other.

LITTLE JACK'S solution calls for a word of praise, as he has written out what really is an algebraical proof *in words*, without representing any of his facts as equations. If it is all his own, he will make a good algebraist in the time to come. I beg to thank SIMPLE SUSAN for some kind words of sympathy, to the same effect as those received from OLD CAT.

HECLA and MARTREB are the only two who have used a method *certain* either to produce the answer, or else to prove it impossible : so they must share between them the highest honours.

CLASS LIST.

I.

HECLA.   MARTREB.

II.

§ 1 (2 *steps*).   § 2 (3 *steps*).

ADELAIDE.   A. A.

CLIFTON C. . . . .   A CHRISTMAS CAROL.

E. K. C.   AFTERNOON TEA.

GUY.   AN APPRECIATIVE SCHOOLMA'AM.

L'INCONNU.   BABY.

LITTLE JACK.   BALBUS.

NIL DESPERANDUM.   BOG-OAK.

SIMPLE SUSAN.   THE RED QUEEN.

YELLOW-HAMMER.   WALL-FLOWER.

WOOLLY ONE.   § 5 (6 *steps*).

§ 3 (4 *steps*).   BAY LAUREL.

HAWTHORN.   BRADSHAW OF THE FUTURE.

JORAM.   § 6 (9 *steps*).

S. S. G.   OLD KING COLE.

§ 4 (5 *steps*).   § 7 (14 *steps*).

A STEPNEY COACH.   THESEUS.

ANSWERS TO CORRESPONDENTS.

I HAVE received several letters on the subjects of Knots II. and VI., which lead me to think some further explanation desirable.

In Knot II., I had intended the numbering of the houses to begin at one corner of the Square, and this was assumed by most, if not all, of the competitors. TROJANUS however says "assuming, in default of any information, that the street enters the square in the middle of each side, it may be supposed that the numbering begins at a street." But surely the other is the more natural assumption?

In Knot VI., the first Problem was of course a mere *ieu de mots*, whose presence I thought excusable in a series of Problems whose aim is to entertain rather than to instruct: but it has not escaped the contemptuous criticisms of two of my correspondents, who seem to think that Apollo is in duty bound to keep his bow always on the stretch. Neither of them has guessed it: and this is true human nature. Only the other day—the 31st of September, to be quite exact— I met my old friend Brown, and gave him a riddle I had just heard. With one great effort of his colossal mind, Brown guessed it. "Right!" said I. "Ah," said

he, "it's very neat—very neat. And it isn't an answer
that would occur to everybody. Very neat indeed." A
few yards further on, I fell in with Smith and to him
I propounded the same riddle. He frowned over it for
a minute, and then gave it up. Meekly I faltered out
the answer. "A poor thing, sir !" Smith growled, as
he turned away. "A very poor thing ! I wonder you
care to repeat such rubbish !" Yet Smith's mind is, if
possible, even more colossal than Brown's.

The second Problem of Knot VI. is an example in
ordinary Double Rule of Three, whose essential feature
is that the result depends on the variation of several
elements, which are so related to it that, if all but one
be constant, it varies as that one : hence, if none be
constant, it varies as their product. Thus, for example,
the cubical contents of a rectangular tank vary as its
length, if breadth and depth be constant, and so on ;
hence, if none be constant, it varies as the product of
the length, breadth, and depth.

When the result is not thus connected with the
varying elements, the Problem ceases to be Double
Rule of Three and often becomes one of great complexity.

To illustrate this, let us take two candidates for a
prize, *A* and *B*, who are to compete in French, German,
and Italian :

(*a*) Let it be laid down that the result is to depend

on their *relative* knowledge of each subject, so that,
whether their marks, for French, be "1, 2" or "100,
200," the result will be the same : and let it also be
laid down that, if they get equal marks on 2 papers,
the final marks are to have the same ratio as those of
the 3rd paper. This is a case of ordinary Double
Rule of Three. We multiply A's 3 marks together,
and do the same for B. Note that, if A gets a single
"0," his final mark is "0," even if he gets full marks
for 2 papers while B gets only one mark for each paper.
This of course would be very unfair on A, though a
correct solution under the given conditions.

(*b*) The result is to depend, as before, on *relative*
knowledge ; but French is to have twice as much
weight as German or Italian. This is an unusual form
of question. I should be inclined to say "the
resulting ratio is to be nearer to the French ratio than
if we multiplied as in (*a*), and so much nearer that it
would be necessary to use the other multipliers *twice*
to produce the same result as in (*a*) :" *e.g.* if the
French Ratio were $\frac{9}{10}$, and the others $\frac{4}{9}$, $\frac{1}{9}$ so that
the ultimate ratio, by method (*a*), would be $\frac{2}{45}$, I
should multiply instead by $\frac{2}{3}$, $\frac{1}{3}$, giving the result, $\frac{1}{5}$
which is nearer to $\frac{9}{10}$ than if he had used method (*a*).

(*c*) The result is to depend on *actual* amount of
knowledge of the 3 subjects collectively. Here we have

to ask two questions. (1) What is to be the "unit" (*i.e.* "standard to measure by") in each subject? (2) Are these units to be of equal, or unequal value? The usual "unit" is the knowledge shown by answering the whole paper correctly; calling this "100," all lower amounts are represented by numbers between "0" and "100." Then, if these units are to be of equal value, we simply add *A*'s 3 marks together, and do the same for *B*.

(*d*) The conditions are the same as (*c*), but French is to have double weight. Here we simply double the French marks, and add as before.

(*e*) French is to have such weight, that, if other marks be equal, the ultimate ratio is to be that of the French paper, so that a "0" in this would swamp the candidate: but the other two subjects are only to affect the result collectively, by the amount of knowledge shown, the two being reckoned of equal value. Here I should add *A*'s German and Italian marks together, and multiply by his French mark.

But I need not go on: the problem may evidently be set with many varying conditions, each requiring its own method of solution. The Problem in Knot VI. was meant to belong to variety (*a*), and to make this clear, I inserted the following passage:

"Usually the competitors differ in one point only. Thus, last year, Fifi and Gogo made the same number of

scarves in the trial week, and they were equally light;
but Fifi's were twice as warm as Gogo's, and she was
pronounced twice as good."

What I have said will suffice, I hope, as an answer
to BALBUS, who holds that (*a*) and (*c*) are the only
possible varieties of the problem, and that to say "We
cannot use addition, therefore we must be intended to
use multiplication," is "no more illogical than, from
knowledge that one was not born in the night, to infer
that he was born in the daytime"; and also to FIFEE,
who says "I think a little more consideration will
show you that our 'error of *adding* the proportional
numbers together for each candidate instead of *multiplying*' is no error at all." Why, even if addition *had*
been the right method to use, not one of the writers (I
speak from memory) showed any consciousness of the
necessity of fixing a "unit" for each subject. "No
error at all!" They were positively steeped in
error!

One correspondent (I do not name him, as the
communication is not quite friendly in tone) writes
thus:—"I wish to add, very respectfully, that I think
it would be in better taste if you were to abstain from
the very trenchant expressions which you are ac-
customed to indulge in when criticising the answer. That
such a tone must not be" ("be not"?) "agreeable to

the persons concerned who have made mistakes may possibly have no great weight with you, but I hope you will feel that it would be as well not to employ it, *unless you are quite certain of being correct yourself.*" The only instances the writer gives of the "trenchant expressions" are "hapless" and "malefactors." I beg to assure him (and any others who may need the assurance : I trust there are none) that all such words have been used in jest, and with no idea that they could possibly annoy any one, and that I sincerely regret any annoyance I may have thus inadvertently given. May I hope that in future they will recognise the distinction between severe language used in sober earnest, and the "words of unmeant bitterness," which Coleridge has alluded to in that lovely passage beginning "A little child, a limber elf"? If the writer will refer to that passage, or to the preface to "Fire, Famine, and Slaughter," he will find the distinction, for which I plead, far better drawn out than I could hope to do in any words of mine.

The writer's insinuation that I care not how much annoyance I give to my readers I think it best to pass over in silence ; but to his concluding remark I must entirely demur. I hold that to use language likely to annoy any of my correspondents would not be in the least justified by the plea that I was "quite certain of being correct." I trust that the knot-untiers and I are not on such terms as those !

I beg to thank *G. B.* for the offer of a puzzle—which, however, is too like the old one "Make four 9's into 100."

ANSWERS TO KNOT VIII.

§ 1. THE PIGS.

Problem.—Place twenty-four pigs in four sties so that, as you go round and round, you may always find the number in each sty nearer to ten than the number in the last.

Answer.—Place 8 pigs in the first sty, 10 in the second, nothing in the third, and 6 in the fourth: 10 is nearer ten than 8; nothing is nearer ten than 10; 6 is nearer ten than nothing; and 8 is nearer ten than 6.

This problem is noticed by only two correspondents. BALBUS says "it certainly cannot be solved mathematically, nor do I see how to solve it by any verbal quibble." NOLENS VOLENS makes Her Radiancy change the direction of going round; and even then is obliged to add "the pigs must be carried in front of her"!

---

§ 2. THE GRURMSTIPTHS.

Problem.—Omnibuses start from a certain point, both ways, every 15 minutes. A traveller, starting on

foot along with one of them, meets one in $12\frac{1}{2}$ minutes :
when will he be overtaken by one?

Answer.—In $6\frac{1}{4}$ minutes.

Solution.—Let "a" be the distance an omnibus goes
in 15 minutes, and "x" the distance from the starting-
point to where the traveller is overtaken. Since the
omnibus met is due at the starting-point in $2\frac{1}{2}$ minutes,
it goes in that time as far as the traveller walks in $12\frac{1}{2}$;
i.e. it goes 5 times as fast. Now the overtaking omnibus
is "a" behind the traveller when he starts, and therefore
goes "$a + x$" while he goes "x." Hence $a + x = 5\,x$;
i.e. $4\,x = a$, and $x = \frac{a}{4}$. This distance would be traversed
by an omnibus in $\frac{15}{4}$ minutes, and therefore by the
traveller in $5 \times \frac{15}{4}$. Hence he is overtaken in $18\frac{3}{4}$
minutes after starting, *i.e.* in $6\frac{1}{4}$ minutes after meeting
the omnibus.

Four answers have been received, of which two are
wrong. DINAH MITE rightly states that the overtaking
omnibus reached the point where they met the other
omnibus 5 minutes after they left, but wrongly concludes
that, going 5 times as fast, it would overtake them in
another minute. The travellers are 5-minutes-walk ahead

of the omnibus, and must walk 1-4th of this distance
farther before the omnibus overtakes them, which will
be 1-5th of the distance traversed by the omnibus in the
same time : this will require $1\frac{1}{4}$ minutes more. NOLENS
VOLENS tries it by a process like "Achilles and the
Tortoise." He rightly states that, when the overtaking
omnibus leaves the gate, the travellers are 1-5th of "a"
ahead, and that it will take the omnibus 3 minutes to
traverse this distance ; "during which time" the travellers,
he tells us, go 1-15th of "a" (this should be 1-25th).
The travellers being now 1-15th of "a" ahead, he
concludes that the work remaining to be done is for the
travellers to go 1-60th of "a," while the omnibus goes
1-12th. The *principle* is correct, and might have been
applied earlier.

CLASS LIST.

I.

BALBUS.   DELTA.

ANSWERS TO KNOT IX.

§ 1.   THE BUCKETS.

Problem.—Lardner states that a solid, immersed in a fluid, displaces an amount equal to itself in bulk. How can this be true of a small bucket floating in a larger one?

Solution.—Lardner means, by "displaces," "occupies a space which might be filled with water without any change in the surroundings." If the portion of the floating bucket, which is above the water, could be annihilated, and the rest of it transformed into water, the surrounding water would not change its position: which agrees with Lardner's statement.

———

Five answers have been received, none of which explains the difficulty arising from the well-known fact that a floating body is the same weight as the displaced fluid. HECLA says that "only that portion of the smaller bucket which descends below the original level of the water can be properly said to be immersed, and only an equal bulk of water is displaced." Hence, according to

HECLA, a solid, whose weight was equal to that of an equal bulk of water, would not float till the whole of it was below "the original level" of the water: but, as a matter of fact, it would float as soon as it was all under water. MAGPIE says the fallacy is "the assumption that one body can displace another from a place where it isn't," and that Lardner's assertion is incorrect, except when the containing vessel "was originally full to the brim." But the question of floating depends on the present state of things, not on past history. OLD KING COLE takes the same view as HECLA. TYMPANUM and VINDEX assume that "displaced" means "raised above its original level," and merely explain how it comes to pass that the water, so raised, is less in bulk than the immersed portion of bucket, and thus land themselves—or rather set themselves floating—in the same boat as HECLA.

I regret that there is no Class-list to publish for this Problem.

§ 2. BALBUS' ESSAY.

Problem.—Balbus states that if a certain solid be immersed in a certain vessel of water, the water will rise through a series of distances, two inches, one inch, half an inch, &c., which series has no end. He concludes that the water will rise without limit. Is this true?

Solution.—No. This series can never reach 4 inches,

since, however many terms we take, we are always short of 4 inches by an amount equal to the last term taken.

Three answers have been received—but only two seem to me worthy of honours.

TYMPANUM says that the statement about the stick "is merely a blind, to which the old answer may well be applied, *solvitur ambulando*, or rather *mergendo.*" I trust TYMPANUM will not test this in his own person, by taking the place of the man in Balbus' Essay! He would infallibly be drowned.

OLD KING COLE rightly points out that the series, 2, 1, &c., is a decreasing Geometrical Progression: while VINDEX rightly identifies the fallacy as that of "Achilles and the Tortoise."

CLASS LIST.

I.

OLD KING COLE.   VINDEX.

---

§ 3. THE GARDEN.

Problem.—An oblong garden, half a yard longer than wide, consists entirely of a gravel-walk, spirally arranged, a yard wide and 3,630 yards long   Find the dimensions of the garden.

Answer.—60, 60½.

Solution.—The number of yards and fractions of a yard traversed in walking along a straight piece of walk, is evidently the same as the number of square-yards and fractions of a square-yard, contained in that piece of walk : and the distance, traversed in passing through a square-yard at a corner, is evidently a yard. Hence the area of the garden is 3,630 square-yards : *i.e.*, if x be the width, $x\,(x\,+\,\tfrac{1}{2}) = 3,630$. Solving this Quadratic, we find $x = 60$. Hence the dimensions are 60, 60½.

Twelve answers have been received—seven right and five wrong.

C. G. L., NABOB, OLD CROW, and TYMPANUM assume that the number of yards in the length of the path is equal to the number of square-yards in the garden. This is true, but should have been proved. But each is guilty of darker deeds. C. G. L.'s "working" consists of dividing 3,630 by 60. Whence came this divisor, oh Segiel ? Divination ? Or was it a dream ? I fear this solution is worth nothing. OLD CROW'S is shorter, and so (if possible) worth rather less. He says the answer "is at once seen to be 60 × 60½"! NABOB'S calculation is short, but "as rich as a Nabob" in error. He says that the square root of 3,630, multiplied by 2, equals the

length plus the breadth.   That is $60\cdot25 \times 2 = 120\frac{1}{2}$.
His first assertion is only true of a *square* garden.   His
second is irrelevant, since $60\cdot25$ is *not* the square-root of
3,630!   Nay, Bob, this will *not* do!   TYMPANUM says
that, by extracting the square-root of 3,630, we get 60
yards with a remainder of $\dfrac{30}{60}$, or half-a-yard, which we
add so as to make the oblong $60 \times 60\frac{1}{2}$.   This is very
terrible: but worse remains behind.   TYMPANUM proceeds
thus:—"But why should there be the half-yard at all?
Because without it there would be no space at all for
flowers.   By means of it, we find reserved in the very
centre a small plot of ground, two yards long by half-
a-yard wide, the only space not occupied by walk."   But
Balbus expressly said that the walk "used up the whole
of the area."   Oh, TYMPANUM!   My tympa is exhausted:
my brain is num!   I can say no more.

HECLA indulges, again and again, in that most fatal
of all habits in computation—the making *two* mistakes
which cancel each other.   She takes x as the width of
the garden, in yards, and $x + \frac{1}{2}$ as its length, and makes
her first "coil" the sum of $x-\frac{1}{2}, x - \frac{1}{2}, x-1, x - 1$, *i.e.*
$4\,x - 3$: but the fourth term should be $x - 1\frac{1}{2}$, so that
her first coil is $\frac{1}{2}$ a yard too long.   Her second coil is
the sum of $x - 2\frac{1}{2}, x - 2\frac{1}{2}, x - 3, x - 3$: here the first
term should be $x - 2$ and the last $x - 3\frac{1}{2}$: these two

mistakes cancel, and this coil is therefore right. And the same thing is true of every other coil but the last, which needs an extra half-yard to reach the *end* of the path : and this exactly balances the mistake in the first coil. Thus the sum total of the coils comes right though the working is all wrong.

Of the seven who are right, DINAH MITE, JANET, MAGPIE, and TAFFY make the same assumption as C. G. L. and Co. They then solve by a Quadratic. MAGPIE also tries it by Arithmetical Progression, but fails to notice that the first and last "coils" have special values.

ALUMNUS ETONÆ attempts to prove what C. G. L. assumes by a particular instance, taking a garden 6 by 5½. He ought to have proved it generally : what is true of one number is not always true of others. OLD KING COLE solves it by an Arithmetical Progression. It is right, but too lengthy to be worth as much as a Quadratic.

VINDEX proves it very neatly, by pointing out that a yard of walk measured along the middle represents a square yard of garden, "whether we consider the straight stretches of walk or the square yards at the angles, in which the middle line goes half a yard in one direction and then turns a right angle and goes half a yard in another direction."

CLASS LIST.

I.

VINDEX.

II.

ALUMNUS ETONÆ.   OLD KING COLE.

III.

DINAH MITE.   MAGPIE.
JANET.   TAFFY.

ANSWERS TO KNOT X.

§ 1. THE CHELSEA PENSIONERS.

Problem.—If 70 per cent. have lost an eye, 75 per cent. an ear, 80 per cent. an arm, 85 per cent. a leg: what percentage, *at least*, must have lost all four?

Answer.—Ten.

Solution.—(I adopt that of POLAR STAR, as being better than my own). Adding the wounds together, we get $70 + 75 + 80 + 85 = 310$, among 100 men; which gives 3 to each, and 4 to 10 men. Therefore the least percentage is 10.

Nineteen answers have been received. One is "5," but, as no working is given with it, it must, in accordance with the rule, remain "a deed without a name." JANET makes it "35 and $\frac{7}{10}$ths." I am sorry she has misunderstood the question, and has supposed that those who had lost an ear were 75 per cent. *of those who had lost an eye;* and so on. Of course, on this supposition, the percentages must all be multiplied together. This she has done correctly, but I can give her no honours, as I do not think the question will fairly bear her interpretation, THREE SCORE AND TEN makes it " 19 and $\frac{3}{8}$ths." Her solution has given me—I will not say " many anxious days and sleepless nights," for I wish to be strictly truthful, but —some trouble in making any sense at all of it. She makes the number of " pensioners wounded once " to be 310 (" per cent., " I suppose !): dividing by 4, she gets 77 and a half as " average percentage : " again dividing by 4. she gets 19 and $\frac{3}{8}$ths as " percentage wounded four times." Does she suppose wounds of different kinds to " absorb " each other, so to speak ? Then, no doubt, the *data* are equivalent to 77 pensioners with one wound each, and a half-pensioner with a half-wound. And does she then suppose these concentrated wounds to be *transferable*, so that $\frac{3}{4}$ths of these unfortunates can obtain perfect health by handing over their wounds to the remaining $\frac{1}{4}$th ? Granting these suppositions, her answer is right ; or rather, *if* the question had been " A road is covered with one inch of gravel, along 77 and a half per cent. of it. How much of it could be covered 4 inches deep with the same material ? " her answer *would* have been right. But alas, that *wasn't* the question ! DELTA makes some most amazing assumptions : "let every one who has not lost an eye have lost an ear," " let every one who has not lost both eyes and ears have lost an arm."

Her ideas of a battle-field are grim indeed. Fancy a warrior who would continue fighting after losing both eyes, both ears, and both arms! This is a case which she (or "it?") evidently considers *possible*.

Next come eight writers who have made the unwarrantable assumption that, because 70 per cent. have lost an eye, *therefore* 30 per cent. have *not* lost one, so that they have *both* eyes. This is illogical. If you give me a bag containing 100 sovereigns, and if in an hour I come to you (my face *not* beaming with gratitude nearly so much as when I received the bag) to say "I am sorry to tell you that 70 of these sovereigns are bad," do I thereby guarantee the other 30 to be good? Perhaps I have not tested them yet. The sides of this illogical octagon are as follows, in alphabetical order:—ALGERNON BRAY, DINAH MITE, G. S. C., JANE E., J. D. W., MAGPIE (who makes the delightful remark "therefore 90 per cent. have two of something," recalling to one's memory that fortunate monarch, with whom Xerxes was so much pleased that "he gave him ten of everything!"), S. S. G., and TOKIO

BRADSHAW OF THE FUTURE and T. R. do the question in a piecemeal fashion—on the principle that the 70 per cent. and the 75 per cent., though commenced at opposite ends of the 100, must overlap by *at least* 45 per cent.; and so on. This is quite correct working, but not, I think, quite the best way of doing it.

The other five competitors will, I hope, feel themselves sufficiently glorified by being placed in the first class, without my composing a Triumphal Ode for each!

CLASS LIST.

I.

OLD CAT.	POLAR STAR.
OLD HEN.	SIMPLE SUSAN.

WHITE SUGAR.

II.

BRADSHAW OF THE FUTURE.	T. R.

III.

ALGERNON BRAY.	J. D. W.
DINAH MITE.	MAGPIE.
G. S. C.	S. S. G.
JANE E.	TOKIO.

§ 2. CHANGE OF DAY.

I must postpone, *sine die*, the geographical problem —partly because I have not yet received the statistics I am hoping for, and partly because I am myself so entirely puzzled by it; and when an examiner is himself dimly hovering between a second class and a third how is he to decide the position of others?

§ 3. THE SONS' AGES.

Problem.—" At first, two of the ages are together equal
to the third. A few years afterwards, two of them
are together double of the third. When the number
of years since the first occasion is two-thirds of the sum
of the ages on that occasion, one age is 21. What are
the other two ?

Answer.—" 15 and 18."

Solution.—Let the ages at first be $x, y, (x+y)$. Now, if
$a+b=2c$, then $(a-n)+(b-n)=2(c-n)$, whatever be
the value of n. Hence the second relationship, if *ever* true,
was *always* true. Hence it was true at first. But it cannot be true that x and y are together double of $(x+y)$.
Hence it must be true of $(x+y)$, together with x or y;
and it does not matter which we take. We assume,
then, $(x+y)+x=2y$; *i.e.* $y=2x$. Hence the three ages
were, at first, $x, 2x, 3x$; and the number of years, since
that time is two-thirds of $6x$, *i.e.* is $4x$. Hence the
present ages are $5x, 6x, 7x$. The ages are clearly *integers*,
since this is only " the year when one of my sons comes
of age." Hence $7x=21$, $x=3$, and the other ages are
15, 18.

Eighteen answers have been received. One of the writers merely asserts that the first occasion was 12 years ago, that the ages were then 9, 6, and 3; and that on the second occasion they were 14, 11, and 8! As a Roman father, I *ought* to withhold the name of the rash writer; but respect for age makes me break the rule: it is THREE SCORE AND TEN. JANE E. also asserts that the ages at first were 9, 6, 3: then she calculates the present ages, leaving the *second* occasion unnoticed. OLD HEN is nearly as bad; she "tried various numbers till I found one that fitted *all* the conditions"; but merely scratching up the earth, and pecking about, is *not* the way to solve a problem, oh venerable bird! And close after OLD HEN prowls, with hungry eyes, OLD CAT, who calmly assumes, to begin with, that the son who comes of age is the *eldest*. Eat your bird, Puss, for you will get nothing from me!

There are yet two zeroes to dispose of. MINERVA assumes that, on *every* occasion, a son comes of age; and that it is only such a son who is "tipped with gold." Is it wise thus to interpret " now, my boys, calculate your ages, and you shall have the money " ? BRADSHAW OF THE FUTURE says "let" the ages at first be 9, 6, 3, then assumes that the second occasion was 6 years afterwards, and on these baseless assumptions brings out the right

answers. Guide *future* travellers, an thou wilt: thou
art no Bradshaw for *this* Age!

Of those who win honours, the merely "honourable"
are two. DINAH MITE ascertains (rightly) the relationship between the three ages at first, but then *assumes* one
of them to be "6," thus making the rest of her solution
tentative. M. F. C. does the algebra all right up to the
conclusion that the present ages are $5z$, $6z$, and $7z$;
it then assumes, without giving any reason, that
$7z = 21$.

Of the more honourable, DELTA attempts a novelty—
to discover *which* son comes of age by elimination: it
assumes, successively, that it is the middle one, and that
it is the youngest; and in each case it *apparently* brings
out an absurdity. Still, as the proof contains the
following bit of algebra, "$63 = 7x + 4y$; $\therefore 21 = x + 4$
sevenths of y," I trust it will admit that its proof is not
quite conclusive. The rest of its work is good. MAGPIE
betrays the deplorable tendency of her tribe—to appropri-
ate any stray conclusion she comes across, without having
any *strict* logical right to it. Assuming A, B, C, as the
ages at first, and D as the number of the years that have
elapsed since then, she finds (rightly) the 3 equations,
$2A = B$, $C = B + A$, $D = 2B$. She then says "supposing
that $A = 1$, then $B = 2$, $C = 3$, and $D = 4$. Therefore for
A, B, C, D, four numbers are wanted which shall be to

each other as $1:2:3:4$." It is in the "therefore" that I detect the unconscientiousness of this bird. The conclusion *is* true, but this is only because the equations are "homogeneous" (*i.e.* having one "unknown" in each term), a fact which I strongly suspect had not been g ᵔsped—I beg pardon, clawed—by her. Were I to lay this little pitfall, "$A+1=B$, $B+1=C$; supposing $A=1$, then $B=2$, and $C=3$. *Therefore* for A, B, C, three numbers are wanted which shall be to one another as $1:2:3$," would you not flutter down into it, oh MAGPIE, as amiably as a Dove ? SIMPLE SUSAN is anything but simple to *me*. After ascertaining that the 3 ages at first are as $3:2:1$, she says "then, as two-thirds of their sum, added to one of them, $=21$, the sum cannot exceed 30, and consequently the highest cannot exceed 15." I suppose her (mental) argument is something like this :—"two-thirds of sum, + one age, $=21$; $\therefore$ sum, + 3 halves of one age, $=31$ and a half. But 3 halves of one age cannot be less than 1 and-a-half (here I perceive that SIMPLE SUSAN would on no account present a guinea to a new-born baby !) hence the sum cannot exceed 30." This is ingenious, but her proof, after that, is (as she candidly admits) "clumsy and roundabout." She finds that there are 5 possible sets of ages, and eliminates four of them. Suppose that, instead of 5, there had been 5 million possible sets ? Would SIMPLE SUSAN have courageously ordered in the necessary gallon of ink and ream of paper?

The solution sent in by C. R. is, like that of SIMPLE SUSAN, partly tentative, and so does not rise higher than being Clumsily Right.

Among those who have earned the highest honours, ALGERNON BRAY solves the problem quite correctly, but adds that there is nothing to exclude the supposition that all the ages were *fractional*. This would make the number of answers infinite. Let me meekly protest that I *never* intended my readers to devote the rest of their lives to writing out answers! E. M. RIX points out that, if fractional ages be admissible, any one of the three sons might be the one "come of age"; but she rightly rejects this supposition on the ground that it would make the problem indeterminate. WHITE SUGAR is the only one who has detected an oversight of mine: I had forgotten the possibility (which of course ought to be allowed for) that the son, who came of age that *year*, need not have done so by that *day*, so that he *might* be only 20. This gives a second solution, viz., 20, 24, 28. Well said, pure Crystal! Verily, thy "fair discourse hath been as sugar"!

ANSWERS TO KNOT X.   151

CLASS LIST.

I.

ALGERNON BRAY.	S. S. G.
AN OLD FOGEY.	TOKIO.
E. M. RIX.	T. R.
G. S. C.	WHITE SUGAR.

II.

C. R.	MAGPIE.
DELTA.	SIMPLE SUSAN.

III.

DINAH MITE.	M. F. C.

I have received more than one remonstrance on my assertion, in the Chelsea Pensioners' problem, that it was illogical to assume, from the *datum* "70 p. c. have lost an eye," that 30 p. c. have *not*. ALGERNON BRAY states, as a parallel case, "suppose Tommy's father gives him 4 apples, and he eats one of them, how many has he left?" and says "I think we are justified in answering, 3." I think so too. There is no "must" here, and the *data* are evidently meant to fix the answer *exactly:* but, if the question were set me "how many *must* he have left?", I should understand the *data* to be that his father gave him 4 *at least*, but *may* have given him more.

I take this opportunity of thanking those who have sent, along with their answers to the Tenth Knot, regrets that there are no more Knots to come, or petitions that I should recall my resolution to bring them to an end. I am most grateful for their kind words; but I think it wisest to end what, at best, was but a lame attempt. "The stretched metre of an antique song" is beyond my compass; and my puppets were neither distinctly *in* my life (like those I now address), nor yet (like Alice and the Mock Turtle) distinctly *out* of it. Yet let me at least fancy, as I lay down the pen, that I carry with me into my silent life, dear reader, a farewell smile from your unseen face, and a kindly farewell pressure from your unfelt hand! And so, good night! Parting is such sweet sorrow, that I shall say "good night!" till it be morrow.

THE END

A CATALOG OF SELECTED DOVER
BOOKS IN ALL FIELDS OF INTEREST

DRAWINGS OF REMBRANDT, edited by Seymour Slive. Updated Lippmann, Hofstede de Groot edition, with definitive scholarly apparatus. All portraits, biblical sketches, landscapes, nudes. Oriental figures, classical studies, together with selection of work by followers. 550 illustrations. Total of 630pp. 9⅛ × 12¼.
21485-0, 21486-9 Pa., Two-vol. set $25.00

GHOST AND HORROR STORIES OF AMBROSE BIERCE, Ambrose Bierce. 24 tales vividly imagined, strangely prophetic, and decades ahead of their time in technical skill: "The Damned Thing," "An Inhabitant of Carcosa," "The Eyes of the Panther," "Moxon's Master," and 20 more. 199pp. 5⅜ × 8½. 20767-6 Pa. $3.95

ETHICAL WRITINGS OF MAIMONIDES, Maimonides. Most significant ethical works of great medieval sage, newly translated for utmost precision, readability. Laws Concerning Character Traits, Eight Chapters, more. 192pp. 5⅜ × 8½.
24522-5 Pa. $4.50

THE EXPLORATION OF THE COLORADO RIVER AND ITS CANYONS, J. W. Powell. Full text of Powell's 1,000-mile expedition down the fabled Colorado in 1869. Superb account of terrain, geology, vegetation, Indians, famine, mutiny, treacherous rapids, mighty canyons, during exploration of last unknown part of continental U.S. 400pp. 5⅜ × 8½. 20094-9 Pa. $6.95

HISTORY OF PHILOSOPHY, Julián Marías. Clearest one-volume history on the market. Every major philosopher and dozens of others, to Existentialism and later. 505pp. 5⅜ × 8½. 21739-6 Pa. $8.50

ALL ABOUT LIGHTNING, Martin A. Uman. Highly readable non-technical survey of nature and causes of lightning, thunderstorms, ball lightning, St. Elmo's Fire, much more. Illustrated. 192pp. 5⅜ × 8½. 25237-X Pa. $5.95

SAILING ALONE AROUND THE WORLD, Captain Joshua Slocum. First man to sail around the world, alone, in small boat. One of great feats of seamanship told in delightful manner. 67 illustrations. 294pp. 5⅜ × 8½. 20326-3 Pa. $4.95

LETTERS AND NOTES ON THE MANNERS, CUSTOMS AND CONDITIONS OF THE NORTH AMERICAN INDIANS, George Catlin. Classic account of life among Plains Indians: ceremonies, hunt, warfare, etc. 312 plates. 572pp. of text. 6⅛ × 9¼. 22118-0, 22119-9 Pa. Two-vol. set $15.90

ALASKA: The Harriman Expedition, 1899, John Burroughs, John Muir, et al. Informative, engrossing accounts of two-month, 9,000-mile expedition. Native peoples, wildlife, forests, geography, salmon industry, glaciers, more. Profusely illustrated. 240 black-and-white line drawings. 124 black-and-white photographs. 3 maps. Index. 576pp. 5⅜ × 8½. 25109-8 Pa. $11.95

THE BOOK OF BEASTS: Being a Translation from a Latin Bestiary of the Twelfth Century, T. H. White. Wonderful catalog real and fanciful beasts: manticore, griffin, phoenix, amphivius, jaculus, many more. White's witty erudite commentary on scientific, historical aspects. Fascinating glimpse of medieval mind. Illustrated. 296pp. 5⅜ × 8¼. (Available in U.S. only) 24609-4 Pa. $5.95

FRANK LLOYD WRIGHT: ARCHITECTURE AND NATURE With 160 Illustrations, Donald Hoffmann. Profusely illustrated study of influence of nature—especially prairie—on Wright's designs for Fallingwater, Robie House, Guggenheim Museum, other masterpieces. 96pp. 9¼ × 10¾. 25098-9 Pa. $7.95

FRANK LLOYD WRIGHT'S FALLINGWATER, Donald Hoffmann. Wright's famous waterfall house: planning and construction of organic idea. History of site, owners, Wright's personal involvement. Photographs of various stages of building. Preface by Edgar Kaufmann, Jr. 100 illustrations. 112pp. 9¼ × 10.
23671-4 Pa. $7.95

YEARS WITH FRANK LLOYD WRIGHT: Apprentice to Genius, Edgar Tafel. Insightful memoir by a former apprentice presents a revealing portrait of Wright the man, the inspired teacher, the greatest American architect. 372 black-and-white illustrations. Preface. Index. vi + 228pp. 8¼ × 11. 24801-1 Pa. $9.95

THE STORY OF KING ARTHUR AND HIS KNIGHTS, Howard Pyle. Enchanting version of King Arthur fable has delighted generations with imaginative narratives of exciting adventures and unforgettable illustrations by the author. 41 illustrations. xviii + 313pp. 6⅛ × 9¼. 21445-1 Pa. $5.95

THE GODS OF THE EGYPTIANS, E. A. Wallis Budge. Thorough coverage of numerous gods of ancient Egypt by foremost Egyptologist. Information on evolution of cults, rites and gods; the cult of Osiris; the Book of the Dead and its rites; the sacred animals and birds; Heaven and Hell; and more. 956pp. 6⅛ × 9¼.
22055-9, 22056-7 Pa., Two-vol. set $21.90

A THEOLOGICO-POLITICAL TREATISE, Benedict Spinoza. Also contains unfinished *Political Treatise*. Great classic on religious liberty, theory of government on common consent. R. Elwes translation. Total of 421pp. 5⅜ × 8½.
20249-6 Pa. $6.95

INCIDENTS OF TRAVEL IN CENTRAL AMERICA, CHIAPAS, AND YUCATAN, John L. Stephens. Almost single-handed discovery of Maya culture; exploration of ruined cities, monuments, temples; customs of Indians. 115 drawings. 892pp. 5⅜ × 8½. 22404-X, 22405-8 Pa., Two-vol. set $15.90

LOS CAPRICHOS, Francisco Goya. 80 plates of wild, grotesque monsters and caricatures. Prado manuscript included. 183pp. 6⅜ × 9⅜. 22384-1 Pa. $4.95

AUTOBIOGRAPHY: The Story of My Experiments with Truth, Mohandas K. Gandhi. Not hagiography, but Gandhi in his own words. Boyhood, legal studies, purification, the growth of the Satyagraha (nonviolent protest) movement. Critical, inspiring work of the man who freed India. 480pp. 5⅜ × 8½. (Available in U.S. only)
24593-4 Pa. $6.95

ILLUSTRATED DICTIONARY OF HISTORIC ARCHITECTURE, edited by Cyril M. Harris. Extraordinary compendium of clear, concise definitions for over 5,000 important architectural terms complemented by over 2,000 line drawings. Covers full spectrum of architecture from ancient ruins to 20th-century Modernism. Preface. 592pp. 7½ × 9⅝. 24444-X Pa. $14.95

THE NIGHT BEFORE CHRISTMAS, Clement Moore. Full text, and woodcuts from original 1848 book. Also critical, historical material. 19 illustrations. 40pp. 4⅝ × 6. 22797-9 Pa. $2.50

THE LESSON OF JAPANESE ARCHITECTURE: 165 Photographs, Jiro Harada. Memorable gallery of 165 photographs taken in the 1930's of exquisite Japanese homes of the well-to-do and historic buildings. 13 line diagrams. 192pp. 8⅜ × 11¼. 24778-3 Pa. $8.95

THE AUTOBIOGRAPHY OF CHARLES DARWIN AND SELECTED LETTERS, edited by Francis Darwin. The fascinating life of eccentric genius composed of an intimate memoir by Darwin (intended for his children); commentary by his son, Francis; hundreds of fragments from notebooks, journals, papers; and letters to and from Lyell, Hooker, Huxley, Wallace and Henslow. xi + 365pp. 5⅜ × 8. 20479-0 Pa. $5.95

WONDERS OF THE SKY: Observing Rainbows, Comets, Eclipses, the Stars and Other Phenomena, Fred Schaaf. Charming, easy-to-read poetic guide to all manner of celestial events visible to the naked eye. Mock suns, glories, Belt of Venus, more. Illustrated. 299pp. 5¼ × 8¼. 24402-4 Pa. $7.95

BURNHAM'S CELESTIAL HANDBOOK, Robert Burnham, Jr. Thorough guide to the stars beyond our solar system. Exhaustive treatment. Alphabetical by constellation: Andromeda to Cetus in Vol. 1; Chamaeleon to Orion in Vol. 2; and Pavo to Vulpecula in Vol. 3. Hundreds of illustrations. Index in Vol. 3. 2,000pp. 6⅛ × 9¼. 23567-X, 23568-8, 23673-0 Pa., Three-vol. set $37.85

STAR NAMES: Their Lore and Meaning, Richard Hinckley Allen. Fascinating history of names various cultures have given to constellations and literary and folkloristic uses that have been made of stars. Indexes to subjects. Arabic and Greek names. Biblical references. Bibliography. 563pp. 5⅜ × 8½. 21079-0 Pa. $7.95

THIRTY YEARS THAT SHOOK PHYSICS: The Story of Quantum Theory, George Gamow. Lucid, accessible introduction to influential theory of energy and matter. Careful explanations of Dirac's anti-particles, Bohr's model of the atom, much more. 12 plates. Numerous drawings. 240pp. 5⅜ × 8½. 24895-X Pa. $4.95

CHINESE DOMESTIC FURNITURE IN PHOTOGRAPHS AND MEASURED DRAWINGS, Gustav Ecke. A rare volume, now affordably priced for antique collectors, furniture buffs and art historians. Detailed review of styles ranging from early Shang to late Ming. Unabridged republication. 161 black-and-white drawings, photos. Total of 224pp. 8⅜ × 11¼. (Available in U.S. only) 25171-3 Pa. $12.95

VINCENT VAN GOGH: A Biography, Julius Meier-Graefe. Dynamic, penetrating study of artist's life, relationship with brother, Theo, painting techniques, travels, more. Readable, engrossing. 160pp. 5⅜ × 8½. (Available in U.S. only) 25253-1 Pa. $3.95

HOW TO WRITE, Gertrude Stein. Gertrude Stein claimed anyone could understand her unconventional writing—here are clues to help. Fascinating improvisations, language experiments, explanations illuminate Stein's craft and the art of writing. Total of 414pp. 4⅝ × 6⅜. 23144-5 Pa. $5.95

ADVENTURES AT SEA IN THE GREAT AGE OF SAIL: Five Firsthand Narratives, edited by Elliot Snow. Rare true accounts of exploration, whaling, shipwreck, fierce natives, trade, shipboard life, more. 33 illustrations. Introduction. 353pp. 5⅜ × 8½. 25177-2 Pa. $7.95

THE HERBAL OR GENERAL HISTORY OF PLANTS, John Gerard. Classic descriptions of about 2,850 plants—with over 2,700 illustrations—includes Latin and English names, physical descriptions, varieties, time and place of growth, more. 2,706 illustrations. xlv + 1,678pp. 8½ × 12¼. 23147-X Cloth. $75.00

DOROTHY AND THE WIZARD IN OZ, L. Frank Baum. Dorothy and the Wizard visit the center of the Earth, where people are vegetables, glass houses grow and Oz characters reappear. Classic sequel to *Wizard of Oz.* 256pp. 5⅜ × 8.
24714-7 Pa. $4.95

SONGS OF EXPERIENCE: Facsimile Reproduction with 26 Plates in Full Color, William Blake. This facsimile of Blake's original "Illuminated Book" reproduces 26 full-color plates from a rare 1826 edition. Includes "The Tyger," "London," "Holy Thursday," and other immortal poems. 26 color plates. Printed text of poems. 48pp. 5¼ × 7. 24636-1 Pa. $3.50

SONGS OF INNOCENCE, William Blake. The first and most popular of Blake's famous "Illuminated Books," in a facsimile edition reproducing all 31 brightly colored plates. Additional printed text of each poem. 64pp. 5¼ × 7.
22764-2 Pa. $3.50

PRECIOUS STONES, Max Bauer. Classic, thorough study of diamonds, rubies, emeralds, garnets, etc.: physical character, occurrence, properties, use, similar topics. 20 plates, 8 in color. 94 figures. 659pp. 6⅛ × 9¼.
21910-0, 21911-9 Pa., Two-vol. set $15.00

ENCYCLOPEDIA OF VICTORIAN NEEDLEWORK, S. F. A. Caulfeild and Blanche Saward. Full, precise descriptions of stitches, techniques for dozens of needlecrafts—most exhaustive reference of its kind. Over 800 figures. Total of 679pp. 8⅛ × 11. Two volumes. Vol. 1 22800-2 Pa. $11.95
Vol. 2 22801-0 Pa. $11.95

THE MARVELOUS LAND OF OZ, L. Frank Baum. Second Oz book, the Scarecrow and Tin Woodman are back with hero named Tip, Oz magic. 136 illustrations. 287pp. 5⅜ × 8½. 20692-0 Pa. $5.95

WILD FOWL DECOYS, Joel Barber. Basic book on the subject, by foremost authority and collector. Reveals history of decoy making and rigging, place in American culture, different kinds of decoys, how to make them, and how to use them. 140 plates. 156pp. 7⅞ × 10¾. 20011-6 Pa. $8.95

HISTORY OF LACE, Mrs. Bury Palliser. Definitive, profusely illustrated chronicle of lace from earliest times to late 19th century. Laces of Italy, Greece, England, France, Belgium, etc. Landmark of needlework scholarship. 266 illustrations. 672pp. 6⅛ × 9¼. 24742-2 Pa. $14.95

ILLUSTRATED GUIDE TO SHAKER FURNITURE, Robert Meader. All furniture and appurtenances, with much on unknown local styles. 235 photos. 146pp. 9 × 12. 22819-3 Pa. $7.95

WHALE SHIPS AND WHALING: A Pictorial Survey, George Francis Dow. Over 200 vintage engravings, drawings, photographs of barks, brigs, cutters, other vessels. Also harpoons, lances, whaling guns, many other artifacts. Comprehensive text by foremost authority. 207 black-and-white illustrations. 288pp. 6 × 9. 24808-9 Pa. $8.95

THE BERTRAMS, Anthony Trollope. Powerful portrayal of blind self-will and thwarted ambition includes one of Trollope's most heartrending love stories. 497pp. 5⅜ × 8½. 25119-5 Pa. $8.95

ADVENTURES WITH A HAND LENS, Richard Headstrom. Clearly written guide to observing and studying flowers and grasses, fish scales, moth and insect wings, egg cases, buds, feathers, seeds, leaf scars, moss, molds, ferns, common crystals, etc.—all with an ordinary, inexpensive magnifying glass. 209 exact line drawings aid in your discoveries. 220pp. 5⅜ × 8½. 23330-8 Pa. $4.50

RODIN ON ART AND ARTISTS, Auguste Rodin. Great sculptor's candid, wide-ranging comments on meaning of art; great artists; relation of sculpture to poetry, painting, music; philosophy of life, more. 76 superb black-and-white illustrations of Rodin's sculpture, drawings and prints. 119pp. 8⅜ × 11¼. 24487-3 Pa. $6.95

FIFTY CLASSIC FRENCH FILMS, 1912–1982: A Pictorial Record, Anthony Slide. Memorable stills from Grand Illusion, Beauty and the Beast, Hiroshima, Mon Amour, many more. Credits, plot synopses, reviews, etc. 160pp. 8¼ × 11. 25256-6 Pa. $11.95

THE PRINCIPLES OF PSYCHOLOGY, William James. Famous long course complete, unabridged. Stream of thought, time perception, memory, experimental methods; great work decades ahead of its time. 94 figures. 1,391pp. 5⅜ × 8½. 20381-6, 20382-4 Pa., Two-vol. set $19.90

BODIES IN A BOOKSHOP, R. T. Campbell. Challenging mystery of blackmail and murder with ingenious plot and superbly drawn characters. In the best tradition of British suspense fiction. 192pp. 5⅜ × 8½. 24720-1 Pa. $3.95

CALLAS: PORTRAIT OF A PRIMA DONNA, George Jellinek. Renowned commentator on the musical scene chronicles incredible career and life of the most controversial, fascinating, influential operatic personality of our time. 64 black-and-white photographs. 416pp. 5⅜ × 8¼. 25047-4 Pa. $7.95

GEOMETRY, RELATIVITY AND THE FOURTH DIMENSION, Rudolph Rucker. Exposition of fourth dimension, concepts of relativity as Flatland characters continue adventures. Popular, easily followed yet accurate, profound. 141 illustrations. 133pp. 5⅜ × 8½. 23400-2 Pa. $3.50

HOUSEHOLD STORIES BY THE BROTHERS GRIMM, with pictures by Walter Crane. 53 classic stories—Rumpelstiltskin, Rapunzel, Hansel and Gretel, the Fisherman and his Wife, Snow White, Tom Thumb, Sleeping Beauty, Cinderella, and so much more—lavishly illustrated with original 19th century drawings. 114 illustrations. x + 269pp. 5⅜ × 8½. 21080-4 Pa. $4.50

SUNDIALS, Albert Waugh. Far and away the best, most thorough coverage of ideas, mathematics concerned, types, construction, adjusting anywhere. Over 100 illustrations. 230pp. 5⅜ × 8½. 22947-5 Pa. $4.50

PICTURE HISTORY OF THE NORMANDIE: With 190 Illustrations, Frank O. Braynard. Full story of legendary French ocean liner: Art Deco interiors, design innovations, furnishings, celebrities, maiden voyage, tragic fire, much more. Extensive text. 144pp. 8⅜ × 11¾. 25257-4 Pa. $9.95

THE FIRST AMERICAN COOKBOOK: A Facsimile of "American Cookery," 1796, Amelia Simmons. Facsimile of the first American-written cookbook published in the United States contains authentic recipes for colonial favorites—pumpkin pudding, winter squash pudding, spruce beer, Indian slapjacks, and more. Introductory Essay and Glossary of colonial cooking terms. 80pp. 5⅜ × 8½. 24710-4 Pa. $3.50

101 PUZZLES IN THOUGHT AND LOGIC, C. R. Wylie, Jr. Solve murders and robberies, find out which fishermen are liars, how a blind man could possibly identify a color—purely by your own reasoning! 107pp. 5⅜ × 8½. 20367-0 Pa. $2.50

THE BOOK OF WORLD-FAMOUS MUSIC—CLASSICAL, POPULAR AND FOLK, James J. Fuld. Revised and enlarged republication of landmark work in musico-bibliography. Full information about nearly 1,000 songs and compositions including first lines of music and lyrics. New supplement. Index. 800pp. 5⅜ × 8¼. 24857-7 Pa. $14.95

ANTHROPOLOGY AND MODERN LIFE, Franz Boas. Great anthropologist's classic treatise on race and culture. Introduction by Ruth Bunzel. Only inexpensive paperback edition. 255pp. 5⅜ × 8½. 25245-0 Pa. $5.95

THE TALE OF PETER RABBIT, Beatrix Potter. The inimitable Peter's terrifying adventure in Mr. McGregor's garden, with all 27 wonderful, full-color Potter illustrations. 55pp. 4¼ × 5½. (Available in U.S. only) 22827-4 Pa. $1.75

THREE PROPHETIC SCIENCE FICTION NOVELS, H. G. Wells. *When the Sleeper Wakes, A Story of the Days to Come* and *The Time Machine* (full version). 335pp. 5⅜ × 8½. (Available in U.S. only) 20605-X Pa. $5.95

APICIUS COOKERY AND DINING IN IMPERIAL ROME, edited and translated by Joseph Dommers Vehling. Oldest known cookbook in existence offers readers a clear picture of what foods Romans ate, how they prepared them, etc. 49 illustrations. 301pp. 6⅛ × 9¼. 23563-7 Pa. $6.50

SHAKESPEARE LEXICON AND QUOTATION DICTIONARY, Alexander Schmidt. Full definitions, locations, shades of meaning of every word in plays and poems. More than 50,000 exact quotations. 1,485pp. 6½ × 9¼. 22726-X, 22727-8 Pa., Two-vol. set $27.90

THE WORLD'S GREAT SPEECHES, edited by Lewis Copeland and Lawrence W. Lamm. Vast collection of 278 speeches from Greeks to 1970. Powerful and effective models; unique look at history. 842pp. 5⅜ × 8½. 20468-5 Pa. $11.95

THE BLUE FAIRY BOOK, Andrew Lang. The first, most famous collection, with many familiar tales: Little Red Riding Hood, Aladdin and the Wonderful Lamp, Puss in Boots, Sleeping Beauty, Hansel and Gretel, Rumpelstiltskin; 37 in all. 138 illustrations. 390pp. 5⅜ × 8½.   21437-0 Pa. $5.95

THE STORY OF THE CHAMPIONS OF THE ROUND TABLE, Howard Pyle. Sir Launcelot, Sir Tristram and Sir Percival in spirited adventures of love and triumph retold in Pyle's inimitable style. 50 drawings, 31 full-page. xviii + 329pp. 6½ × 9¼.   21883-X Pa. $6.95

AUDUBON AND HIS JOURNALS, Maria Audubon. Unmatched two-volume portrait of the great artist, naturalist and author contains his journals, an excellent biography by his granddaughter, expert annotations by the noted ornithologist, Dr. Elliott Coues, and 37 superb illustrations. Total of 1,200pp. 5⅜ × 8.
                                                                          Vol. I 25143-8 Pa. $8.95
                                                                          Vol. II 25144-6 Pa. $8.95

GREAT DINOSAUR HUNTERS AND THEIR DISCOVERIES, Edwin H. Colbert. Fascinating, lavishly illustrated chronicle of dinosaur research, 1820's to 1960. Achievements of Cope, Marsh, Brown, Buckland, Mantell, Huxley, many others. 384pp. 5¼ × 8¼.   24701-5 Pa. $6.95

THE TASTEMAKERS, Russell Lynes. Informal, illustrated social history of American taste 1850's–1950's. First popularized categories Highbrow, Lowbrow, Middlebrow. 129 illustrations. New (1979) afterword. 384pp. 6 × 9.
                                                                          23993-4 Pa. $6.95

DOUBLE CROSS PURPOSES, Ronald A. Knox. A treasure hunt in the Scottish Highlands, an old map, unidentified corpse, surprise discoveries keep reader guessing in this cleverly intricate tale of financial skullduggery. 2 black-and-white maps. 320pp. 5⅜ × 8½. (Available in U.S. only)   25032-6 Pa. $5.95

AUTHENTIC VICTORIAN DECORATION AND ORNAMENTATION IN FULL COLOR: 46 Plates from "Studies in Design," Christopher Dresser. Superb full-color lithographs reproduced from rare original portfolio of a major Victorian designer. 48pp. 9¼ × 12¼.   25083-0 Pa. $7.95

PRIMITIVE ART, Franz Boas. Remains the best text ever prepared on subject, thoroughly discussing Indian, African, Asian, Australian, and, especially, Northern American primitive art. Over 950 illustrations show ceramics, masks, totem poles, weapons, textiles, paintings, much more. 376pp. 5⅜ × 8. 20025-6 Pa. $6.95

SIDELIGHTS ON RELATIVITY, Albert Einstein. Unabridged republication of two lectures delivered by the great physicist in 1920–21. *Ether and Relativity* and *Geometry and Experience.* Elegant ideas in non-mathematical form, accessible to intelligent layman. vi + 56pp. 5⅜ × 8½.   24511-X Pa. $2.95

THE WIT AND HUMOR OF OSCAR WILDE, edited by Alvin Redman. More than 1,000 ripostes, paradoxes, wisecracks: Work is the curse of the drinking classes, I can resist everything except temptation, etc. 258pp. 5⅜ × 8½.   20602-5 Pa. $4.50

ADVENTURES WITH A MICROSCOPE, Richard Headstrom. 59 adventures with clothing fibers, protozoa, ferns and lichens, roots and leaves, much more. 142 illustrations. 232pp. 5⅜ × 8½.   23471-1 Pa. $3.95

PLANTS OF THE BIBLE, Harold N. Moldenke and Alma L. Moldenke. Standard reference to all 230 plants mentioned in Scriptures. Latin name, biblical reference, uses, modern identity, much more. Unsurpassed encyclopedic resource for scholars, botanists, nature lovers, students of Bible. Bibliography. Indexes. 123 black-and-white illustrations. 384pp. 6 × 9. 25069-5 Pa. $8.95

FAMOUS AMERICAN WOMEN: A Biographical Dictionary from Colonial Times to the Present, Robert McHenry, ed. From Pocahontas to Rosa Parks, 1,035 distinguished American women documented in separate biographical entries. Accurate, up-to-date data, numerous categories, spans 400 years. Indices. 493pp. 6½ × 9¼. 24523-3 Pa. $9.95

THE FABULOUS INTERIORS OF THE GREAT OCEAN LINERS IN HISTORIC PHOTOGRAPHS, William H. Miller, Jr. Some 200 superb photographs capture exquisite interiors of world's great "floating palaces"—1890's to 1980's: *Titanic, Ile de France, Queen Elizabeth, United States, Europa,* more. Approx. 200 black-and-white photographs. Captions. Text. Introduction. 160pp. 8⅞ × 11¾. 24756-2 Pa. $9.95

THE GREAT LUXURY LINERS, 1927–1954: A Photographic Record, William H. Miller, Jr. Nostalgic tribute to heyday of ocean liners. 186 photos of Ile de France, Normandie, Leviathan, Queen Elizabeth, United States, many others. Interior and exterior views. Introduction. Captions. 160pp. 9 × 12. 24056-8 Pa. $9.95

A NATURAL HISTORY OF THE DUCKS, John Charles Phillips. Great landmark of ornithology offers complete detailed coverage of nearly 200 species and subspecies of ducks: gadwall, sheldrake, merganser, pintail, many more. 74 full-color plates, 102 black-and-white. Bibliography. Total of 1,920pp. 8⅝ × 11¼. 25141-1, 25142-X Cloth. Two-vol. set $100.00

THE SEAWEED HANDBOOK: An Illustrated Guide to Seaweeds from North Carolina to Canada, Thomas F. Lee. Concise reference covers 78 species. Scientific and common names, habitat, distribution, more. Finding keys for easy identification. 224pp. 5⅜ × 8½. 25215-9 Pa. $5.95

THE TEN BOOKS OF ARCHITECTURE: The 1755 Leoni Edition, Leon Battista Alberti. Rare classic helped introduce the glories of ancient architecture to the Renaissance. 68 black-and-white plates. 336pp. 8⅜ × 11¼. 25239-6 Pa. $14.95

MISS MACKENZIE, Anthony Trollope. Minor masterpieces by Victorian master unmasks many truths about life in 19th-century England. First inexpensive edition in years. 392pp. 5⅜ × 8½. 25201-9 Pa. $7.95

THE RIME OF THE ANCIENT MARINER, Gustave Doré, Samuel Taylor Coleridge. Dramatic engravings considered by many to be his greatest work. The terrifying space of the open sea, the storms and whirlpools of an unknown ocean, the ice of Antarctica, more—all rendered in a powerful, chilling manner. Full text. 38 plates. 77pp. 9¼ × 12. 22305-1 Pa. $4.95

THE EXPEDITIONS OF ZEBULON MONTGOMERY PIKE, Zebulon Montgomery Pike. Fascinating first-hand accounts (1805–6) of exploration of Mississippi River, Indian wars, capture by Spanish dragoons, much more. 1,088pp. 5⅜ × 8½. 25254-X, 25255-8 Pa. Two-vol. set $23.90

CATALOG OF DOVER BOOKS

A CONCISE HISTORY OF PHOTOGRAPHY: Third Revised Edition, Helmut Gernsheim. Best one-volume history—camera obscura, photochemistry, daguerreotypes, evolution of cameras, film, more. Also artistic aspects—landscape, portraits, fine art, etc. 281 black-and-white photographs. 26 in color. 176pp. 8⅜ × 11¼. 25128-4 Pa. $12.95

THE DORÉ BIBLE ILLUSTRATIONS, Gustave Doré. 241 detailed plates from the Bible: the Creation scenes, Adam and Eve, Flood, Babylon, battle sequences, life of Jesus, etc. Each plate is accompanied by the verses from the King James version of the Bible. 241pp. 9 × 12. 23004-X Pa. $8.95

HUGGER-MUGGER IN THE LOUVRE, Elliot Paul. Second Homer Evans mystery-comedy. Theft at the Louvre involves sleuth in hilarious, madcap caper. "A knockout."—Books. 336pp. 5⅜ × 8½. 25185-3 Pa. $5.95

FLATLAND, E. A. Abbott. Intriguing and enormously popular science-fiction classic explores the complexities of trying to survive as a two-dimensional being in a three-dimensional world. Amusingly illustrated by the author. 16 illustrations. 103pp. 5⅜ × 8½. 20001-9 Pa. $2.25

THE HISTORY OF THE LEWIS AND CLARK EXPEDITION, Meriwether Lewis and William Clark, edited by Elliott Coues. Classic edition of Lewis and Clark's day-by-day journals that later became the basis for U.S. claims to Oregon and the West. Accurate and invaluable geographical, botanical, biological, meteorological and anthropological material. Total of 1,508pp. 5⅜ × 8½.
21268-8, 21269-6, 21270-X Pa. Three-vol. set $25.50

LANGUAGE, TRUTH AND LOGIC, Alfred J. Ayer. Famous, clear introduction to Vienna, Cambridge schools of Logical Positivism. Role of philosophy, elimination of metaphysics, nature of analysis, etc. 160pp. 5⅜ × 8½. (Available in U.S. and Canada only) 20010-8 Pa. $2.95

MATHEMATICS FOR THE NONMATHEMATICIAN, Morris Kline. Detailed, college-level treatment of mathematics in cultural and historical context, with numerous exercises. For liberal arts students. Preface. Recommended Reading Lists. Tables. Index. Numerous black-and-white figures. xvi + 641pp. 5⅜ × 8½.
24823-2 Pa. $11.95

28 SCIENCE FICTION STORIES, H. G. Wells. Novels, *Star Begotten* and *Men Like Gods,* plus 26 short stories: "Empire of the Ants," "A Story of the Stone Age," "The Stolen Bacillus," "In the Abyss," etc. 915pp. 5⅜ × 8½. (Available in U.S. only)
20265-8 Cloth. $10.95

HANDBOOK OF PICTORIAL SYMBOLS, Rudolph Modley. 3,250 signs and symbols, many systems in full; official or heavy commercial use. Arranged by subject. Most in Pictorial Archive series. 143pp. 8⅛ × 11. 23357-X Pa. $5.95

INCIDENTS OF TRAVEL IN YUCATAN, John L. Stephens. Classic (1843) exploration of jungles of Yucatan, looking for evidences of Maya civilization. Travel adventures, Mexican and Indian culture, etc. Total of 669pp. 5⅜ × 8½.
20926-1, 20927-X Pa., Two-vol. set $9.90

DEGAS: An Intimate Portrait, Ambroise Vollard. Charming, anecdotal memoir by famous art dealer of one of the greatest 19th-century French painters. 14 black-and-white illustrations. Introduction by Harold L. Van Doren. 96pp. 5⅜ × 8½.
25131-4 Pa. $3.95

PERSONAL NARRATIVE OF A PILGRIMAGE TO ALMANDINAH AND MECCAH, Richard Burton. Great travel classic by remarkably colorful personality. Burton, disguised as a Moroccan, visited sacred shrines of Islam, narrowly escaping death. 47 illustrations. 959pp. 5⅜ × 8½. 21217-3, 21218-1 Pa., Two-vol. set $17.90

PHRASE AND WORD ORIGINS, A. H. Holt. Entertaining, reliable, modern study of more than 1,200 colorful words, phrases, origins and histories. Much unexpected information. 254pp. 5⅜ × 8½. 20758-7 Pa. $5.95

THE RED THUMB MARK, R. Austin Freeman. In this first Dr. Thorndyke case, the great scientific detective draws fascinating conclusions from the nature of a single fingerprint. Exciting story, authentic science. 320pp. 5⅜ × 8½. (Available in U.S. only) 25210-8 Pa. $5.95

AN EGYPTIAN HIEROGLYPHIC DICTIONARY, E. A. Wallis Budge. Monumental work containing about 25,000 words or terms that occur in texts ranging from 3000 B.C. to 600 A.D. Each entry consists of a transliteration of the word, the word in hieroglyphs, and the meaning in English. 1,314pp. 6⅜ × 10.
23615-3, 23616-1 Pa., Two-vol. set $27.90

THE COMPLEAT STRATEGYST: Being a Primer on the Theory of Games of Strategy, J. D. Williams. Highly entertaining classic describes, with many illustrated examples, how to select best strategies in conflict situations. Prefaces. Appendices. xvi + 268pp. 5⅜ × 8½. 25101-2 Pa. $5.95

THE ROAD TO OZ, L. Frank Baum. Dorothy meets the Shaggy Man, little Button-Bright and the Rainbow's beautiful daughter in this delightful trip to the magical Land of Oz. 272pp. 5⅜ × 8. 25208-6 Pa. $4.95

POINT AND LINE TO PLANE, Wassily Kandinsky. Seminal exposition of role of point, line, other elements in non-objective painting. Essential to understanding 20th-century art. 127 illustrations. 192pp. 6½ × 9¼. 23808-3 Pa. $4.50

LADY ANNA, Anthony Trollope. Moving chronicle of Countess Lovel's bitter struggle to win for herself and daughter Anna their rightful rank and fortune—perhaps at cost of sanity itself. 384pp. 5⅜ × 8½. 24669-8 Pa. $6.95

EGYPTIAN MAGIC, E. A Wallis Budge. Sums up all that is known about magic in Ancient Egypt: the role of magic in controlling the gods, powerful amulets that warded off evil spirits, scarabs of immortality, use of wax images, formulas and spells, the secret name, much more. 253pp. 5⅜ × 8½. 22681-6 Pa. $4.50

THE DANCE OF SIVA, Ananda Coomaraswamy. Preeminent authority unfolds the vast metaphysic of India: the revelation of her art, conception of the universe, social organization, etc. 27 reproductions of art masterpieces. 192pp. 5⅜ × 8½.
24817-8 Pa. $5.95

CHRISTMAS CUSTOMS AND TRADITIONS, Clement A. Miles. Origin, evolution, significance of religious, secular practices. Caroling, gifts, yule logs, much more. Full, scholarly yet fascinating; non-sectarian. 400pp. 5⅜ × 8½.
23354-5 Pa. $6.50

THE HUMAN FIGURE IN MOTION, Eadweard Muybridge. More than 4,500 stopped-action photos, in action series, showing undraped men, women, children jumping, lying down, throwing, sitting, wrestling, carrying, etc. 390pp. 7⅞ × 10⅝.
20204-6 Cloth. $19.95

THE MAN WHO WAS THURSDAY, Gilbert Keith Chesterton. Witty, fast-paced novel about a club of anarchists in turn-of-the-century London. Brilliant social, religious, philosophical speculations. 128pp. 5⅜ × 8½.
25121-7 Pa. $3.95

A CEZANNE SKETCHBOOK: Figures, Portraits, Landscapes and Still Lifs, Paul Cezanne. Great artist experiments with tonal effects, light, mass, other qualities in over 100 drawings. A revealing view of developing master painter, precursor of Cubism. 102 black-and-white illustrations. 144pp. 8¾ × 6⅜.
24790-2 Pa. $5.95

AN ENCYCLOPEDIA OF BATTLES: Accounts of Over 1,560 Battles from 1479 B.C. to the Present, David Eggenberger. Presents essential details of every major battle in recorded history, from the first battle of Megiddo in 1479 B.C. to Grenada in 1984. List of Battle Maps. New Appendix covering the years 1967–1984. Index. 99 illustrations. 544pp. 6½ × 9¼.
24913-1 Pa. $14.95

AN ETYMOLOGICAL DICTIONARY OF MODERN ENGLISH, Ernest Weekley. Richest, fullest work, by foremost British lexicographer. Detailed word histories. Inexhaustible. Total of 856pp. 6½ × 9¼.
21873-2, 21874-0 Pa., Two-vol. set $17.00

WEBSTER'S AMERICAN MILITARY BIOGRAPHIES, edited by Robert McHenry. Over 1,000 figures who shaped 3 centuries of American military history. Detailed biographies of Nathan Hale, Douglas MacArthur, Mary Hallaren, others. Chronologies of engagements, more. Introduction. Addenda. 1,033 entries in alphabetical order. xi + 548pp. 6½ × 9¼. (Available in U.S. only)
24758-9 Pa. $11.95

LIFE IN ANCIENT EGYPT, Adolf Erman. Detailed older account, with much not in more recent books: domestic life, religion, magic, medicine, commerce, and whatever else needed for complete picture. Many illustrations. 597pp. 5⅜ × 8½.
22632-8 Pa. $8.95

HISTORIC COSTUME IN PICTURES, Braun & Schneider. Over 1,450 costumed figures shown, covering a wide variety of peoples: kings, emperors, nobles, priests, servants, soldiers, scholars, townsfolk, peasants, merchants, courtiers, cavaliers, and more. 256pp. 8⅜ × 11¼.
23150-X Pa. $7.95

THE NOTEBOOKS OF LEONARDO DA VINCI, edited by J. P. Richter. Extracts from manuscripts reveal great genius; on painting, sculpture, anatomy, sciences, geography, etc. Both Italian and English. 186 ms. pages reproduced, plus 500 additional drawings, including studies for *Last Supper, Sforza* monument, etc. 860pp. 7⅞ × 10¾. (Available in U.S. only) 22572-0, 22573-9 Pa., Two-vol. set $25.90

THE ART NOUVEAU STYLE BOOK OF ALPHONSE MUCHA: All 72 Plates from "Documents Decoratifs" in Original Color, Alphonse Mucha. Rare copyright-free design portfolio by high priest of Art Nouveau. Jewelry, wallpaper, stained glass, furniture, figure studies, plant and animal motifs, etc. Only complete one-volume edition. 80pp. 9⅜ × 12¼. 24044-4 Pa. $8.95

ANIMALS: 1,419 COPYRIGHT-FREE ILLUSTRATIONS OF MAMMALS, BIRDS, FISH, INSECTS, ETC., edited by Jim Harter. Clear wood engravings present, in extremely lifelike poses, over 1,000 species of animals. One of the most extensive pictorial sourcebooks of its kind. Captions. Index. 284pp. 9 × 12.
23766-4 Pa. $9.95

OBELISTS FLY HIGH, C. Daly King. Masterpiece of American detective fiction, long out of print, involves murder on a 1935 transcontinental flight—"a very thrilling story"—NY Times. Unabridged and unaltered republication of the edition published by William Collins Sons & Co. Ltd., London, 1935. 288pp. 5⅜ × 8½. (Available in U.S. only) 25036-9 Pa. $4.95

VICTORIAN AND EDWARDIAN FASHION: A Photographic Survey, Alison Gernsheim. First fashion history completely illustrated by contemporary photographs. Full text plus 235 photos, 1840–1914, in which many celebrities appear. 240pp. 6½ × 9¼. 24205-6 Pa. $6.00

THE ART OF THE FRENCH ILLUSTRATED BOOK, 1700–1914, Gordon N. Ray. Over 630 superb book illustrations by Fragonard, Delacroix, Daumier, Doré, Grandville, Manet, Mucha, Steinlen, Toulouse-Lautrec and many others. Preface. Introduction. 633 halftones. Indices of artists, authors & titles, binders and provenances. Appendices. Bibliography. 608pp. 8⅜ × 11¼. 25086-5 Pa. $24.95

THE WONDERFUL WIZARD OF OZ, L. Frank Baum. Facsimile in full color of America's finest children's classic. 143 illustrations by W. W. Denslow. 267pp. 5⅜ × 8½. 20691-2 Pa. $5.95

FRONTIERS OF MODERN PHYSICS: New Perspectives on Cosmology, Relativity, Black Holes and Extraterrestrial Intelligence, Tony Rothman, et al. For the intelligent layman. Subjects include: cosmological models of the universe; black holes; the neutrino; the search for extraterrestrial intelligence. Introduction. 46 black-and-white illustrations. 192pp. 5⅜ × 8½. 24587-X Pa. $6.95

THE FRIENDLY STARS, Martha Evans Martin & Donald Howard Menzel. Classic text marshalls the stars together in an engaging, non-technical survey, presenting them as sources of beauty in night sky. 23 illustrations. Foreword. 2 star charts. Index. 147pp. 5⅜ × 8½. 21099-5 Pa. $3.50

FADS AND FALLACIES IN THE NAME OF SCIENCE, Martin Gardner. Fair, witty appraisal of cranks, quacks, and quackeries of science and pseudoscience: hollow earth, Velikovsky, orgone energy, Dianetics, flying saucers, Bridey Murphy, food and medical fads, etc. Revised, expanded In the Name of Science. "A very able and even-tempered presentation."—The New Yorker. 363pp. 5⅜ × 8.
20394-8 Pa. $6.50

ANCIENT EGYPT: ITS CULTURE AND HISTORY, J. E Manchip White. From pre-dynastics through Ptolemies: society, history, political structure, religion, daily life, literature, cultural heritage. 48 plates. 217pp. 5⅜ × 8½. 22548-8 Pa. $4.95

SIR HARRY HOTSPUR OF HUMBLETHWAITE, Anthony Trollope. Incisive, unconventional psychological study of a conflict between a wealthy baronet, his idealistic daughter, and their scapegrace cousin. The 1870 novel in its first inexpensive edition in years. 250pp. 5⅜ × 8½. 24953-0 Pa. $5.95

LASERS AND HOLOGRAPHY, Winston E. Kock. Sound introduction to burgeoning field, expanded (1981) for second edition. Wave patterns, coherence, lasers, diffraction, zone plates, properties of holograms, recent advances. 84 illustrations. 160pp. 5⅜ × 8¼. (Except in United Kingdom) 24041-X Pa. $3.50

INTRODUCTION TO ARTIFICIAL INTELLIGENCE: SECOND, EN-LARGED EDITION, Philip C. Jackson, Jr. Comprehensive survey of artificial intelligence—the study of how machines (computers) can be made to act intelli-gently. Includes introductory and advanced material. Extensive notes updating the main text. 132 black-and-white illustrations. 512pp. 5⅜ × 8½. 24864-X Pa. $8.95

HISTORY OF INDIAN AND INDONESIAN ART, Ananda K. Coomaraswamy. Over 400 illustrations illuminate classic study of Indian art from earliest Harappa finds to early 20th century. Provides philosophical, religious and social insights. 304pp. 6⅝ × 9⅜. 25005-9 Pa. $8.95

THE GOLEM, Gustav Meyrink. Most famous supernatural novel in modern European literature, set in Ghetto of Old Prague around 1890. Compelling story of mystical experiences, strange transformations, profound terror. 13 black-and-white illustrations. 224pp. 5⅜ × 8½. (Available in U.S. only) 25025-3 Pa. $5.95

ARMADALE, Wilkie Collins. Third great mystery novel by the author of *The Woman in White* and *The Moonstone*. Original magazine version with 40 illustrations. 597pp. 5⅜ × 8½. 23429-0 Pa. $9.95

PICTORIAL ENCYCLOPEDIA OF HISTORIC ARCHITECTURAL PLANS, DETAILS AND ELEMENTS: With 1,880 Line Drawings of Arches, Domes, Doorways, Facades, Gables, Windows, etc., John Theodore Haneman. Sourcebook of inspiration for architects, designers, others. Bibliography. Captions. 141pp. 9 × 12. 24605-1 Pa. $6.95

BENCHLEY LOST AND FOUND, Robert Benchley. Finest humor from early 30's, about pet peeves, child psychologists, post office and others. Mostly unavailable elsewhere. 73 illustrations by Peter Arno and others. 183pp. 5⅜ × 8½. 22410-4 Pa. $3.95

ERTÉ GRAPHICS, Erté. Collection of striking color graphics: *Seasons, Alphabet, Numerals, Aces* and *Precious Stones*. 50 plates, including 4 on covers. 48pp. 9⅜ × 12¼. 23580-7 Pa. $6.95

THE JOURNAL OF HENRY D. THOREAU, edited by Bradford Torrey, F. H. Allen. Complete reprinting of 14 volumes, 1837–61, over two million words; the sourcebooks for *Walden*, etc. Definitive. All original sketches, plus 75 photographs. 1,804pp. 8½ × 12¼. 20312-3, 20313-1 Cloth., Two-vol. set $80.00

CASTLES: THEIR CONSTRUCTION AND HISTORY, Sidney Toy. Traces castle development from ancient roots. Nearly 200 photographs and drawings illustrate moats, keeps, baileys, many other features. Caernarvon, Dover Castles, Hadrian's Wall, Tower of London, dozens more. 256pp. 5⅜ × 8¼. 24898-4 Pa. $5.95

CATALOG OF DOVER BOOKS

AMERICAN CLIPPER SHIPS: 1833–1858, Octavius T. Howe & Frederick C. Matthews. Fully-illustrated, encyclopedic review of 352 clipper ships from the period of America's greatest maritime supremacy. Introduction. 109 halftones. 5 black-and-white line illustrations. Index. Total of 928pp. 5⅜ × 8½.
25115-2, 25116-0 Pa., Two-vol. set $17.90

TOWARDS A NEW ARCHITECTURE, Le Corbusier. Pioneering manifesto by great architect, near legendary founder of "International School." Technical and aesthetic theories, views on industry, economics, relation of form to function, "mass-production spirit," much more. Profusely illustrated. Unabridged translation of 13th French edition. Introduction by Frederick Etchells. 320pp. 6⅛ × 9¼. (Available in U.S. only)
25023-7 Pa. $8.95

THE BOOK OF KELLS, edited by Blanche Cirker. Inexpensive collection of 32 full-color, full-page plates from the greatest illuminated manuscript of the Middle Ages, painstakingly reproduced from rare facsimile edition. Publisher's Note. Captions. 32pp. 9⅜ × 12¼.
24345-1 Pa. $4.95

BEST SCIENCE FICTION STORIES OF H. G. WELLS, H. G. Wells. Full novel *The Invisible Man*, plus 17 short stories: "The Crystal Egg," "Aepyornis Island," "The Strange Orchid," etc. 303pp. 5⅜ × 8½. (Available in U.S. only)
21531-8 Pa. $4.95

AMERICAN SAILING SHIPS: Their Plans and History, Charles G. Davis. Photos, construction details of schooners, frigates, clippers, other sailcraft of 18th to early 20th centuries—plus entertaining discourse on design, rigging, nautical lore, much more. 137 black-and-white illustrations. 240pp. 6⅛ × 9¼.
24658-2 Pa. $5.95

ENTERTAINING MATHEMATICAL PUZZLES, Martin Gardner. Selection of author's favorite conundrums involving arithmetic, money, speed, etc., with lively commentary. Complete solutions. 112pp. 5⅜ × 8½.
25211-6 Pa. $2.95

THE WILL TO BELIEVE, HUMAN IMMORTALITY, William James. Two books bound together. Effect of irrational on logical, and arguments for human immortality. 402pp. 5⅜ × 8½.
20291-7 Pa. $7.50

THE HAUNTED MONASTERY and THE CHINESE MAZE MURDERS, Robert Van Gulik. 2 full novels by Van Gulik continue adventures of Judge Dee and his companions. An evil Taoist monastery, seemingly supernatural events; overgrown topiary maze that hides strange crimes. Set in 7th-century China. 27 illustrations. 328pp. 5⅜ × 8½.
23502-5 Pa. $5.95

CELEBRATED CASES OF JUDGE DEE (DEE GOONG AN), translated by Robert Van Gulik. Authentic 18th-century Chinese detective novel; Dee and associates solve three interlocked cases. Led to Van Gulik's own stories with same characters. Extensive introduction. 9 illustrations. 237pp. 5⅜ × 8½.
23337-5 Pa. $4.95

Prices subject to change without notice.
Available at your book dealer or write for free catalog to Dept. GI, Dover Publications, Inc., 31 East 2nd St., Mineola, N.Y. 11501. Dover publishes more than 175 books each year on science, elementary and advanced mathematics, biology, music, art, literary history, social sciences and other areas.